"I caught a fish! My very first!" Ella cried.

Nate couldn't help but grin at her excitement. "Your papa never took you fishing?" he asked.

"No." Nate knew by the way her lips tightened that he'd strayed onto dangerous ground.

"Well, now I have to catch up to you," he said, keeping his tone light. "My honor as an experienced fisherman is at stake."

By the time they left, they had a stringerful of fish. Ella had laughed and enjoyed herself more than he'd imagined her capable of. *Had no one ever shown her how to have fun?*

"Thanks for taking me." She reached for the stringer. "I guess I'll see you later…"

"*Tsk-tsk*, Miss Ella, did you think I was going to leave you with the nasty job of cleaning the fish after I had the fun of catching them with you?" Nate told himself it was mere chivalry, and not the fact that he wanted to earn more of her brilliant smiles.

She gazed up at him. "You'd do that for me?" she breathed, eyes wide and luminous.

"Sure," he said, feeling as if there wasn't much he couldn't do under the effect of her grateful smile.

Books by Laurie Kingery

Love Inspired Historical

Hill Country Christmas
The Outlaw's Lady
*Mail Order Cowboy
*The Doctor Takes a Wife
*The Sheriff's Sweetheart
*The Rancher's Courtship
*The Preacher's Bride
*Hill Country Cattleman
*The Preacher's Bride Claim
*A Hero in the Making

*Brides of Simpson Creek

LAURIE KINGERY

makes her home in central Ohio, where she is a "Texan in exile." Formerly writing as Laurie Grant for the Harlequin Historical line and other publishers, she is the author of eighteen previous books and the 1994 winner of a Readers' Choice Award in the Short Historical category. She has also been nominated for Best First Medieval and Career Achievement in Western Historical Romance by *RT Book Reviews*. When not writing her historicals, she loves to travel, read, participate on Facebook and Shoutlife and write her blog at www.lauriekingery.com.

A Hero in the Making

LAURIE KINGERY

HARLEQUIN LOVE INSPIRED HISTORICAL

Recycling programs
for this product may
not exist in your area.

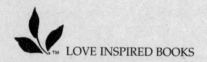

™ LOVE INSPIRED BOOKS

ISBN-13: 978-0-373-28270-8

A HERO IN THE MAKING

Copyright © 2014 by Laurie A. Kingery

www.Harlequin.com

Printed in U.S.A.

Be not forgetful to entertain strangers:
for thereby some have entertained angels unawares.
—*Hebrews* 13:2

To Tom, my own "jack of all trades" and master of many. I'm so lucky to spend my life with you!

And to Ella Lorene (Hill) Schroeder, my mother, for whom my heroine is named.

Chapter One

Simpson Creek, Texas
September 1869

"Could I interest you in a sandwich, cowboy? Maybe a bowl of chili?"

Ella Justiss didn't like the look of the man who leaned on the counter, studying her instead of the menu posted behind her. He had a scraggly scruff of a beard, narrow, calculating eyes and smelled of sweat, stale whiskey and the cheroots that peeked out of his shirt pocket.

"So here's where Detwiler keeps his best gal!" the drifter crowed, staring at her with red-rimmed eyes. "I knew he had to have somethin' better than the ones he's got out there servin' rotgut. What's your name, pretty gal?"

Pretty? Me? The drifter must have drunk a powerful lot of the saloon's whiskey before coming to her little café in the back of the building. "Whoa, cowboy, I think you misunderstood. I'm not one of the saloon girls. See the sign?" she said, pointing behind her. "I'm selling food, cold tea, lemonade and coffee, nothing else." There was no one else in the café at the moment, and nothing between her and the drifter but a long, battered and scratched pecan-wood countertop with a narrow opening at one end so she could bring orders out to the tables. She'd have to leave its safety and go right by him to reach the saloon or out into the alley behind her café. And something in his avid gaze told her she'd never make it past him, that he might try to force his way behind the counter. Then she could be trapped between the stove and the wall.

"Are you hungry? Would you like something to eat?" she prompted, keeping her voice natural, hoping to distract him.

His eyes went narrower still, and she knew she'd said the wrong thing.

"Oh, I'm hungry, all right, gal. An' you look purdy enough to eat. C'mere." Before she could think to back away or try to call for George Detwiler, the saloonkeeper, the stranger made a grab for her, pulling her out from behind the counter, snaking an arm around her waist and hauling her toward him.

Suddenly she was a frightened child back in the asylum at night, waking at the sound of the creaking of the floorboards in the darkness. Her eyes strained to see through the gloom, but she couldn't make out what had roused her. Around her, she could hear snores from some of the cots, the quiet breathing of children from others. And then there was a hand over her mouth...

Ella could never remember further than that. She didn't know why confrontations with overfriendly customers made her think of the asylum, but they always did. Her stomach clenched, as it always did when this half memory paid a visit.

"Stop it!" she screamed. "George, help me!" She

boxed her assailant's ears and clawed at his face as he succeeded in pulling her out of her sanctuary, but she might as well have pounded on a tree trunk.

The stranger guffawed, amused by her attempts to free herself, and clamped a smelly hand over her mouth, muffling her screams. "Settle down, woman, I jes' wanna kiss… You don' weigh any more'n a minute, you know that?"

Oh, yes, she knew folks said she was thin as a fiddle string and short as an ant's eyebrow, and now her size was a distinct liability in the fight. The tinkly piano music in the saloon had probably drowned out her cries. Detwiler would never hear her in time to come to her aid.

Dimly she was aware of the door opening behind her, but she was too busy fending off her attacker, who had begun to paw at the neckline of her dress, to pay any attention to what the sound might mean. Then all at once she was free, and the drifter, his nose bloodied, had fallen heavily on his backside, out cold. Ella found herself looking into the clear blue eyes of yet another stranger.

This one was as well favored as the drifter had been ugly, with a lock of curly light brown hair falling over his forehead.

"You all right, ma'am?" he asked, his Southern drawl like a caress.

"Yes, I think so… Thank you," she said fervently. "You came along at just the right time. I knew the saloonkeeper wouldn't hear me over his piano…" Ella glanced uneasily at her unconscious attacker lying just a few feet from her, wondering if he would come around and launch himself at her again.

"Don't worry about him," the newcomer said, following her gaze. "He'll be out for a while, and when he wakes up, his head will ache too much to think of bothering you. I'll get the saloonkeeper and we'll drag him out of here." He left for a moment, and when he returned, he had Detwiler in tow.

"*Again,* Miss Ella?" Detwiler said, glancing from her unconscious attacker to Ella and back again.

She nodded. "I'm afraid so, George."

Detwiler said nothing more to her, just grunted as he reached under the man's shoulders, and with the newcomer hoisting the attacker's booted feet, and Ella holding the back door open, the two men hauled the drifter into the alley. She knew they would leave him in front of the saloon, and hopefully, he wouldn't find his way back.

When they returned, Detwiler trudged back into the saloon, leaving Ella once more alone with her rescuer. As much as Ella had wanted to scuttle back behind the counter, she had been too shaky to move, and she still stood clutching the doorknob.

"You get a lot of that sort of thing, men bothering you like that?"

Her rescuer look concerned, but what was he going to do about it? She nodded and tried to look unperturbed, despite the fact that she was still shaking inside. *If this man hadn't come along...* And being alone with this man now, without the counter between them, made her nearly as uneasy as the drifter had.

"Not usually as bad as that," she said, hoping she sounded calm. "Guess it was too much to hope that some fellows wouldn't get the wrong idea from my little café being in the back of the saloon." It couldn't be helped—it wasn't as if she had the funds to buy a lot and erect a building on it. Using the back room of George

Detwiler's saloon for her little eatery and paying him a small sum that covered rent and provisions was supposed to be a temporary measure until the profits would enable her to have her own café, but it seemed she'd be old and gray by the time that happened.

She could think of that later. Meanwhile, she owed this stranger some sort of thanks for his timely intervention.

"Can I offer you a cup of coffee, mister? And a sandwich?" Ella asked, though she couldn't help wincing inwardly at the loss of the three bits it would cost her to give away what she was supposed to be selling.

"Thank you, but I'll pay for two sandwiches, since I came in with money to buy food anyway," he told her. "I'll eat one now, but would you wrap up the other sandwich for a friend, please?" Suiting his action to his words, he sprinkled some coins onto the countertop. "You could tell me your name."

"Ella," she said. "Ella Justiss."

"Nice to meet you, Miss Ella. I'm Nate Bohannan."

After making the first beef sandwich and pouring his coffee, she studied the man from under her lashes as he ate. He wasn't one of the local ranch hands, and he wasn't dressed like a cowboy. He wore black trousers, a clean white shirt and a silver brocade vest with a gold watch fob. All of his clothes were clean and well cared for, if a little well-worn. If it weren't for the fancy vest, she might have thought him a doctor, or maybe a preacher. He was well-spoken and polite, but the vest revealed a showier side to his character than a man of one of those professions.

"What brings you to Simpson Creek, Mr. Bohannan, if I may ask?" she said as she fashioned the second sandwich for his unseen friend. "Are you a gambler, by any chance?" Detwiler operated a faro table at night, so maybe the man had come to try his luck.

Bohannan threw back his head and laughed. It was a hearty laugh, as if he enjoyed a good sense of humor. "No, I'm not a gambler, though you might say our business is a kind of gamble. I'm the assistant to Mr. Robert Salali. He runs the Cherokee Medicine Show, and we're visiting your fair town to sell his amazing product."

"'Salali?' Is he Indian? Or is that some kind of foreign name?" she asked.

Bohannan smiled as he answered. "As American as you and I, though he was given the Cherokee name Salali by a Cherokee chief. He considers it an honor and uses it for his medicine business. Say, Miss Ella, why don't you come see the medicine show. The bottled medicine he sells is a wondrous potion. It'll cure whatever ails a body—though looking at *you,* I'd say you're not troubled by lumbago, catarrh or rheumatism," he said with a wink of a twinkling blue eye.

What was it about this man that made her want to laugh and smile at everything he said, despite her unease with his charm? It was more than the gratitude inspired by his rescue.

"No, I'm not subject to those complaints," she said, trying to sound tart but failing miserably.

"It's good for lots of other things," he assured her. "Things that might not be apparent on the surface. Melancholy, dyspepsia…"

"Fortunately, I'm in good health, but I have to watch my pennies too carefully to spend money on such things," she told him. "I want to open my own restaurant someday, one not attached to a saloon." She had no idea why she was sharing her dream with a man who was next to a stranger to her, a man who sent disquieting emotions zinging through her.

"A completely worthy ambition," he agreed. "But come see the presentation, won't you? It's entertaining, if nothing else. Salali puts on a good show." He'd finished his sandwich—wolfed it down, more like. "Our wagon's pulled up in front of the mercantile. And you just might think of a need for our wonderful Cherokee medicine."

Entertaining? Ella couldn't remember when she'd last been entertained. Life was hard for an honest woman on her own. "What's in this amazing medicine of yours?" she asked, letting her skepticism reveal itself.

"Ah, but that'd be telling," he said with a wink. "Suffice it to say, a little of this, a little of that, and all good for what ails a person."

"You'd better be glad our Dr. Walker and his wife are off in Austin this week," she told him. "He doesn't hold with quackery. Says calomel is poison, and most of the other things in patent medicines are, too."

Bohannon regarded her seriously, though amusement danced in those blue eyes. He held up a hand and looked straight at her. "On my mother's grave, I swear that there's no calomel or any other harmful thing in Salali's Cherokee Marvelous Medicine."

"When does the show start?"

He smiled, a smile that wrapped itself around her soul, a smile that made her regret her long-held beliefs about men, and think that this man just might be the exception. Reaching inside his vest pocket, he brought out a gold pocket watch.

"In fifteen minutes," he said. "Thanks for the sandwiches and that fine coffee, Miss Ella Justiss."

"You're welcome. Come back for supper, if you like. My fried chicken is the best in San Saba County."

"I just might do that," he said. He picked up the wrapped sandwich and exited through the saloon.

If she wanted to take a few minutes out to watch a medicine show, she could, Ella told herself. She'd been her own boss since leaving her job at the hotel restaurant and Mrs. Powell, the tyrannical cook who'd made her life miserable. She didn't do business in midafternoon, anyway—those looking for a bite to eat at noon had already found it, either at her café or the hotel restaurant, and no one was seeking supper yet.

Ella locked the door to the alley, just in case the drifter woke up and tried to find his way back inside, then reached into the cigar box that held the pitifully paltry revenue from the day so far and emptied it into her reticule.

She went into the empty saloon and caught sight of Detwiler sitting on a chair at the piano, picking out a tune she didn't know, though she *did* recognize the fact that the piano badly needed tuning. So George had been the one playing at the time the drifter had been attacking her.

He looked up as she approached. "Sorry about what happened, Miss Ella. Guess I shoulda known that fellow was too shifty-eyed to let him go back there, what with you bein' alone."

She forced a bright smile to her lips. "No harm done, George. Mr. Bohannan intervened."

"Seemed like a nice fella, even if he is one a' them snake-oil salesmen." Now the saloonkeeper's eyes turned apologetic as he cleared his throat. "I'm not sure our arrangement's gonna work out, Miss Ella, from the number of times I've had to step in and keep some yahoo from botherin' ya. I don't want anything…bad t' happen to ya, after all."

Desperation gripped her with icy fingers. She could *not* lose the use of Detwiler's back room, not when she had nowhere else to run her café. And there was very little in the way of other work for a decent woman if one was not a wife, like some of the ex-Spinsters, or a schoolteacher, like Spinsters' Club member Louisa Wheeler.

"Please, George," she said, clasping her hands together. "I'll only need the space until I can get my own place," she said, refusing to think about how long that would take. "I can't go back to the hotel—Mrs. Powell's already hired Daisy Henderson to wait tables in the restaurant." Even if her job had not already been taken, it would be too galling to submit to the cook's bullying again. Nor did she want to move on to yet another town.

Detwiler sighed. "All right. You kin stay for the time bein'. I know ya don't have any other good options. I'll try to keep a better eye on your customers. Maybe we could rig up some kinda bell rope that would ring behind the bar or somethin' if you get another bad'un."

Ella smothered a snort. As noisy as it got at times in the saloon, she could probably fire a cannon back there and he wouldn't be able to hear it. But it was nice knowing Detwiler cared about her safety, at least. She knew him to be a decent man. Even the women who served the whiskey in his saloon weren't compelled to do anything more, and if they took customers upstairs, that was entirely up to them. Detwiler took no cut of it. And Detwiler had given her a chance to go into business for herself instead of remaining under Mrs. Powell's bullying thumb at the hotel.

"Thanks," she said. "I'm just going to go down the

street for a few minutes and see the Cherokee Medicine Show. I'll be back before anyone's likely to mosey in looking for supper."

"Gonna buy ya some snake oil, eh?" Detwiler asked with a chuckle.

"Hardly," she said, and pushed through the batwing doors to the outside.

Down the street she could see a buckboard with an extralong wagon bed pulled up in front of the mercantile. The wagon bed was gaily painted in emerald-green with navy trim and an inscription along the side in fancy script lettering. As she drew closer, she saw that the inscription read The Cherokee Marvelous Medicine Show. In the middle of the wagon bed stood a narrow podium, with a box on either side stacked full of amber bottles—no doubt the famous Cherokee elixir.

Then she saw Nate emerge from the other side of the wagon, holding a stool and a banjo he'd evidently brought out from storage beneath the wagon. She watched as he placed the stool to one side of the podium, laid the banjo on one of the boxes and, using the front wheel of the wagon, climbed gracefully aboard. He settled himself on the stool and picked up the banjo. For a moment, he tried each of the strings, adjusting one or two as needed at the end of the neck, then began strumming a few chords. Then his fingers began flying over the frets and strings as he played a rollicking tune that reminded her of a minstrel show she'd once seen in New Orleans.

Why, he's really good, she marveled. She hadn't expected him to have such musical talent.

She was distracted then by a flash of color down the street, and made out a swarthy, strangely dressed man in some sort of outlandish striped turban and matching waist sash, pacing up and down the street, hold-ing a speaking trumpet to his lips. He cried, "Come one, come all, and learn of the marvelous, wondrous, extraordinary medicine first discovered by Cherokee healers. Hear about the amazing cures this medicine has brought about, from dreaded diseases like consumption, dropsy and apoplexy, to the everyday ills of catarrh, melancholia and piles!"

Everywhere up and down Main Street, people turned around and heads poked out of shops to see what was going on, including a fellow at the barbershop whose face was half shaved, half covered in thick white lather. Not much happened out of the ordinary in Simpson Creek, Texas, and its inhabitants didn't want to miss it when it did.

So this was Robert Salali, the man Nate Bohannan had said he worked for.

Salali strode to the end of Main Street, calling through his speaking trumpet, and Ella saw the post-master emerge from the post office and Sheriff Bishop and Deputy Menendez amble out from the jail. The medicine-show man was obviously in his element, drawing the crowd with his singsong pitch and stopping to exchange remarks with individual townspeople, even chucking a baby held by a young mother under the chin.

When Salali headed back toward the wagon-bed stage, Ella heard Delbert Perry, the town's handyman, ask him, "How much is this amazing medicine, mister? Does it cure a bad liver?"

"Yes, my friend, it'll underange a deranged liver faster than a crow can fly from here to San Saba. As for the price, come listen to our show and we'll sell it to you at a discount for being the first person to ask, but I promise you, it'll be the best money you ever spent!"

Ella couldn't help chuckling at the idea of an under-anged liver. Everyone knew Delbert Perry had been the town drunk before he'd gotten right with the Lord, and he hadn't touched a drop of liquor since then, but years of hard living had taken its toll, leaving him with a permanently veiny, reddened nose and a paunch that was at odds with his skinny arms and legs.

Bohannan spotted her then, and flashed an intimate smile and a wink that had Ella blushing and wishing she was wearing something besides her plain, service-able dark blue skirt and waist.

Don't be silly, she told herself sternly. Why should she give two hoots about what a charming stranger working for a medicine-show man thought of her? He'd be gone tomorrow and she'd never see him again. And she had a goal to accomplish that didn't include falling for the wiles of a smooth talker like Bohannan, even if he had saved her from that drifter. She should be using this time to bread chicken for her supper customers, and not be out here on the street lollygagging when she had no intention of wasting her pennies on this quackery. She hoped Perry wouldn't buy any, either; these nos-trums were usually half alcohol and it might cost him his hard-won sobriety.

Despite her reservations, though, Ella joined the crowd gathering in front of the medicine wagon. She might as well see the show, since that was what she'd come out for.

Bohannan strummed faster, escalating the music to a frenzied pace. Then just as suddenly, he stopped and laid the banjo aside, then stood and faced the crowd.

The only noise was the buzzing of horseflies plagu-ing the rumps of the horses tied up to a nearby hitch-ing rail.

He leaned forward, making eye contact with everyone in the crowd in turn, until Ella found herself holding her breath. Even the flies seemed to cease buzzing.

"I'm Nathan Bohannan, and it is my honor and privilege to be the one to introduce you to the purveyor of the amazing elixir of health, Cherokee Marvelous Medicine. And now, direct from a secret Cherokee fortress in the Smoky Mountains of Tennessee, I give you Robert Salali! Let's have a round of applause to welcome him, shall we, folks?"

Chapter Two

Now the medicine-show man ascended to the wagon bed via a set of steps that Bohannan had apparently placed there for him. He carried himself like royalty ascending to the throne instead of a gaudily painted wagon.

The medicine-show man paused a moment, surveying the crowd before him with a lordly air, a king in front of his subjects, as if he wore ermine-trimmed robes instead of buckskin trousers and a navy blue tunic. Around his neck was a necklace strung with what looked like alternating bear and panther claws. An eagle feather stuck out of the back of his striped turban. Raven-black hair brushed his shoulders.

He certainly had a *presence,* Ella thought before he had spoken so much as a single word.

When he opened his mouth at last, a torrent of syllables poured out, all of them strange and foreign to her ears. "I am Robert Salali," he proclaimed, switching to English. "What I said in the Cherokee tongue is this—I bring you greetings in the name of the Cherokee Nation."

Ella could not place his accent. It was neither Yankee nor a Southern drawl nor quite foreign.

"How did I come by the knowledge of this astonishing medicine, you may be wondering?" Salali said. "It is quite a tale. I saved a Cherokee chief from an agonizing death at the claws of a fierce, enormous bear. In gratitude, the chief gave me this necklace, these articles of Cherokee clothing and the knowledge of the ingredients of the elixir. He said I could share the elixir with those I wished, or keep it to myself. 'But how could I be so selfish?' I asked him. 'Ah, you have a great soul,' the chief told me. 'So I will give you a new surname, which means "Generous Heart" and you may share the elixir as you choose. It is a gesture of friendship to our white brothers.'"

"They must be more neighborly Injuns than the Comanches, then," somebody muttered, and there were answering chuckles.

"That must mean this medicine's free, I reckon!" hooted one of the town's graybeards.

Salali smiled and raised his arm majestically to quiet his audience. "Not free, no, for what is free is often not valued, and the ingredients of our amazing Cherokee medicine do cost money to obtain. I must charge a pittance or I would not be able to produce it as a service to mankind." He pulled out a rolled scroll of parchment from his pants pocket, and with a flourish, undid the red satin ribbon that bound it and handed it to Bohannan. "My assistant will read some testimonials from satisfied customers," he said.

Ella listened as Bohannan read accounts of a woman cured of cataplectic hysteria—whatever that was—who had come back to her right mind and made her husband a hearty breakfast the very next day after starting to take Cherokee Marvelous Medicine, a boy cured of lameness, a man cured of heart seizures, a woman of insomnia. Nothing in his tone hinted at the cynicism he'd revealed earlier to her when he'd said the medicine man "put on a good show."

Ella heard the townspeople around her speculating as to whether the medicine would heal this ailment or that. She looked around, and though several reached into pockets or reticules for money to buy, others looked as unconvinced as she was.

Then Robert Salali spoke again, his expression solemn. "Though I can see there are many doubters among you, I will still provide the medicine for the paltry sum of only fifty cents for a pint bottle. Fifty cents for the most amazing medicine of all time, folks! I would advise you to act quickly if you are interested. In other towns near here, the elixir has gone very fast, and we are only here for this one day."

In no time the citizens of Simpson Creek surged forward, surrounding him and the makeshift stage upon which Salali stood, clamoring for the medicine and holding out coins. She watched as Salali took the money and Bohannan handed out the bottles. Ella turned away in disgust after seeing Delbert Perry buy a bottle and walk away with an expression of bliss on his simple features. Would he be back at the saloon tomorrow, buying whiskey with his hard-earned money?

How could Bohannan help Salali prey on innocent folks this way? Rescuing her earlier had been a gentlemanly thing to do, but his actions now proved Nate Bohannan and his employer were no better than thieves.

When she turned, she saw her friend Kate Patterson standing on the boardwalk beside the wagon. She must have come out from behind the counter of the mercantile where she worked with her aunt, its proprietress, to watch the show. There was probably no one in the mercantile while this unusual diversion took place outside.

"Kate, how are you?" Ella said, smiling at her friend. "You're not going to buy that stuff, are you?"

Kate giggled. "Of course not! I don't need it for anything, but my aunt's buying a bottle," she said, indicating Mrs. Patterson wading through the throng toward Bohannan. "She suffers from rheumatism, you know, and what Dr. Walker's prescribed so far hasn't helped much."

"Well, you'll have to let me know if it works for her," Ella said.

"The man helping Salali certainly is a nice-looking fellow, isn't he?" Kate said.

Even as Ella followed her friend's gaze, she saw Bohannan raise one empty crate triumphantly. "One box gone, Mr. Salali!" he called.

But there were still pint amber bottles in the other crate, and now those who had not bought a bottle surged forward, panicked that they might have missed their chance. Ella saw the medicine-show man could hardly keep up with the flow of coins.

"He is handsome, even if he's helping to peddle snake oil," Ella said. "He came to the café to buy sandwiches a little while ago. Say, I need to get started on my supper menu—why don't you come over to the café and we can have lemonade while I cook the chicken for supper? I'll tell you all about how he rescued me," she said with a tantalizing wink.

It had been too long since she and Kate had had a cozy chat, now that Kate had a beau. For once *she* would have something interesting to talk about—she would not just be listening to Kate tell about what her beau had said and done. Ella would enjoy telling the other girl about the stranger's saving her from the drifter, even if she no longer believed in his sincerity.

Kate's eyes widened. "He rescued you? From what? It sounds thrilling! Oh, but I can't. I promised my aunt I'd help her tend the store the rest of the afternoon since Gabe and I are going for a ride tonight in his buggy."

Ella took an involuntary step backward, keeping her smile pasted on her face, even if her friend's words had caused pain and jealousy to ping through her. Ever since the barbecue and dance the Spinsters' Club had held this summer at Gilmore House, the mayor's palatial home, her friend Kate had been oh-so-busy with Gabe Bryant, a lawyer who practiced in Simpson Creek. She was always stepping out with him, getting ready to step out with him or thinking about the marriage proposal she hoped would come soon.

Ella sighed inwardly. She didn't begrudge Kate her beau, and she was happy for her, Ella told herself. She'd had a good time at the barbecue herself, and had danced nearly every dance with the gents who had attended. But after that evening, her lackluster life went on as before.

"Can you spare a few minutes to come into the mercantile and tell me about it?" Kate asked. "I've got to admit, you've got me intrigued," she said, her gaze darting between Ella and Bohannan. The other crate was now empty also and Bohannan appeared to be consoling disappointed townsfolk.

"No, I really have to start working on supper," Ella said. "I'm sure I'll see you sometime," she said, keeping her tone carefree as she turned to go. "It really wasn't that important."

She crossed the street diagonally to the saloon, and back to the hardscrabble reality of her existence.

* * *

"You made a good haul today," Nate said to Salali as he parked the medicine-show wagon under a tree in the meadow across from Simpson Creek's white-clapboard church. "Sold every bottle. You'll have to make some more before we go to any more towns." He unhitched the horses, hobbling them before he let the geldings loose to graze, and saw that Robert had taken a cross-legged seat under one of the live oak trees, pulled off his striped turban and thrown it onto a nearby bush.

I'd faint dead away if he ever offered to help with the unhitching, or at least thank me, Nate thought. But he reminded himself that under the terms of their "deal," *he* was responsible for the horses and wagon, and assisting Salali when the latter did shows, so he supposed his employer really didn't owe him any help. Nate's "pay," in return, was his meals and, eventually, a ride as far as Council Bluffs, Iowa, where he planned to take the new Transcontinental Railroad to California.

In California he could finally *be* somebody. He'd loved his father, who'd raised him alone after his mother died when he was only a baby. But all his life he had wanted to become something more than his father had been, a jack-of-all-trades who'd taken Nate to a series of small towns to live. Cal Bohannan had been content with that. Nate wasn't.

His cousin on his mother's side, Russell Blake, had gone to San Francisco and had become the proprietor of a grand hotel, and moved in influential circles in that thriving town. He said he planned to run for mayor in the next election, and he'd offered Nate the chance to become his partner in the hotel, with a further promise to introduce him to the powerful men he counted as friends. Nate could become a powerful man, too.

But would he ever get to San Francisco? So far, Salali didn't seem to be in any hurry to even get out of Texas.

The day after Nate met Salali, they'd put on a show in some small east Texas town, and he'd been impressed with the man's effortless showmanship and his personal magnetism—and the way coins poured into his hands in exchange for pint bottles of the elixir. Salali seemed inexhaustible.

Nate wasn't so impressed anymore. Now that he had someone else to do the hard work of taking care of the horse and the wagon, navigating their journey from town to town and obtaining their vittles, Salali became a different person between shows. He seemed to feel his sole contribution to the success of the medicine show should be mixing up the elixir—a combination of laudanum, sassafras and ginseng roots, actual snake oil, and at least half alcohol—when the supply ran low.

"Mmm," Salali muttered, his mouth full of the sandwich he'd given Nate the money to buy before the show.

"Good sandwich? You should have seen the pretty girl who made it for you," Nate said. "Did you see her in the crowd? Tiny and dark-haired, with big brown eyes?"

Salali shook his head and mumbled something through a last mouthful of sandwich that might have been a disinterested "no."

"Why don't we go back to her café for some supper tonight? The food's cheaper than in the hotel, and you could meet Miss Ella. I'm sure she'd be right fascinated to make your acquaintance." *And I could see her again.* He didn't know why that was so important; after all, he wasn't about to abandon his goal of reaching San Francisco to take root in Simpson Creek. But there was something so compelling about the plucky, hardworking Ella...

"She wasn't fascinated enough to buy any," his employer muttered.

Nate shrugged. "She's had to mind her pennies. She wants to build her own restaurant so she doesn't have to use the back room of the saloon anymore. What do you care that she didn't buy any elixir? We sold 'em all."

He wished he could take back the words after he saw Salali's eyes light up when he said "saloon." Within days of their meeting, Nate had discovered his employer had two vices, gambling and whiskey. But what other choice had Nate had, on foot in the middle of nowhere after his horse had broken a leg and he'd had to put him down? Hot and sweaty from carrying his banjo, saddlebags and saddle, he'd come across the medicine-show wagon, broken down about five miles from where Nate's horse had put his leg in a hole. Nate had repaired the broken axle for the medicine-show man, and regretted the deal he'd made with him ever since.

After Salali's last drunken binge, he'd begged Nate to keep him from succumbing to his vices again.

Evidently he'd forgotten that now, however, for he said, "That saloon got poker? Faro? Why don't I go make us a stake gambling while you see your sweetheart? I won't drink, I promise. Or maybe just one whiskey, just to wet my whistle. What d'ya say, Nate-boy?"

It was a familiar wheedle, and one Nate had resolved to ignore forever more. When Salali gambled, he drank then lost every penny in his pockets. Then he'd lie around in a drunken stupor for the next day, and wake up cranky as a wet rattlesnake.

Sorrowful and repentant after his last binge, he'd agreed to let Nate hold on to their money after a show, so Nate resolved to stick to his guns and do just that. The money was safe in its secret hiding place on the wagon. Even if it meant neither he nor his employer had anything more to eat today than the last of the buffalo jerky, he wasn't going to let Salali get close to temptation. If they went to town, Salali would have to agree to go into the café via the back entrance, not through the saloon. He figured the medicine-show man wouldn't agree, but Nate would have liked to see Ella Justiss again, even for a brief time.

"I can't let you do that, *compadre,*" Nate said firmly. "You told me not to let you gamble away the profits, or drink liquor, and I'm sticking to that." He tried to ignore the way Salali's eyes glared at him in thwarted anger. "If you won't agree to only visit the café, we'll stay right here. I'm just doing what you asked me to do, remember?"

Salali yawned widely, as if he didn't care one way or the other. "Think I'll take me a siesta," he muttered.

Maybe he'd change his mind about supper when he woke up, Nate thought. "Think I'll take a nap, too," he said, but he was talking to empty air. The medicine-show man was already snoring.

His employer had once admitted to him while drunk that his lately adopted surname, Salali, meant "Squirrel" in the Cherokee tongue, not "Generous Heart." But there was nothing of the industrious planning-for-winter rodent or of generosity in Robert Salali, and Nate had to wonder why the chief had given it to him—and what he'd really done for the Indian. He didn't believe for a minute that story of Salali killing a bear—the man was much too indolent. As Nate spread his blanket under the wagon to take advantage of the shade, he wondered what the Cherokee word for "lazy" was.

Someday soon, he and Salali would have to part ways, he thought, settling himself on his blanket and listening to his employer snore. Their arrangement wasn't working. At the speed they were meandering through Texas, it would take years for Nate to reach Iowa, and the business opportunity in San Francisco that had been promised to him would have vanished.

It was evening when Nate awoke. He saw that Salali was already stirring around, his turban back in place, his clothes brushed. Hope rose in Nate that his employer had seen the sense of what he'd said, and decided to accompany him to supper—if it wasn't already too late, he thought, wondering what time the petite pretty woman closed her establishment.

"You going to Ella's café with me?" Nate asked. "I'll bet it'll be the best supper we've had in a long time." He stepped up to the cabinet on the side of the wagon and used the comb and mirror that he kept there to spruce up a little. Maybe he ought to give himself a quick shave, he thought, after glancing at his beard-shadowed face, and pulled out his razor and a bowl, which he'd fill with water from the burbling creek just a few feet away.

"No," Salali said, a challenging note in his voice. "I'm going to go play faro and drink as much whiskey as I please, and don't think you're going to tell me different."

Nate shrugged, trying to tamp down the anger that boiled within him. There was no arguing with Salali when he got this way, but he didn't have to make it easy. Surely if he remained firm, his employer would thank him one day. "I don't know how you're going to do that," he said, taking the bowl and striding toward the creek. "You don't know where the money we made today is, and I'm not about to tell you."

He heard Salali following him, and figured he was

going to try to wheedle him into changing his mind. He never saw the other man raise his arm, but a second later, he felt a crushing blow to the back of his head and felt himself falling. The fading light of dusk went black.

Ella had just dressed and was heading out the back steps of the boardinghouse the next morning with a basket full of eggs to scramble and a covered dish of bacon to fry for her café's breakfast offering when she saw Detwiler trudging across the street toward her, looking as if he'd lost his last friend. His normally hound dog–droopy features were saggier than usual, and his eyes red-rimmed, as if he'd just been weeping.

Unease gripped her. While not of an overly cheerful nature, he was normally an even-tempered man. She hurried forward, alarm clenching her insides. "George, what's wrong?"

"They wrecked the place, Miss Ella, that d— 'scuse me, Miss Ella, them awful snake-oil salesmen."

Ella froze. *"W-wrecked it?* What are you saying?"

"Tore it up. Ever'thing inside is all smashed, 'cludin' your café. Sheriff noticed a broken front window, and found it all smashed up inside. He came out to the house and notified me, and I just came from seein' the damage. I'm ruined, Miss Ella. We're both ruined."

Ella felt a coldness wash over her despite the early warmth of the morning. She set the covered dish down on the doorstep, afraid her trembling hands would drop it in the next second. What Detwiler was saying didn't make sense.

"You're saying they wrecked it, but the sheriff didn't find it till this morning? How do you know both of those men did it?" *And why am I already trying to protect them?* she wondered, even as she began to run down the alley past the hotel toward the saloon. *No, this couldn't have happened. Not my café!*

Detwiler followed her. "That medicine-show man, the one in the outlandish clothes, came into the saloon last night, set down at the faro table and proceeded to get booze-blind drunk. He got mad when he lost his money an' I told him he had to leave. He told me he was gonna lay a Cherokee curse on me, mumbled some a' that foreign gibberish an' left."

"He left? So why do you think he and the other man did the damage? Was the other man with him when he was gambling?" She looked behind her, and saw Detwiler shake his head.

"Nope, I didn't see that other fella, but it had to have been both of 'em. Wait'll you see it, Miss Ella. That Salali character couldn't've done that much by hisself."

They'd emerged onto Main Street, and Ella picked up her skirt hem and ran the rest of the way.

From outside the batwing doors, nothing looked amiss, but inside it was another story.

Everything had been destroyed. Chairs and tables were splintered and lay on their sides at odd angles. The huge mirror behind the bar bore a crazy quilt of cracks radiating out from a hole in the middle. The painting of a scantily clad reclining woman that hung above it had been gashed so that the canvas now hung in pathetic strips from the gilt frame. The once-magnificent mahogany bar had deep scrapes furrowing it, as if someone had gouged it with a Bowie knife. The two girls who served whiskey in the saloon huddled along the side of the bar, their faces a study in misery, their garish-colored costumes pathetic in this scene of destruction. In the middle of the floor lay the feather of a golden eagle—just like the one that had been stuck in Robert Salali's turban.

All this Ella took in at a horrified glance as she dashed to the back door of the saloon and into her café. She hoped desperately that George had been exaggerating about her café, at least. Maybe the drunken medicine-show man had only broken into the pie safe and found the half loaf of bread and the cookies she'd had left from yesterday.

But George hadn't overstated the situation at all. The pecan countertop was cracked in half, and the three tables and half a dozen chairs lay in splintered pieces, as if a mad bull had been let loose in this small room. Her crockery lay in shards. The empty pie safe gaped open, its decorative tinwork door hanging by one hinge.

"Why?" It was a cry ripped from her heart. How could the Lord have allowed this to happen, knowing how hard she'd worked to achieve this much, all on her own, and how much more she wanted to accomplish? How could she go on now? Her pitiful savings couldn't replace what she had lost.

"I'm sorry about this, Miss Ella," Detwiler said behind her.

She whirled around, even as stinging tears began to cascade down her cheeks. "What about those women out there?" she demanded, pointing an accusatory arm at the saloon behind Detwiler. "Wouldn't they have heard something going on from upstairs and gone to get the sheriff?"

"They weren't here," he told her. "They've got a room over on Lee Street," he said. "They don't always sleep here, unless…"

Ella knew what he wasn't saying, and appreciated

his discretion. But now she couldn't think of what to do. She felt frozen in place.

"Sheriff Bishop's gone to get his deputy," he told her. "Somebody saw them two swindlers campin' t'other side a' the creek yesterday. Bishop's going out there with the deputy to see if they're still there."

"Well, I'm going with them," she said as fury swamped the grief and fear within her. "And when I see that—that scoundrel Bohannan, I'm gonna punch him right in the nose. The medicine man, too."

Chapter Three

A horsefly buzzing around Nate Bohannan's left ear woke him. Instantly he regretted returning to awareness, for it felt like an anvil had been dropped on his head and was still bouncing on it. Opening a cautious eye, he saw that it was early morning, and he was lying in the open meadow. *Strange.* He usually slept under the wagon. The ground at his fingertips dropped away, and he heard a gurgling splash below. Gingerly, he raised himself up on his elbows, and was rewarded with rocketing pain that left him retching onto the grass beside him.

Once the spasm passed, he felt a tad better and was able to cast a bleary look around him. Had Salali been attacked, too? Was his partner lying somewhere nearby, beaten insensible or worse?

He was alone in the meadow. The horses and the medicine wagon were gone. There was no sign of Salali. Where was he?

Then he caught sight of the tin bowl that he used for shaving, lying in the grass a few feet to his right, next to the skillet. It all came back to him then. He'd been about to fill the bowl with water and shave before walking into town to eat at the café, and the two of them had been arguing about Salali's intention to drink and gamble. And then...blackness.

He felt a wave of dizziness as realization hit him. Salali had hit him over the head—probably with the skillet—and taken everything, including the contents of his back pockets, his banjo, the horses and the wagon. And the money concealed in the wagon. He had vanished, leaving Nate Bohannan with only the clothes on his back and a tin bowl.

He let a curse fly then. What in the name of blazes was he going to do now?

Had Salali fled in the direction of his hideout, where he kept the ingredients to make the elixir? If so, he must be counting on Nate not having the wherewithal to follow in time to catch up with him there, for Nate knew where it was—just two or three days' ride to the southeast, a makeshift hut hidden atop a limestone hill. Nate guessed he'd probably left right after he'd knocked Nate unconscious, and if that was so, maybe someone in Simpson Creek had seen him, and the direction he was heading.

The one thing Salali hadn't remembered to do was to relieve Nate of his gold pocket watch—probably because when he fell, he'd sprawled face-first on the ground, on top of it. The weight of it still rested reassuringly in his breast pocket. It was all he had to purchase a horse and saddle, but perhaps there was a way to avoid selling it. It was worth way more than the price of a horse and saddle, after all, and it was his only inheritance from his father. He might not want to be like him, but the old man had loved him.

Maybe he could arrange to borrow a horse and revenge himself against that thieving charlatan. Just how he'd pay Salali back when he caught up with him, he hadn't yet decided, but he'd have plenty of time to cogitate on it while he pursued him.

Now that he'd made his decision, time was of the essence. He levered himself to his feet, swaying slightly, feeling the earth beneath his feet tilt as if he was on the deck of a storm-tossed ship. Nausea still churned his stomach, and he blinked to clear his vision. He turned toward the bridge that lay across the creek.

And saw four very angry-looking people heading straight for him.

He blinked again, sure his headache was making him hallucinate, for one of them was Miss Ella, the proprietress of that café. Why was she making a bee-line for him, her hands doubled into fists and thunder in her dark eyes?

The other three were men, and the only one he recognized was the stocky saloonkeeper he'd met yesterday. Judging by the tin stars on their shirts, the remaining men were lawmen. Sweet mercy, what had Salali done?

"I'm Sheriff Bishop, and this is my deputy, Luis Menendez. You Nate Bohannan?" asked the older of the two lawmen, his tone hard as granite.

Nate nodded, the motion sending waves of vertigo surging over him again. "What's this about, Sheriff?" he asked, keeping his gaze averted from Ella.

"Did you and that partner of yours willfully destroy the inside of the Simpson Creek Saloon, along with Miss Ella's café in the back of it?"

Nate closed his eyes, feeling his desire for revenge against the medicine-show man multiply tenfold. Not only had Salali robbed him blind, but by the sound of things, he'd gone on a tear in town, too.

Bishop must have taken his closed eyes as an admission of guilt, for the next thing Nate knew, the deputy had taken advantage of it to swoop behind him, grab his forearms and clamp a set of come-alongs around his wrists. His eyes flew open. "No," he breathed. "I didn't… And he's n-not my partner. We had a deal—"

"You're under arrest," Bishop said, his eyes as cold as if he'd just condemned Nate to hang. "Come with us peaceably now, or I'll let Miss Ella slug you in the nose as she's been threatening to do. Destroying the saloon's bad enough, but what kind of man wrecks a lady's business?"

Nate let himself look at Ella then—anything to escape the implacable, hawk-eyed stare of the sheriff, and the equally accusing gaze of his deputy. But looking into the wrath-mixed-with-hurt eyes of Ella Justiss was worse, for tears flooded down her cheeks. Even though he hadn't done what he was charged with, he felt lower than a snake's belly just for having been associated with the scoundrel that had done the damage.

"I didn't do it, Sheriff," he said. "I've been robbed, too. Salali laid me out with a frying pan last evening and took everything I had—the wagon, the horses, the profits—and skedaddled. I only just came to, as a matter of fact." He felt guilty not mentioning the pocket watch, but if he was able to talk his way out of the charges, he was going to need it.

"You expect us to believe that?" Bishop demanded.

Dizzy again, Nate closed his eyes. "It's the truth. The last thing I remember before being hit over the head was arguing with Salali about going into town. I wanted to go have some supper at Miss Ella's café, since I'd had a sandwich there before the show and it was mighty tasty." He darted a glance at Miss Ella then, hoping to find some softening in her eyes, but there was none.

"Salali wanted to go drink and gamble at the saloon. I didn't want him to because whiskey and my employer don't mix well—"

Without warning, the deputy's fingers roughly probed the back of Nate's head, sending fresh waves of sickening pain piercing through his skull.

"There *is* a lump back here, Sheriff," the deputy confirmed in a Spanish-accented voice.

"Let me see…"

That was the last thing Nate heard before he passed out again.

When Nate woke, he was lying on a straw-tick mattress facing the bars of a jail cell. From *inside*. He groaned. Surely locking up a man when he was insensible was against the law somehow.

"You gonna live?" a woman's scorn-laced voice inquired.

A dark skirt and small, laced-up boots hovered into his line of sight. When his gaze traveled upward, he recognized Miss Ella staring down at him through the bars.

"I'm not sure," he said honestly, still feeling the pounding in his head, but it had diminished, somehow, as if the hammer pounding the anvil was only hitting the end of the anvil, rather than right in the middle.

"*Humph.* Mighty convenient, I'd say, passing out like that."

He stared at her, his headache and her disbelief making him even testier than he might otherwise be under the circumstances. "For the sheriff, maybe. Why would you care? I'm behind bars anyway, aren't I?"

She ignored that. "Dr. Walker says as long as you woke up, you aren't gonna die. Oh, yes, Sheriff Bishop had the doctor check your noggin all right and proper. You're awake, so I guess you'll survive."

Having to put up with the lash of Ella Justiss's tongue, along with the pain in his head, was surely more than any man ought to have to bear. "Where's the sheriff? I want to talk to him," he said.

"You'll just have to wait. The sheriff and his deputy went to see if they could catch up with that snake-oil-selling fraud and I agreed to sit with you—since I don't have a café to run, thanks to your friend."

Nate doubted they'd catch Salali. If the scoundrel had taken to the road right after wrecking the saloon and café, he must have gotten a good head start. Salali wasn't fool enough to dawdle after a spree like that, nor would he stick to the main roads.

"The sheriff'll never catch him," he muttered.

"I wouldn't be so sure," Ella argued. "And that tall tale your friend was spouting about saving the Indian chief from a bear—that was all made-up moondust, wasn't it? And he was just spouting gibberish, not real Cherokee, wasn't he?"

"Probably," he admitted. "Woman, if you're just going to torment me unmercifully till the sheriff gets back, get the rope and the lynch mob and put an end to my misery. I hurt too much to listen to you carp at me."

That stopped her. She had the grace to look ashamed. "D-doctor said I was to give you this when you woke, if you were still in pain," she said, reaching for a cup sitting on a nearby bench.

"What is it? Poison, to finish me off?" he said, eyeing it, and her, balefully.

"No, it's not, and how dare you accuse the good doctor of such a thing? It's willow-bark tea, and his wife brewed it herself. It'll help your headache, though maybe you deserve to keep it."

Despite what she'd said, she held it out to him. The bars were just wide enough to pass the cup through. He noticed she was careful not to let their fingers touch.

The remedy was bitter, but he drank it all.

"Well, since you're awake and all, I'm going to go help Mr. Detwiler clear up the mess your friend made," Ella said, turning to go.

"He's not my friend," he ground out. "I was tired of his drinking and his gambling and I was about to part company with him, though I hadn't told him yet." The truth was, he rued the day he'd met Salali and been in such a hurry to find a cheap way to get to the railroad, that he'd thrown in with the man. If he hadn't taken the easy way out of his transportation problem, he would now not have to atone for what Salali had done. "Besides," he added, standing and gripping the bars. "How can you just leave? You're supposed to be guarding me, aren't you?"

She shrugged. "Sheriff said I could, soon as you were awake. It's not as if you could escape, anyway."

He didn't know why the idea of her leaving bothered him so. Hadn't he just been complaining about the way she had plagued him?

"But I'm hungry," he said, hoping he looked pitiful enough that she wouldn't laugh at him. "I haven't eaten anything since that sandwich you sold me for lunch yesterday, and—" he glanced out of the cell's one high window "—it's got to be at least noon, I reckon."

"Then it's a pity your friend destroyed my café, isn't it?" she retorted sweetly. "It's not as if the hotel cook's going to feed you. Mrs. Powell doesn't give anything away."

He played his last card. "Doesn't the Bible say you're supposed to feed the hungry? Sure it does—remember the passage where it says 'I was in prison, and you visited me'? You did the visiting part, Miss Ella. Don't you reckon you could take pity on a poor hungry man and do the feeding part, too?"

She studied him, chewing on her lip. "Anyone can quote scripture, Mr. Bohannan," she said. "I could quote 'Man does not live by bread alone,' but I'll just give you part of the breakfast I had planned to serve at the café this morning. It's a wonder some stray dog didn't find it first, but my friend Maude rescued the makings from where I left them on the back step of the boardinghouse and went ahead and cooked them. I had some, and I'll fetch you a portion. The rest is for the sheriff and his deputy when they get back."

Ella went over to the desk that occupied the center of the sheriff's office part of the jail, removed the cover from a dish and scooped up a hearty helping of bacon and eggs onto a tin plate she got off a shelf. She tossed a couple of biscuits onto it and passed it under the bottom bar, along with a cup of water from the pitcher on the desk. Then, as he murmured his thanks, she went out the door without another word.

The eggs and bacon were cold, but it was food, and soon the ache in his belly had subsided. The ache in his head had faded to a dull whisper, too.

Now all he could do was wait for Sheriff Bishop and his deputy to return. He doubted they'd have Salali with them when they did. And if he was being realistic, by the time he was freed, it was unlikely he'd able to catch up with Salali, either. The wily charlatan would be gone by the time he was able to make his way to the canyon hideout.

He wasn't sleepy, even now that his belly was full, so it seemed he would have an indefinite amount of time to contemplate what he *would* do after he was freed—assuming they didn't try to hold him responsible for what his erstwhile employer had done.

He wanted to stick to his original plan and to shake the dust of Simpson Creek off his boots as soon as possible. Somehow he'd get a horse, even if he had to stay here long enough to earn the price of it. He'd head for the railroad terminus at Council Bluffs, taking jobs along the way to earn the price of a ticket to San Francisco. He'd never work in a medicine show—he didn't want to be someone's shill ever again.

Fortunately he had more cards in his deck. His father had passed along a number of skills to his son before he'd died. Nate hadn't valued them then—he'd been too full of big plans and as little common sense as most wet-behind-the-ears young'uns possessed.

Something about Miss Ella's stricken face as she spoke about the wreck of her café nagged at him. He couldn't leave until he assured himself she would be all right. Surely she had parents who would take her in, or relatives, or friends. Maybe even someone who could afford to help her rebuild. Perhaps she had a beau who'd been pressing her to marry him, yet some stubborn independent streak had driven her to prove she could take care of herself. Perhaps this incident would force her to be practical and marry the man. A young woman should be cooking in her own kitchen, with babies crawling at her feet, and a hungry husband on the way home for supper. Serving sandwiches to rowdy cowboys and saddle tramps was for some plain old maid or a widow, not for a pretty thing like Ella Justiss.

That was it. If Bishop let him go, he'd linger just long enough to ensure himself that Miss Ella had some reasonable options. Then he was San Francisco bound.

Chapter Four

Ella parted the batwing doors of the saloon and walked inside. She'd expected that Detwiler would have made some start at cleaning up the mess, but the ruined tables and chairs, the broken glass, were still strewn everywhere. George Detwiler, Dolly and Trudy were sitting on the floor along the wall, sniffling and swollen-eyed, staring dully ahead of them.

"What're y'all doing?" Ella demanded. "Don't you think you should at least sweep up the broken glass?"

Detwiler studied her with doleful eyes. "Won't make no diff'rence, Miss Ella. How'm I gonna fix all this? Those medicine-show swindlers took what was in the till an' every whiskey bottle they didn't drink. I don't have anything t'sell, even if customers were willing to stand while they drink."

Ella looked around. "You still have the piano," she said, spotting it against the far wall. Amazingly, it had escaped the destruction. Had Robert Salali possessed some innate respect for a musical instrument that had caused him to leave the piano alone during his destructive spree?

"Ain't no one gonna pay to come hear me play," he said.

It was true—Detwiler could only pick out a few tunes poorly.

"Well, you can't leave the place like this," she said, making a sweeping gesture at the piles of splintered wood and glass. "Unless you're planning on tearing it down and selling your lot."

At her words, the two saloon girls set up a keening wail. If there was no saloon, they had no livelihood, any more than Detwiler did.

"Come on," she said. "Get the brooms out and let's start cleaning up. We could at least separate the trash and firewood from what could be repaired. Some of those tables and chairs just need new legs, looks like."

"An' who's gonna repair them?" he asked, though without heat. "I'm no carpenter."

"Hank Dayton's got a lathe at the mill," Dolly mumbled. "I seen it once."

"What does that matter?" Detwiler muttered. "Hank Dayton's a skinflint who doesn't give anything away. I don't know how to operate a lathe."

"So we need someone who does," Ella said, going behind the bar and fetching the two brooms that were propped in the corner. She handed Detwiler one of them. "Let's get started clearing this mess, and maybe one of us will think of something."

"You girls kin go home," Detwiler said to Dolly and Trudy. "I'll let you know what I'm going to do—soon's I figure it out."

Ella didn't try to stop them. There were only two brooms, and the women hadn't seemed inclined to do more than sit and blubber. She started sweeping, intending to leave the café till last, for she was too afraid

Detwiler would give way to despair again if she left him on his own.

Lord, if you're up there, we could use some help. She'd never quite believed that the Deity was interested in aiding Ella Justiss, or He would have done so years ago at the asylum, but she figured she'd offer Him the opportunity, at least.

She left Detwiler to clean his saloon while she went to do the same with her café. She had soon swept the debris into the center of her area and came back to help Detwiler with his larger one. For a time both of them plied their brooms in silence, but as the afternoon went on, the interruptions began—the saloon's faithful customers stopping in to see if the rumor was true that there was no whiskey or poker games to be had in Simpson Creek because of the vandalism in the saloon. Ella ignored them and kept sweeping, but Detwiler stopped to tell each of his customers what had happened. Ella rather thought he was enjoying the sympathy gained with each encounter, but as these patrons began to build up inside the saloon, chattering with each other over where they would have to go to get their whiskey and card games, and doing nothing to help, even Detwiler began to get testy. Ella was past exasperated at having to ask gents to move while she swept the areas they had been standing in.

Finally, to Ella's relief, Detwiler roared an order for all of them to leave, saying he'd put up a sign when the saloon was open again. Then he took a piece of a broken table, and a brush and bootblacking he'd dug up from who knew where and handed them to Ella.

"Your book learnin's probably better than mine, Miss Ella," he said. "Write on the bottom a' this tabletop Closed Till Further Notice, an' I'll prop it up outside."

If George only knew how haphazard her "book learning" had been, Ella thought as she bent to her task. The asylum orphans' schooling had been hit-or-miss, since they couldn't attend if they were needed to work in the laundry or the kitchens or the superintendent's wife's garden. But when Ella *was* able to go to class, she'd paid attention with a desperate intensity, for she'd known even then it was her ticket to a better life.

Detwiler had returned after placing the sign outside and Ella was sweeping piles of broken glass into a dustpan when the sound of footsteps had them both looking up. Ella recognized Faith Chadwick, the preacher's wife, and wondered what she was doing here.

"Mr. Detwiler, the sheriff told us what happened here. I'm so sorry," Faith said.

He'd been stacking broken table and chair legs into a pile like firewood, but now he straightened. "Thank you, ma'am. Yes, it surely is going to be a trial to replace all this."

Faith looked troubled, but shifted her gaze to Ella. "I wonder if I might speak to you privately, Ella."

Ella wondered what she wanted but gestured for the preacher's wife to follow her to the café. "I'd ask you to sit down, Faith," she said, ruefully gesturing at the splintered tables and chairs that littered the tiny area, "but as you can see, that's impossible just now."

Faith nodded, surveying the wreckage. "That's what I've come to speak to you about."

Ella gazed at her curiously. She and the pastor's wife had worked together on Spinsters' Club projects back before Faith and Reverend Gil Chadwick had married, but Ella didn't know her very well.

And that was her own fault, Ella realized. She'd kind of had a chip on her shoulder when she'd first joined the group because she was the only one who rarely made it to meetings and Spinsters' Club events because of having to work so much—first in the hotel restaurant and lately, in her own establishment.

"I'd like to help you get started again," Faith said. "I have a small table in the parlor that we don't use often, Ella, which I can loan to you, and I happened to pass the mayor's wife on the way here, and she said she also has a couple of small tables, as well as some dishes and silverware she wants to give you outright. She had her own household before marrying the mayor, of course, so she no longer needs them."

Ella couldn't believe her ears. It was a God-sent answer to her dilemma. "Thank you, Faith," she breathed. "It's an answer to a prayer!"

The preacher's wife blinked as if the remark had really touched her. "We're happy to be able to help, Ella dear. It's what church members do for one another. Gil will be over with those things in a few minutes. He's borrowing a horse and buckboard from the livery."

"Can't you read the sign? The saloon's closed till further notice!" Detwiler's voice boomed from the saloon.

Faith flinched and the two women exchanged a glance. Ella could guess the preacher's wife was wishing she could help George somehow, too, but it wouldn't be fitting for the church to help a saloon owner resume selling spirits and promoting card playing and other activities the church couldn't approve of.

"Perhaps I shouldn't say this, but I can't help wishing you didn't have to conduct your business in the back of the saloon, Ella dear," Faith said.

Ella sighed. She knew the preacher's wife meant well, and her arranging to get Ella the furniture, dishes and silverware to resume business was certainly a blessing. But what choice did she have? She was glad Faith didn't know about the drifter who had manhandled her only yesterday.

"Yes, I know it's far from ideal," Ella admitted. "And believe me, I'm trying my best to earn enough to set up my café elsewhere."

"I know," Faith said, surprising her with a hug before she could back away. "I'm going to pray about it, and see if God will send you a solution."

"Thanks—for the prayer and the things you and Mrs. Gilmore are giving me." *Praying won't hurt,* Ella thought, *though it's never seemed to help me very much.*

Ella went back into the saloon, feeling guilty about her good fortune. She would be back in business by tomorrow, while Detwiler was still trying to figure out how to replace his whiskey and his furniture. But when she told the saloonkeeper about Faith Chadwick's generous offer, the man showed no envy.

"She's a good Christian woman," he said. "Reckon there's nothing more I can do here. I'll see if I can help the preacher load up those things and drive 'em over here so he don't have to come."

Ella watched him go. She couldn't help wishing someday *her* good works would be worthy of notice. It seemed as if she spent so much time working to survive that she had no energy left for higher goals.

Well, she wasn't perfect, but at least she didn't consort with thieves, like that slick fellow Nate Bohannan, she thought.

As if summoned by her thoughts, Bohannan walked through the batwing doors.

"What are *you* doing here?" she demanded, glaring at him. "There's nothing left to ruin!" she added, making a sweeping gesture that included the pile of damaged furniture. She thought she saw Bohannan flinch at the sight. Then she saw Sheriff Bishop behind him. "Did you catch that thieving medicine-show man, Sheriff?" she asked. "Is that why you're back?"

"No, we didn't see a trace of him, so I came back, but Menendez stayed out to keep trying to pick up his trail. He's also going to let the sheriffs of the nearby towns know in case he shows up there," Bishop said. "I just thought Mr. Bohannan might like to help you clean up, but I see you've mostly finished that. Sorry I didn't get back in time so he could do more."

"Thanks for the thought, Sheriff," Ella said, "but what the saloon needs now is a carpenter." She nodded toward the broken tables and chairs. "Mrs. Chadwick and Mrs. Gilmore are going to give me what I need to reopen my café, but that won't help Mr. Detwiler. You don't happen to have anyone with carpentry skills in your other jail cell, do you?" she added. It was an attempt at a joke, but she was surprised to see Bohannan's gaze sharpen.

He strode over to survey the pile. "Miss Ella, it just so happens I'm kind of a jack-of-all-trades, and carpentry is one of my skills," Bohannan told her over his shoulder. "I could fix everything in the saloon and your café for room and board. The only problem is, I don't have any tools. I'd need a saw, a lathe, a hammer, nails…"

"Hank Dayton has a lathe at his mill," Sheriff Bishop murmured.

"But he'd probably charge for the use of it," Ella countered, remembering the conversation between Detwiler and Dolly.

"Maybe not," Bishop mused, a half smile on his face. "As sheriff, I just happen to know Hank's one of the saloon's best customers. I could pay him a visit, persuade him it's in his best interest to donate the use of his lathe so Nate, here, could make new table legs. And if I'm very persuasive, maybe he'll even loan George some planking and sawhorses for temporary tables."

"But Bohannan's under arrest," Ella reminded the sheriff. "Or are you letting him work off his sentence by fixing the damage he—that is, his employer—inflicted on this place?" she asked, allowing her voice to suggest that she still didn't believe he was completely innocent.

"Sentence? He's not under arrest anymore," Bishop said blandly.

"He's not?"

"I'm not?" Ella and Bohannan asked in unison. Ella's voice was indignant, while Bohannan's held notes of disbelief and gratitude.

Bishop nodded, and turned to Ella. "He's convinced me he didn't know anything about what Salali was planning to do, so I can't hold him any longer. I would've advised him to ride on out of here and stay out of trouble, but that Salali scoundrel robbed him, too, Miss Ella. So what he's offering is a favor to George Detwiler—and to you, since he'll fix your café, too."

"I wonder if he'd be offering to stay and help if he had any way to leave," she retorted, glaring at Bohannan.

Something—she wasn't sure if it was hurt or anger—sparked in those blue eyes as he returned her stare, but when he replied, his voice was even.

"I'm sorry you don't trust me, Miss Ella."

"No, I don't," she retorted. "You may not have wrecked the saloon, but I saw how willing you were to help fleece the townspeople of their hard-earned money to sell a bottle of worthless—maybe even dangerous—

liquid. How do I know you won't try to fleece Mr. Detwiler too?"

"I don't believe there was anything harmful in the Cherokee Marvelous Medicine, Miss Ella," he said.

She noticed he didn't try to insist that it was helpful, though.

"And it's true I might not have offered if I had a dollar in my pockets and a horse to ride out of here," he went on. "But my carpentry skills will speak for themselves, and I hope I'll be able to prove you have nothing to fear from me while I'm here."

She couldn't seem to escape that penetrating gaze of his.

Sheriff Bishop cleared his throat. "Reckon there's no time like the present to make that visit to the lumber mill."

She stiffened. The sheriff was going to leave her alone with Bohannan?

"Sheriff Bishop, surely you should speak to Mr. Detwiler before you do that," she protested. "It'll be up to him whether he decides to take Mr. Bohannan up on his very *kind* offer." She was aware of Bohannan's eyes on her, and his infuriating grin.

As if on cue, they heard a wagon pull up outside, and a moment later Detwiler came through the bat wings, carrying a small parlor table.

Bishop quickly informed the saloonkeeper about Bohannan's being cleared of the charges, his offer to help repair the saloon and his own intended visit to the lumber mill.

First, Detwiler was incredulous, then whooped and slapped Bohannan on the back. "If you ain't an answer to a prayer, I don't know what is! Sure, you kin have room an' board, can't he, Miss Ella?"

Ella knew she was being asked because the "board" part of the offer would have to come from her. What could she say but yes? Hopefully, the fellow wouldn't be there to eat into her profits for very long.

"'Course, the poker players won't like it too much, bein' so close together an' all, but I'll designate one table as bein' for poker and the players in one game can sit at opposite ends of the table from the players in another. Don't usually have more than a coupla games goin' at a time, anyhow. The first table you repair will be for faro, Mr. Bohannan. Must admit, it'll be good to have someone here at night to watch over the place when I leave," Detwiler enthused, and then the two men went to help the preacher bring in the chairs and boxes of dishes and silverware for the café.

After removing the debris from the café and salvaging what could be repaired, they left Ella alone to arrange the tables and chairs as she saw fit, and to put away the dishes, silverware and cups the preacher's and mayor's wives had sent. By the time she had the donated things set up to her satisfaction, she found that the sheriff had indeed succeeded in convincing the lumber mill owner to loan some planking and sawhorses, and the men were already setting them up. And Dayton had also agreed to let Bohannan use his lathe to repair the saloon's wrecked furniture. The hotel had contributed a few cast-off chairs from its storeroom, as well, so at least the poker players could sit, but the rest would have to stand until the chairs were repaired.

"There!" Detwiler said with a satisfied grin a little while later, clapping his hands together as he looked over the arrangement of the long tables and benches. "That'll do for a spell, I reckon." But he was speaking to Bohannan's back, for he had wandered over to study the piano against the wall.

Curious as to what he might be up to, Ella watched him as he studied the piano, plunking a few keys here and there.

"Nice piano, ain't it?" Detwiler said.

"It would be, but it's out of tune," Bohannan said.

"I used to have someone to play it at night when the saloon was crowded full of fellas playin' poker and drinkin' whiskey, but he moved on not long ago." Detwiler ran his hand along the piano top. "I've got the tuning stuff upstairs—the guy who sold me the piano left 'em—but I dunno how to tune it."

"Reckon I can help you with that, too. Just so happens I can tune a piano," Bohannan murmured.

Ella ground her teeth in frustration at the sight of Detwiler's round face all lit up. George set great store by his piano, and he was looking at Bohannan as if he'd hung the moon.

"Bohannan, this is turning into my lucky day!" Detwiler told him. "Don't suppose you kin play, too? If you'd agree to play for a couple of hours every night when the saloon is busiest, Nate, I could see my way clear to offering you an additional three dollars a week, over and above your room and board."

Ella watched Bohannan's face, which revealed nothing of what he was thinking.

It took an endless minute, but at last he shook his head. "I'm not one to spend my nights in a saloon. But I'll tune your piano, Mr. Detwiler. I can start on that right away."

Ella hadn't thought Bohannan would decline working in the saloon for money, and she felt her respect for him go up half a notch.

Bohannan straightened and turned from the piano. "So now that you have the problem of the furniture solved, what else do you need in order to open the saloon for business again?"

"Some glasses and whiskey. I buy the whiskey from a saloon in San Saba—the proprietor there orders extra for me." Detwiler turned to Ella. "Miss Ella, would you please go down to the mercantile and see if Mrs. Patterson would consider putting a case of glassware on my account? If we can get the saloon back in business, tell her I could settle with her in a few days."

Ella nodded. Anything to get away from these two men who had suddenly become allies and fast friends.

"Do you have any money saved up so you could go to San Saba and get some whiskey?" Bohannan asked Detwiler. "There's still a lot of daylight left. If you got some whiskey, and assuming the mercantile will give Miss Ella some glasses, you could have the saloon open by tomorrow."

Detwiler beamed as he dug through his pockets. "I reckon I got enough to buy some whiskey, all right—enough to get started, at any rate. I'll go fetch it, by gum!" He clapped Bohannan on the back again. "How did I ever get by without you, Nate?"

How indeed? Ella wondered sourly to herself. When would Detwiler remember that before Bohannan and Salali had come to town, the saloon had been intact and he had gotten along just fine?

To add to her ire, the two men never even noticed when she left.

Chapter Five

"Why, sure, George can pay me later for the glass-ware," Mrs. Patterson replied. "His mama would never speak to me again if I didn't give him credit. How about you, Ella? Don't you need some new plates and glasses? I heard that medicine-show man broke everything in your café, as well as the saloon."

"Mrs. Gilmore was kind enough to give me some extra, thanks," Ella said, and waved at her friend Kate, the proprietress's niece, who was dusting shelves.

Mrs. Patterson lifted a crate of glasses and placed them on the counter. "A saloon never lacks for business, even if we Christian folk wish people wouldn't spend their money on what they buy there," she said. "You take care, Ella. You're a hardworking girl."

Ella thanked her again and picked up the crate, nodding at Kate, who held the door for her. But she had walked only a few feet down the boardwalk when her way was blocked by the rotund form of Mrs. Powell, the cook from the hotel restaurant.

Ella's former boss narrowed her already beady eyes, making her cheeks look even fleshier than before. "*Humph.* It's gonna take a whole lot more than some new glasses to get that saloon runnin' again, and your café, too, from what I hear. You'll be back whinin' for your job any minute now, won't you, Ella?"

"Nope." She wouldn't go back to this woman's bullying if it was the last job in Texas. Mrs. Powell had made Ella's life miserable, and it had given Ella the impetus to start her own establishment sooner than it had probably been wise.

"Well, it's too late if you was to come beggin'," Mrs. Powell cackled. "That Trudy came and pleaded for a job, and I already have Daisy Henderson, too. I wouldn't hire you back anyway, the way you left us high and dry, with the clerk having to do double duty waiting on tables *and* registering hotel guests."

Ella couldn't imagine the lazy, free-and-easy Trudy in a gray waitress uniform, putting up with the cook's rantings. She wouldn't last till the end of the week, especially after she saw the saloon was back in business.

She tamped down her temper with difficulty. "The saloon *and* my café will be back open tomorrow. Now, if you don't mind, this crate is heavy and I have to get back there."

She had the satisfaction of seeing the woman's jaw drop, and knew she was wondering how reopening tomorrow would be possible.

"You're dreamin'—"

"I'll help you carry that crate, Miss Ella," interrupted a voice from the street.

She looked away from her tormentor to see Bohannan crossing toward her, reaching out for the crate.

"Why, thank you," Ella murmured, but she made sure her voice was brisk and businesslike. She hoped to get away from Mrs. Powell before the woman realized who Bohannan was. Ella wasn't sure if the cook had been among the throng flocking to the Cherokee Marvelous Medicine Show yesterday, but if she had been, Ella didn't want Mrs. Powell to figure out the man who had helped Salali fleece the townspeople of their money was the same one helping Detwiler now. The woman loved to gossip more than she loved to breathe, and if her tongue got going, it might slash Detwiler—and her—to ribbons.

Mrs. Powell's eyes narrowed again as Bohannan took the crate from Ella. "Say, ain't you the—"

Nate favored the cook with a quick, dazzling smile. "Good day, ma'am."

Together, they crossed the street to the saloon, with Ella sensing that Mrs. Powell still stared suspiciously at their backs. She knew she should be grateful that Bohannan had rescued her just now—the man had a positive *habit* of coming to the rescue, didn't he? Instead, she said, "I thought you were supposed to be tuning the piano."

Bohannan gave her a sideways glance. "I guess you're not going to thank me for interrupting that dragon's tirade," he said, "but after George left with the wagon for San Saba, I realized he hadn't told me just where in his office he kept the tuning tools. And I didn't feel right about rummaging in there without him or you present. After all, both of you just met me yesterday, and a lot's happened since then."

How did he do that? Ella wondered. How did he have a knack for bringing another person's fears out in the open like that so that the other person felt faintly foolish for having them? He was right—if she'd arrived back at the saloon and found Bohannan rifling through Detwiler's desk in his upper-story office, she'd have been suspicious all over again.

By now Bohannan was backing his way through the saloon's batwing doors, carrying the crate, with Ella following.

"All right, we'll go up to Detwiler's office and I'll stand there while you look for them," she said grudgingly. "Do you know what you're looking for?" She'd never seen a piano tuned, and had no idea what tools he needed.

Bohannan set the crate down at the foot of the stairs. "Sure. I'm hoping he has a tuning fork, a tuning hammer and mutes, at the minimum," he said, climbing the stairs alongside her. "What I furnish is this," he added, tapping his ear.

They reached the top of the stairs. The first room was Detwiler's office, and the two rooms at the other end of the hall were the ones Dolly and Trudy used. The room across the hall from the office was a spare room with a cot, and here was where Bohannan would sleep. How convenient—right across from the room where George Detwiler's safe resided. She'd have to warn the saloonkeeper to start taking his profits home with him at night, for Nate Bohannan might number safecracking among his many skills.

Bohannan paused right outside the office and was looking thoughtfully at her.

"Go ahead," she urged, pointing at the open room, wondering what he was thinking.

"Miss Ella, I'm aware you don't like me," Nate Bohannan said.

She blinked, astonished that he was exposing this feeling of hers, too. She was not going to allow him to make her feel guilty for being wary of him. Only a fool wouldn't be.

"It's not that I don't like you, Mr. Bohannan," she

retorted crisply. "I don't *trust* you. Not any farther than I could throw you."

"Yet George Detwiler does," he pointed out.

She gave a mirthless laugh. "So it's up to me to stay on my guard, since Mr. Detwiler trusts way too soon."

"What is he to you, anyway?" he asked. "You don't call him uncle, or Pa—he's not your beau, is he?"

The idea of George Detwiler being anyone's beau, let alone hers, was so laughable she almost forgot how audacious the question was, coming from this relative stranger.

"You have a lot of nerve, Mr. Bohannan. What business is that of yours?"

Speaking of nerve, she thought, the intensity in those blue eyes was decidedly *un*nerving. She was suddenly aware she was alone in the building with a man she'd just admitted she didn't trust.

He shrugged. "Just wondering, Miss Ella. Since we're going to be working in the same place, more or less, I just thought I'd ask. I like to know what's what."

If the circumstances had been different, she'd have reiterated that it was none of his business and flounced off, but she knew she had a responsibility to Detwiler to watch Bohannan search his office.

She extended her arm, pointing at the office. "Fetch what you need to get in there, Mr. Bohannan, and do it quickly. I have other things to do."

By the time Ella left Bohannan tuning the piano and returned to the boardinghouse, it was already almost suppertime. She would still have to get the ingredients organized for tomorrow's café meals after supper—but considering what had happened today, it was a miracle that she would be able to serve customers tomorrow at all.

"I'll set the table," she told Mrs. Meyer, the boardinghouse proprietress, as the woman stood putting final touches on the beef roast.

"And Ella and I will do the dishes afterward, so you can put your feet up," her fellow boarder Maude added, giving Ella a wink.

"*Ach,* you girls are so good to me," Mrs. Meyer said, shooting each a grateful smile.

"Nonsense, you work too hard," Ella said, but she admitted to herself she had an ulterior motive for taking over the after-supper cleanup. She and Maude could get it done much more quickly than the older woman would, enabling Ella to do her meal preparation for the next day sooner. Normally, she could do it at her café. And while she did the slicing, mixing, seasoning and preliminary cooking, she and Maude could talk about what had happened.

There would be eight at dinner this evening; besides Mrs. Meyer, Maude and Ella, there were the other boarders—Mr. Dixon, the undertaker, a pair of drummers, a stagecoach driver and Delbert Perry—if he showed up. No one had seen him since he'd gone strolling down the street the day before with his bottle of Cherokee Marvelous Medicine, and Mrs. Meyer, Maude and Ella were beginning to worry about what had happened to him. They planned to ask Mr. Dixon to look for him after supper if he didn't make an appearance.

But when Mr. Dixon arrived and sat himself down at his customary place at the foot of the table, he mentioned seeing Delbert shambling into the saloon.

Mrs. Meyer pursed her lips and *tsk-tsked.* "So he's drinking again. He'd better not think he will keep his place in my boardinghouse if he's going to be a drunkard again. I keep a decent establishment."

Another thing to blame Bohannan and Salali for, Ella thought grimly. Bohannan would see firsthand how his phony elixir affected one of his customers, assuming he was still there working on the piano. Not that he would be able to do anything about it. Perry would have to start that long road back to sobriety all over again.

"You've had quite a busy day, from what I hear," Maude said later, after the boardinghouse residents had left the table and Mrs. Meyer had gone out onto the porch to put her feet up.

Ella rolled her eyes. "That's the understatement of the year." She gave Maude a summary of the day's events, ending with Bohannan's being released from jail and agreeing to help repair the furniture and tune the saloon piano.

"Well, that was decent of him to stay and help like that," Maude said. "I guess he has a conscience along with that handsome face."

Ella stared at her friend. "Sounds like he's got you fooled, too." Ella knew Maude had only seen Bohannan once, when he'd been assisting with the medicine show. She hadn't even spoken to him, and she already believed he would do as he said he would. "Well, not me. I've already told him I don't trust him."

"Ella, give the man a chance," Maude said, her tone mild. "He sure didn't have to offer to help. You're always so suspicious of people. And you *did* admit he didn't want to play piano in the saloon."

Ella set her jaw and said nothing. She knew she tended to be untrusting of people's motives, but she had reason to be. Maude hadn't been through what she had. Maude had grown up the treasured only daughter of the town doctor, not a frightened orphan constantly in danger from the adults around her.

Maude may have had an easy childhood, but life hasn't been so easy for her lately, Ella's conscience reminded her. She'd seen her father cut down in the street by Comanche arrows, and she'd had to move to the boardinghouse when Dr. Walker became the doctor and moved into the attached house that went with the job, though she'd never complained.

"I'll give the man a chance," Ella said at last. "But I'm going to watch him like a hawk." She was aware she sounded grudging at best, but she wasn't about to trust someone just because he had twinkling blue eyes that did something funny to her heart.

Nate Bohannan figured it was going to be a long evening. Not only was the old piano resistant to being tuned, but his stomach kept reminding him that he'd only eaten once today, and that had been many hours ago. He wasn't about to seek Ella Justiss out and ask her for an advance on the "board" that was part of the deal. Something told him he was going to have to do something to prove himself, like providing Detwiler with a perfectly tuned piano, before the mistrustful miss with the dark eyes would ever smile at him the way she had when he'd rescued her from the lecherous saddle tramp. No, he was just going to have to wait until morning, when he hoped she would bring over breakfast.

He was just beginning to make progress when an older man dressed in worn, threadbare clothes walked into the saloon, introduced himself as Delbert Perry and asked him if he had any more bottles of Cherokee Marvelous Medicine.

"That sure was some great med'cine," Perry said. "Did me a world a' good." But his eyes told a different story, red-rimmed and anxious, and his hands trembled slightly.

"No, friend, I'm sorry, but we sold every bottle we had yesterday," Nate told him.

"Are you gonna make some more soon?" the other man asked hopefully.

Nate shook his head. "I wasn't the one who made the elixir—it was Mr. Salali, and he's gone. You probably heard what he did here last night."

Perry nodded, looking around him at the unfamiliar benches and sawhorse tables. "Yeah, I don't rightly understand that," he mumbled, his shoulders sagging.

Nate felt a renewed surge of guilt at being part of a shady enterprise. "You know, friend, I'm going to let you in on a little something," he said, lowering his voice as if he were about to impart a valuable secret. "That stuff really didn't do half of what it was supposed to do. You're better off without it."

Perry nodded slowly. "I 'spose you're right, mister. I figured it wouldn't hurt to ask, though." Without another word, he turned and trudged out of the saloon.

Never again, Nate thought. Never again would he get himself involved in something he knew to be dishonest.

Detwiler returned about an hour later, his buckboard loaded with several crates full of whiskey bottles. Nate had just finished tuning the piano, and ran his fingers over the keyboards to demonstrate.

"Sounds mighty fine," the saloonkeeper said. "I ran into a fella on the way back who might be able to come play most nights, so that's taken care of. Now, if you'll just help me carry these crates in, we'll lock up and call it a day."

Just as they'd stashed the last crate in the storeroom behind the bar, Nate's stomach rumbled so loudly that the other man couldn't help hearing it.

He chuckled. "Reckon you worked right on through supper, didn't you? Miss Ella didn't bring you any supper over from the boardinghouse?"

Nate shook his head. "I reckon she thought my meals were supposed to start tomorrow," he said. He didn't want to admit he didn't have even four bits to his name to go buy something to eat at the hotel. "Anyway, I don't think Miss Ella likes me very much, so I didn't want to ask." Not liking him was one thing, but he didn't want to tell the other man what the girl had actually said about not trusting him.

"Shucks, just give her some time. Miss Ella's a bit... shy, let's say, around menfolk she doesn't know, and she had a shock today, too, with what happened. Meanwhile, I'm headed home—Ma's got supper waitin' for me. She always makes plenty, so you come along with me and we'll see you get fed right enough."

"Oh, I don't think that's a good idea," he murmured. Nate could imagine how unwelcome it would be to have a stranger show up for supper, especially a stranger associated with the man who had wrecked the saloon. Detwiler's "Ma" had to be elderly, since the man himself looked to be forty or so.

"Horsefeathers. My ma's like the mother of this town, and she loves having folks to feed," George said. "Come on an' git in the wagon. Our house is just a hop an' a skip down the road leadin' south."

It felt good to be welcome, to belong. It had been a long time since Nate had felt that way.

Chapter Six

Nate was just descending the stairs into the saloon, intending to make an early start at fashioning new table and chair legs using the lathe at the lumber mill, when he heard a key being turned in the door inside the batwing doors. A few seconds later Ella entered, carrying a basket of eggs and a towel-covered bowl on top of a rectangular covered dish. The makings of breakfast, unless he missed his guess. His stomach rumbled in an eager response.

"Good morning, Miss Ella. Can I help you carry those into the café?" He took in her no-nonsense navy skirt and waist, and her equally serious face framed by dark hair braided and caught up in a practical knot at the back of her neck. Inexplicably, he found himself wondering what her hair would look like spread over her shoulders.

"Morning," she said. "No, I've got them, but it would help if you would open the door to the café for me."

When he had let her into the café, she turned to him. "Give me a few minutes, and you can have your breakfast, Mr. Bohannan."

She was back to formality, he noted. "That would

be very nice, Miss Ella. I wasn't sure if 'board' included breakfast or not." He wasn't about to tell her that George's mother had insisted he take a half-dozen leftover biscuits with him when he'd departed from the Detwiler house last night, and that he'd already devoured a couple of them this morning.

He waited until the smells of bacon frying and biscuits baking wafted into the saloon, and returned to the café, taking a chair at one of the tables. While he waited, he watched her efficient movements as she cracked and scrambled the eggs and poured them into a waiting skillet, then set up the plates and silverware for easy serving. He noticed she had brought a towel-wrapped stack of tortillas also.

"For the travelers and cowboys who pass who want something they can take with them and eat on the road," she explained, following his gaze. Then she dished up a generous helping of bacon, eggs and biscuits, and placed them in front of him, along with a small jar of preserves.

"Thank you, Miss Ella. It smells delicious." He dipped his fork into the fluffy eggs, and found that his nose hadn't deceived him. Silence descended as she stared out the window at the street behind the saloon.

"I...I hope you slept well last night, in spite of all that happened yesterday," he said, determined to penetrate her coolness.

Her reply was crisp. "As well as could be expected, under the circumstances."

They heard footsteps coming through the saloon and Detwiler appeared, and Ella dished out food for him, too.

"Mornin', Miss Ella. Ma said it did her heart good to watch you eat last night, Nate," George said with a chuckle.

Nate had been hoping George wouldn't mention his supper at the Detwilers' in front of Ella. It made him look as if he were going from person to person, mooching meals. He darted a quick glance at her, and sure enough, one eyebrow was raised as she poured George coffee. "It was mighty nice of her to invite me," he told George. "Please thank her again."

And then customers started showing up, and Ella got busy serving them, and she didn't appear to notice when Nate left to go to the lumber mill.

He found the mill past the school, nestled on the creek bank, just as Detwiler had said it would be, and located its proprietor, Hank Dayton, as dour and paunchy a man as the saloonkeeper had predicted.

"You'll be Bohannan from the saloon, needin' some two-by-twos and the use of the lathe. Sheriff told me you were comin'," Dayton said as if his customer's presence was something distasteful to be dealt with as soon as possible so he could be alone again. "You know how many you need, and how long to cut 'em?"

"Thirty-two, thirty inches long, just like this one," Nate said, holding out one table leg that had miraculously escaped the carnage. He was glad he'd done his figuring beforehand, for it didn't seem the taciturn Dayton had much patience. Twelve of the table legs were for Ella's tables, the rest for the saloon's. "And I'll need some planks I can trim and join into five sixty-inch round tabletops and four chair seats, but I'll work on the legs first."

Dayton just grunted, wiped his hands on his heavy canvas apron and motioned Bohannan to follow him. "You might as well help me saw until you've got enough to start with."

Within the hour, Nate was hard at work in a little

room off to the side of the main mill building, sanding lengths of wood and angling them at the end that would contact the floor so that the tables wouldn't wobble. He was rusty at first, having used his silver tongue much more of late than he'd used his hands, but before long he discovered a remembered pleasure in turning the wood from rough two-by-twos into smooth pieces fit for table legs.

The tables in the saloon, of course, would be fairly plain and utilitarian—the customers wouldn't care how ornate the table legs were so long as their cards and bottles stayed steady on the tabletop. He was able to fashion those fairly quickly, he discovered, as his hands rediscovered a long-unused skill with the lathe. He thought he might spend a little more time on the tables and chairs he made for the café. The ones Ella had had that day he'd come in and bought the sandwiches had been as plain as those in the saloon—in fact, they probably had been borrowed from there—but the ones on loan from the preacher's wife were full of fancy swirls and spindles and feet like talons clutching balls. Ladies, he knew, liked fancy details.

He imagined presenting Ella with new tables and chair legs that were curved and tapered—cabriole legs, his father had called them. Did his hands still possess enough talent to make such things? *And what will she say if I do?* As he worked, he imagined various ways she might react, then wondered why it mattered to him. He'd be riding on as soon as he'd finished the job, after all.

Nate worked steadily through the day, forgetting to go to the café for his meal at noon and ignoring his back's protest at the long hours bent over the lathe, until he had finished most of the table and chair legs for the saloon. He was startled, therefore, when Dayton wheeled in a low cart laden with planking for him to shape and join into tabletops, and informed him he was ready to lock up and go home for supper.

"Reckon I'll see you tomorrow, then," Nate told him. He would have asked if he could return after supper to work some more if he thought Dayton would trust him in the mill alone, but the man didn't seem like the trusting sort.

"Nope, you won't. Tomorrow's Sunday, and the mill's closed. Reckon you might meet my missus at church, if you're a churchgoin' man—she'll be there with the young'uns, but once she gets those squallin' brats outta the house, that's *my* time to get some extra shut-eye," Dayton announced proudly, as if avoiding church was a virtue.

Tomorrow is Sunday? Nate was surprised once again. He and Salali had kept track of Sundays only to avoid staging medicine shows on that day, for conducting business on the Sabbath was apt to offend decent folks. He couldn't think when he'd last darkened the door of a church.

But if he didn't attend church, what would he do with himself all morning?

Nate figured the noise from the saloon would keep him awake for a while tonight. He wasn't sure how long Detwiler kept his establishment open—it probably depended on the thirst of the clientele on any given evening. Tonight the drinkers and gamblers would no doubt be celebrating the reopening of the saloon. And since it was Saturday, there'd be cowboys in from the ranches enjoying time away from their chores.

No matter how late he went to bed, though, his lids just naturally tended to fly open at dawn. He wasn't one to lie abed like the lumber mill owner.

Did Ella attend church? Did she ever let herself rest that much, or would she be serving breakfast, then dinner, to travelers passing through town? If she *was* a churchgoing woman, what would she say if he were to show up there?

It might go a long way to allay her suspicion of him, to see him warming a pew.

On the other hand, though, would the Lord think him a hypocrite, going to church after living a lie for so long?

Ella just happened to be bringing Detwiler's supper in to him in the saloon—a favor she did so he could continue to be available to any early-evening customers—when Bohannan entered carrying a tied stack of newly turned table and chair legs with him over one shoulder as if he were a conqueror laden with booty. She noted he also carried a brown-paper–wrapped parcel as if he'd made a stop at the mercantile.

Detwiler whistled. "You've been busy," he said admiringly.

Bohannan grinned. "That I have. I'll take them back with me in the morning since I'll need to join them to the tabletops and chair seats when those are done, but I thought I'd make sure you approve of how I'm doing them before they're varnished."

As if Bohannan thought there was anything to disapprove of, Ella thought waspishly, seeing the saloonkeeper run a hand over the even, sanded surfaces of a couple of chair legs.

"*Whoo-ee,* these are smooth as a baby's—" Detwiler darted a hasty glance at Ella "—um, cheek. The only problem with these is they're too *good* for my customers," he added with a chuckle, keeping his voice low so it didn't carry to a couple of cowboys lounging at one of the long tables.

Ella managed to stifle an unladylike snort at the fulsome compliments, but she could see that Bohannan had done quality work.

"Dare I hope there's some of that for me?" Bohannan asked, with a nod toward the plate of roast beef and mashed potatoes she was still holding.

Ella set it down on the bar. "You *should* have had to eat the cold chicken I kept by for you at noontime," she told him tartly. "But you never showed up. I finally ate it myself."

He had the grace to look abashed. "I'm sorry about that, Miss Ella. I got caught up in what I was doing, once I got started at the lathe. Next time, I'll either come back at noon, or maybe take some extra breakfast with me, all right?"

Who could stay irritated at a man who could smile like that? His smile seemed to know the path straight to her heart, unfortunately for her.

"Come on back to the café after you wash up," she said, turning on her heel. Over her shoulder, she added, "By the way, you might want to rinse the sawdust out of your hair while you're at it."

Ten minutes later, freshly shaved, his damp hair curling, he entered the café and sat down at one of the tables. He was wearing a new white shirt, she noted, one that looked like the ready-made ones sold at the mercantile, along with the silver brocade vest he'd had on the first day he came to town. The shirt was what had been in the package he'd been carrying, she realized, remembering that Salali had robbed him of everything but the clothes he'd been wearing. She thought he must have sweet-talked Mrs. Patterson into advancing him the cost of it, since he'd said the medicine-show man had picked his pockets, too.

She managed to refrain from telling him he cleaned up well by busying herself with dishing up his food.

"This is delicious, Miss Ella," he said, looking up from his supper. "Thank you."

"You're welcome," she murmured automatically, but she avoided his eyes. Just then a trio of cowboys came in and sat down at the other table, so she was spared the necessity of making polite conversation with him. But she could feel his gaze on her as she waited on the other men, and he lingered over his meal and a second cup of coffee until the three had finished and left.

But it didn't seem as though he'd been waiting to talk with her, for as soon as her other customers had gone out the door, he arose.

"Reckon I'll go take a walk before I turn in," he said. He paused as if about to say something, then turned and walked out her door.

Had he remained at his table to protect her while the cowboys had been there, since he'd had to rescue her from the saddle tramp the day they'd met? The idea touched her in a way she didn't want to admit.

Half a dozen more diners came in before she was ready to close, and while she served them, the sounds of clinking glasses and rough laughter, as well as the stench of cigar smoke, drifted back into the café. For the thousandth time she wished she had been able to open her café elsewhere. She'd asked Mrs. Patterson, for the mercantile had a back room, and Detwiler had been willing to sell her his stove, but Mrs. Patterson had claimed she planned on expanding the mercantile and couldn't spare the space.

Someday she'd have her café in its own building, she promised herself. Someday.

After turning the card on the back door of the café to Closed, she washed the dishes, but instead of locking up and returning to the boardinghouse as she usually did, Ella found herself dawdling. She wiped down tables and chairs she'd already cleaned while she pictured Bohannan strolling by the creek, watching hungry bluegills jumping at dragonflies, or looking at the little fort that was built in the back lot of Mrs. Detwiler's property, the one that had saved so many townspeople during the Comanche attack a couple of years ago.

If she left now, would she run into him returning from his perambulation? Would he share his impressions of the town?

How silly of her to be thinking that way. He was nothing to her. She should get a jump on Sunday-dinner preparations. She didn't open the café on Sunday morning, preferring to take breakfast at the boardinghouse and get ready for church. She missed some business that way, but probably not much, and she wanted to prepare her heart for what the Lord might say to her through worship.

But she realized suddenly that Bohannan might not know the café was closed on Sunday morning, and would come down expecting breakfast. Why the thought of him going hungry till after church should bother her, she didn't know. He hadn't cared enough to show up at midday, after all. She didn't like feeling responsible for another person, particularly not a male person. When had a man ever worried about her, except for what she could provide for him?

Nevertheless, she found herself slicing roast beef and bread for a sandwich and wrapping it up in a cloth.

There. She'd done the right thing, the Christian thing. She walked quietly out into the saloon, careful not to draw the attention of any of its customers.

She stepped over to Detwiler, who was leaning on the bar, and laid the sandwich beside him.

"This is for Bohannan," Ella told him. "Would you give this to him when he comes back from his walk, please? I forgot to tell him I don't serve breakfast at the café on Sunday. We wouldn't want him to starve before the café opens after church, would we?"

Detwiler grinned as he looked down at it, then back up at her. "*Noooo,* we wouldn't," he said. "That was right considerate of you, Miss Ella."

She felt herself flushing. Why, George Detwiler thought she'd left Bohannan food because she was sweet on the man! She knew that any attempt at denying an accusation the saloonkeeper hadn't actually made, though, might look as if she was protesting too much, so she merely tightened her lips and retraced her steps back through the darkened café and out into the alley, head held high.

"Men are such contrary creatures," she grumbled.

Chapter Seven

Nate donned the shirt he'd bought from the mercantile yesterday, leaving his other everyday shirt hanging on a hook on the wall. He'd used some of Ella's soap and had soaked it in an empty bucket he'd found last night when he returned from his walk and found Miss Ella gone. It'd be dry by the time he returned to work at the lumber mill tomorrow. It had been nice of Detwiler to gift him with the four bits it had cost for the shirt.

Unable to sleep once the saloon fell quiet about midnight, he'd gone down and played the piano he'd tuned, letting his fingers rove over the keys and playing lush romantic tunes like "Jeanie with the Light Brown Hair" and "Beautiful Dreamer." The raucous crowd that had populated the place earlier likely wouldn't have appreciated such music, but this music was more to his taste than "Camptown Races" or the other bouncy tunes he'd recognized from the minstrel shows he'd played with for a time.

He'd gone to bed after that, only to dream of Ella Justiss standing beside him as he'd played. *Fool. Why would she care to listen to me play, let alone gaze adoringly at me while I did so?*

Now he brushed the last crumbs of his breakfast sandwich off his trousers. He'd been surprised when Detwiler had given him the wrapped sandwich last night after the final customer had left, and he hadn't missed the wink the saloonkeeper had bestowed on him.

Obviously the other man thought Miss Ella's action revealed some deeper feelings on her part, but Nate suspected she was just adhering to the "deal"—Detwiler provided lodging, Miss Ella provided food, until Nate finished his part of the bargain. It was nothing more. So why had her making sure he had something for breakfast left him with such a warm feeling?

It was time to go. He'd learned when the church service began from Detwiler, who assured Nate he was welcome to sit with him and his mother. He stepped out into the street, careful to avoid anything that might sully his freshly cleaned boots until he could reach the boardwalk.

The number of townsfolk heading for the church at the east end of town increased as he passed the mercantile and murmured good-morning to Mrs. Patterson and her niece. The proprietress returned his greeting.

No one else spoke to him, but he didn't think much about it until he reached the lawn of the church. There, a wizened old man, standing at the edge of a chattering cluster of people, narrowed his eyes and stared at him, long and deliberately. Then he spat into the grass and jiggled the elbow of a rotund woman next to him.

Nate recognized the cook from the hotel, the one who had berated Ella on the street. The old man pointed right at Nate.

Uh-oh. It'd been a mistake to wear the silver vest, Nate thought. Because of it, the old codger had recognized him as one of the medicine-show salesmen. No doubt he and the woman had bought some of the elixir, and after realizing they'd been sedated for a while but not miraculously cured, they were no longer satisfied customers.

Nate looked away from them, hoping the two wouldn't express their displeasure further. His gaze landed on Ella, who was accompanied by a red-haired lady, entering the churchyard from Travis, the street behind Main Street.

The simple tan, brown-trimmed dress should have been dowdy and plain, but somehow it perfectly complemented Ella's glossy, dark hair and eyes and petite figure.

She looked at him then, as if she'd felt his gaze like a touch.

Nate nodded in her direction, not risking a smile. It was possible that she wouldn't want to acknowledge him away from her café. She gave him a cautious half smile in return.

But the redhead, following Ella's gaze, widened her eyes and started tugging Ella toward him. Ella seemed to be resisting. He was interested to know who would win the struggle, but just then he was struck by a verbal volley from the old man.

"You got your nerve comin' t' church like you done nothin' wrong," he growled, baring yellowed teeth. "Why, I ain't felt right since I sipped the first drop of that evil brew you dare t' call *medicine!*" He spat again, and the viscid stream landed perilously close to Nate's trouser leg.

"Zeke's right," the old woman snarled, emboldened by the man's attack. "That stuff left me weak in the head and so dizzy I could hardly stagger to the doctor's."

Another in the group took up the cry. "You show

up at church like you got a right t'be here, same as the rest of us God-fearin' folks? You ought to be ashamed, mister, after defrauding us of our hard-earned money! My husband slept for fifteen hours straight after he drank that bottle! I liketa never woke him this side of the pearly gates!"

Nate knew before he spoke it would be futile. "He drank the whole bottle? Madam, neither Mr. Salali nor I told him to drink so much at one time," he protested. "In his presentations, my former employer always made it a point to say a person should take no more than a tablespoonful, two at the most, in a day."

Salali shouldn't have made it taste so good, blast his hide. Nate guessed the woman's spouse must have thought if two spoonfuls were good, the whole bottle might work wonders.

"He's defendin' that scalawag!" a stocky middle-aged man crowed. "The very one that wrecked the saloon! This fella was probably in on it."

"I'm not—" Nate began, then shut his mouth. This had been a mistake. He shouldn't have come. Not daring to look to see Ella's reaction, he started to turn on his heel and retreat to the saloon, only to find himself taken by the elbow.

"Now, just a cotton-pickin' minute, y'all. That's not how we treat folks coming to our church," Mrs. Detwiler, still holding on to him, boomed.

Her voice was trumpet-like. Nate half expected the occupants of the graves beneath the weathered tombstones beside the church to emerge in response.

"Mr. Bohannan was a victim of that Salali fella, too," she reminded them. "The Injun-elixir peddler robbed him and left him for dead right over yonder," she added, pointing to the meadow beyond the creek while her eyes roved the complainers as if she dared anyone to disagree.

Nate thought "left him for dead" might be overstating the case, but before he could ponder it further, George Detwiler spoke up. "Yeah, and he's workin' to repair the damage that man did to my establishment. He didn't have t'do that. He could've just skedaddled."

Reverend Chadwick and his wife appeared, seemingly from out of nowhere.

"Mr. Bohannan, you are most welcome to our church," the reverend said, extending his hand.

"Yes, we're happy that you're here," Mrs. Chadwick added, her smile sweet and sincere.

"Thank you, Reverend, Mrs. Chadwick," Nate murmured, and then felt a timid touch on his other arm. He looked down to see Ella standing there, with the red-haired woman next to her.

"Mr. Bohannan, I'd like you to meet my friend, Miss Maude Harkey," she said, her gaze steady, her voice unwavering. "Maude and I would be pleased if you'd sit with us," she said, nodding toward the church door.

The murmuring crowd fell silent.

If Ella had said the moon was made of green cheese, Nate would not have been more astonished.

"I'd be honored, ladies," he said. "Please lead the way."

They settled themselves in a pew in the middle of the small church, Maude first, then Ella, then Nate. Mrs. Detwiler and her son sat on Nate's other side. A solid show of support, Nate thought, amazed by this turn of events.

Ella was looking straight ahead.

"Thank you," he whispered to her. "That was very kind of you both."

She half turned toward him. "I only did what's right," she said evenly. "People aren't supposed to act the way those folks did outside then expect the Lord to hear their prayers."

"I agree," Maude said.

Nor were folks supposed to sell worthless potions and tout them as wonder-working cure-alls, Nate thought, ashamed all over again that he had ever associated himself with the likes of Robert Salali. He didn't deserve his pewmates' support.

He felt even guiltier when the preacher announced his text. "Be not forgetful to entertain strangers, for thereby some have entertained angels unawares."

Had the text been selected beforehand, or was the preacher rebuking those of his congregation who had given Nate such a hard time outside? Either way, he knew he was certainly no angel in disguise.

He caught Ella looking at him out of the corner of her eye, and guessed that she was also thinking he wasn't any such creature. But he met her eyes nonetheless and gave her a deliberate wink—to which she responded with an indignant huff and turned back to stare straight ahead at the preacher.

Caught up in pondering why some citizens of Simpson Creek were being so kind to him, while others had given him what he considered his just deserts before church, he didn't hear much of the rest of the sermon, and before he knew it, the service was over.

As soon as the last notes of the closing hymn died away, Mrs. Detwiler turned to him. "Would you like to come for Sunday dinner? If you're one of those celestial beings the preacher was referrin' to, I don't want to miss another chance to entertain ya, Mr. Bohannan."

"I assure you I'm not," he said, smiling. "May I come

another time? I was planning to partake of one of Miss Ella's delicious dinners," he explained. He turned to Ella, to see what her reaction was to his words, only to find her already scooting out of the pew as if she hadn't even heard him.

"Miss Ella?" he called after her.

"I have to go start dinner at the café," she explained, and kept moving, greeting others who reached out to her, but never pausing to chat.

Next to Nate, Mrs. Detwiler said, "That is one busy gal. I feel sorry for her, havin' to work so hard all the time, with no family in town to lean on. But she doesn't want anyone's sympathy—she just goes on workin' hard. She's a member of the Spinsters' Club an' all, but she hardly ever gets to take part in their activities."

"The…Spinsters' Club?" Nate repeated. "What's that?"

"You ain't heard a' them? Well, I reckon you ain't been in town long enough," George Detwiler said. "It was started by Milly Matthews—Milly Brookfield, she is now. We didn't have no single men here after the war—'ceptin' me, and I ain't no marryin' sort," he added with a chuckle.

"Which I never understood," his mother said. "What man doesn't want to get married and give his ma grand-children?"

"Aw, Ma, none o' these ladies want to marry a saloonkeeper," George protested, then went back to what he'd been saying to Nate. "Anyway, Milly figured she and the others would never git t' marry *and* stay in Simpson Creek less'n they did something, so they started advertisin' for mail-order grooms. They started bringin' eligible bachelors to Simpson Creek. Miss Milly was the first to succeed, marryin' an En-

Laurie Kingery

glishman, of all things. Now several of 'em have gotten hitched."

"There's Milly Brookfield and her husband now," said Mrs. Detwiler, nodding toward a pretty young matron who was holding a little boy while she and a man Nate presumed to be her husband spoke with the preacher and his wife. "Let me start introducin' you to the folks ya haven't met."

"Thanks, but they might not want to meet me, after what my employer did," he said. He wasn't eager to experience a repeat of the confrontation before church. The preacher's "angels unaware" sermon wouldn't really change anyone's mind about him; they might just be more apt to keep their contempt to themselves. Besides, he had wanted to follow Ella to the café and be one of her first customers, before the after-church folks got there. Maybe he could even get her to talk to him before she got busy, so he could determine if her change of heart toward him was permanent.

But Mrs. Detwiler was not to be gainsaid. "Nonsense, the Brookfields were out on their ranch when you an' that Salali fella were sellin' your potion, and even if they hadn't been, neither of them has a mean bone in their bodies. C'mon."

Mrs. Brookfield and her husband, who was indeed English, proved to be just as welcoming and friendly as Mrs. Detwiler had promised. Then a pretty blonde lady, the one who'd been playing the piano during the hymn singing, joined them, and Milly introduced her as her sister, Mrs. Sarah Walker, wife of the town doctor.

"Welcome to Simpson Creek, Mr. Bohannan," Sarah Walker said. "George tells me you're quite the piano player."

"I was still workin' in the office upstairs when you

went down and started playin' last night," Detwiler said with a grin. "You've got talent, Bohannan. And don't look so worried—it's nothing to me if you don't want to play for the yahoos that frequent my establishment. Shorty Ledbetter was glad to get the job playin' for 'em. But he don't have a lick of your ability, you know."

"Perhaps we should let the preacher know you can play, in case I'm unable to some Sunday," Sarah Walker said then.

Nate was astonished that she'd even suggest such a thing. *Nate Bohannan, playing hymns? Surely the church would be hit by lightning.* "Thank you, Mrs. Walker, but I'm not even sure how long I'll be staying in town. And in any case, my ability doesn't extend itself to church music," Nate said.

"Nonsense. I'm sure you could do it, if need be," Sarah Walker said. "Don't hide your light under a bushel basket, Mr. Bohannan. I might be needing some time off in a few months." The color rose in her fair cheeks.

An auburn-haired man, who carried a sleeping baby on his shoulder, smiled proudly down at her, then up at Nate. "Yes, my wife will need to take some time off in a few months, so you might well be needed to play some Sunday mornings then. I'm Nolan Walker," he added, extending his hand.

Nate blinked. The town doctor. He must not know Nate had recently been peddling snake oil. He wouldn't be nearly so cordial if he knew.

Something in Nate compelled him to be honest. "Dr. Walker," he said, shaking the proffered hand. "I'm honored, sir, but I have to confess, I—"

The other man held up his free hand and interrupted. "I know all about the Cherokee Marvelous Medicine you and that other fellow were selling. But I also know that didn't work out so well for you, and you're no longer doing it," Nolan Walker said, looking him steadily in the eye. "Many of us find we have to change course in life, Mr. Bohannan. So we're glad to have you."

Nate got the feeling Dr. Walker was speaking from experience. "Well, I'm not sure how long I'll be here, but—"

Before he could finish his sentence, he was being introduced to someone else, then someone else, and someone else, and by the time he bid farewell to Mrs. Detwiler and her son, he and they were nearly the last ones to leave the churchyard. Without exception, everyone he'd encountered had been kind and friendly—if one didn't count the hotel cook, who walked past him and sniffed, "'Angels unaware'—*humph!*"

And he *didn't* want to count that woman. He'd prefer to think the typical citizen of Simpson Creek was more like the ones he'd met after church, willing to forgive and judge for themselves what sort of man he was, based on his current actions. Willing to give a fellow a fresh start, a clean slate.

Why that mattered to him when he wasn't going to stay, he couldn't say.

Just as he and the Detwilers parted ways, his stomach rumbled for the dozenth time. Sneaking a look at his timepiece, he saw that it was nearly one o'clock. He'd better get a move on, or he'd miss dinner entirely—and the chance to thank Ella for taking his side this morning.

Was this the start of smoother dealings with the prickly girl? He certainly hoped so.

Chapter Eight

Ella hoped Bohannan wouldn't come, hoped that the Detwilers or someone else had taken him under their wing and asked him to Sunday dinner. She didn't want him to think that inviting him to sit with her and Maude meant everything was different between them. She'd never set out to champion a snake-oil peddler—*former* snake-oil peddler, she corrected herself—but neither could she allow him to be verbally torn apart by the likes of old Zeke Carter and Mrs. Powell.

She began to think her wish had been granted when the café filled up and none of the eager, expectant faces was Bohannan's. Dinner was ready to dish out. Folks were lined up at her counter, with the queue stretching out into the alley behind the saloon. Her three tables were occupied.

Most of her customers on Sunday afternoon wanted something that was easy to eat on the road as they travelled home from church, so she had made sandwiches ahead that she could wrap in brown paper and sell along with jars of cold tea. But her tables were always full, too, for others wanted to eat before they set out for their homes, and more cheaply than they could at the hotel.

It was a challenge to keep those at the tables satisfied with refills of their tea or coffee and keep the sandwich line moving at the same time.

I'm just one person, she wanted to protest when a mustachioed man huffed impatiently at a table, holding aloft an empty coffee cup. It wasn't as if she could afford to hire a helper. She needed every penny she could earn if she was ever to break out of this tiny back room of the saloon and have her own establishment. Sunday noontimes always left her feeling as though she'd been trampled by a herd of stampeding cattle. Her apron pocket was considerably heavier with coin, though, by the time she returned to the boardinghouse. At least on Sundays she didn't get the rowdy, drunken customers from the saloon.

She heard a stir of air and a rustling among the queue of waiting customers, but she was too busy wrapping sandwiches to look up. Then suddenly Bohannan stood at the head of the line, next to the woman who was paying for her order.

"Miss Ella—"

"Now see here, Mr. Bohannan, you can't just jump to the head of the line like that," she snapped. "I know you're entitled to a meal, but those in line have been waiting patiently—"

"I'm not trying to ditch the line, Miss Ella," he told her, his tone mild as milk. "I can see you need help, and I want to offer it. We can get everyone served faster if I help you. Do you want me to take the money or serve the food?"

Neither, she started to say. *There is no "we." I can handle this myself, as I always do.* But before she said it, she realized how foolish it would be to refuse. Already those in line were looking hopeful that their hunger could be satisfied more quickly.

"Take the money, please," she said at last. "Two bits for a sandwich, ten cents for a jar of tea, a nickel if they've brought a jar back." Surely she could manage to keep coffee cups refilled and sandwiches made and wrapped up if he was taking the money. At least she could if the little Harding boy would stop dropping his fork and spilling his glass of milk.

Soon she and Bohannan had established a rhythm, and before long the line at the counter had evaporated. Those who'd occupied tables were leaving with satisfied smiles.

He pushed a pile of coins over to her across the counter. "I'm afraid I wasn't able to keep any sort of tally," he said, "but—"

"I'm sure it's correct," she said. Her tone came out more prim than she had intended, as if only her presence had kept him from diverting some of the money to his own pocket. Feeling guilty, Ella softened her voice. "Would you like some dinner, now that you've been kind enough to help me?" She would fill his plate extra full to thank him.

"I wouldn't mind," he said with a grin, "though I'd begun to worry there wouldn't be anything left. You were busier than a barefoot boy on a red-ant hill in here today."

She smiled at the image. "There's plenty of fried chicken and biscuits and mashed potatoes left, as you can see," she said, pointing to the big platters. "Yes, I do quite a good business in here on Sundays—much to Mrs. Powell's dismay," she said with a triumphant grin. "Before my café opened, Simpson Creek folks used to have to wait for a table at the hotel restaurant or eat at home."

He watched as Ella heaped his plate. "Will you sit down and have some, too? You've got to be hungry, yourself," he said.

"I'll eat later," she said. The idea of sitting right across a small table from him and sharing a meal felt much too intimate. "Right now, there are dishes to do." She pointed to the stack of soiled dishes, silverware and cups on the back counter.

"I'll help with those, too. Get some food, Miss Ella, and keep me company."

Ella knew she shouldn't. She should continue to keep some distance between them. She was about to decline politely, when her stomach betrayed her with a growl. She tried to smother it, but she was too late. She blushed.

He grinned. "Sounds like you need some dinner, Miss Ella. Please join me."

She gave in. "All right. Since you were kind enough to help me instead of merely taking your food and leaving."

"It was my pleasure to help," he said as he held her chair for her.

No man had ever held her chair for her. It was ridiculous that he did so here, in her own establishment. Nevertheless, she felt a flush of pleasure as she sat down.

"Besides, it wasn't as if I had to rush off anywhere," Bohannan continued, "since the saloon is closed."

Ella couldn't help smiling at that. "I don't know what saloonkeepers do in other towns, but George Detwiler's mama made him promise to respect the Lord's Day."

"And the mill's closed, too, so I can't even work on the furniture," he said with a shrug.

Goodness, she couldn't remember when she'd had a free afternoon stretching out in front of her like that. Now that she was in business for herself, as soon as she finished cleaning up the dishes from a meal she'd just served, it was time to start working on the next one— day after day.

She wondered what Bohannan would do with his time. It was a beautiful early-fall day, cooler than it had been. Would he take a stroll around Simpson Creek since he didn't have a horse? Or perhaps he'd go upstairs after she left and take a nap. How nice it must be to be able to choose how one spent one's leisure.

If she were the one choosing, a nap would be her choice. It sounded like an unbelievable luxury to just lie down in the middle of the day and let the world go on without her participation.

She wasn't aware she had sighed out loud until he said, "What's the matter, Miss Ella? Is my company that dreary?"

His tone was teasing, not hurt. She didn't dare look up. His blue eyes saw too much.

"Not at all, Mr. Bohannan." She thought about making up something that she had sighed about, but that wouldn't be right. She gathered up their empty dishes and silverware and added them to the pile left by the customers.

"If you must know, I was envying you your leisure this afternoon," she admitted as she brought over the big kettle full of water she'd left heating on the stove for washing the dishes.

"My leisure?" He pulled a length of toweling down from a hook on the wall and stood poised to do the drying.

"Sure. You can do anything you like, but I need to

figure out what I'm going to cook for supper. I don't get too many customers on a Sunday evening, but there are always a few." Including cranky old Zeke Carter, the man who had given Nate such a hard time this morning, she thought with a twinge of irritation. Zeke took Sunday dinner with his married daughter, but he turned up hungry, regular as clockwork, every Sunday evening. "It doesn't look as if there'll be enough chicken left, though I suppose I could fry those chicken livers…" She eyed the bowl full of chicken innards she'd left in a covered dish at the back of the stove, but the idea held little appeal.

"Are there catfish in the creek?" he asked.

For a moment she could only blink at him in confusion. His question seemed like a complete non sequitur. But he must have a reason for asking it. She remembered a time when she'd seen a pair of boys walk past, coming from the creek, with a trio of fish on a stringer. She'd recognized them as catfish from the characteristic barbels around their gaping mouths.

"Yes, I think so, but what does that have to do—"

"What about fried catfish for dinner? Wouldn't that taste good, with some breading and seasoning, maybe some biscuits to go with it?"

"But I don't have any catfish," she said, gaping at him. "Or even a fishing pole, for that matter, and I only have a few hours before—"

"Time enough," he said. "How about we go fishing as soon as we get done with these dishes?"

She could only stare at him. "Me? Go fishing with you? But you don't have any poles," she pointed out.

"George told me he'd stashed some cane poles in the shed out back," he said. "He keeps them in case he ever feels like fishing."

"We don't have any bait," she said, fighting the dangerous appeal that an hour or two spent sitting on the shady bank of Simpson Creek with this man held for her. And the thought of fried catfish, breaded, seasoned and hot off the griddle made her mouth water. There was something so compelling about this man—it made all her common-sense resolutions to avoid him fly out the window.

"Chicken livers are the best catfish bait in the world," he told her.

"But I'm wearing my Sunday best," she said thinking of the grass stains and mud that she'd have to scrub out over Mrs. Meyer's washboard.

If she thought her continued objections would discourage him, he proved her wrong. "Go back to the boardinghouse and change," he told her.

"But by the time—"

"By the time you go change, I can have these dishes redded up and ready to go for supper, *and* I'll be ready and waiting with the poles. Now, scoot," he added, grinning, brandishing the towel as if he meant to snap her with it.

She scooted, fighting an uncharacteristic urge to laugh as she ran out the back door.

Ella was back, dressed in a dark skirt and waist and carrying a folded bit of cloth that she held out to him as he emerged from Detwiler's shed, poles in hand.

"Mrs. Meyer sent this old shirt of her late husband's for you to wear so you wouldn't have to get yours dirty," she said.

"That was right thoughtful of her," he said, taking it from her.

"She says she'll take any fish we—that is, *I*—" she

looked flustered as she corrected herself "—have left over after supper."

The garment was musty smelling, as if it had been put away in a trunk for a score of years. Mr. Meyer must have been a bit wider than him, too, he thought, studying it, but he couldn't afford to be too particular.

Two minutes later, they were walking down the main street of Simpson Creek, poles slung over their shoulders, with Nate carrying the pail full of chicken livers.

"We have to be back by five so I can be ready to serve at six," Ella said, looking slightly anxious. "It was two-thirty on the grandfather clock in the boardinghouse parlor when I left. I don't suppose you have a pocket watch? Oh, no, I'm sorry—I forgot Salali took all your things, Mr. Bohannan," she added quickly. "Forgive my question, please."

He felt a twinge of guilt, thinking of the gold pocket watch that after church he'd hidden away under a loose floorboard in his room above the saloon. If anyone knew he still had a valuable gold pocket watch and chain, they'd wonder why he didn't sell it to repay Detwiler and Ella for the damage to the saloon and café, and he'd have no source of investment money for when he reached California.

"Don't worry, I can keep track of what time it is by looking at the sun," he told her. "But we'll probably catch a mess of catfish in an hour or so and leave the creek in plenty of time."

She still looked doubtful. Evidently his confidence wasn't catching.

"I always heard it was best to go fishing at dawn or dusk," she said as they passed the mercantile. She waved to Mrs. Patterson, who was sweeping the dust from her doorstep.

"It is, but catfish like chicken livers so much they won't mind," he assured her. "Besides, what's the worst that can happen? If we don't catch anything, you could always serve eggs and pancakes, couldn't you?"

"I suppose so…"

They had passed the church and walked another quarter mile downstream so as to be away from a trio of noisy boys who had fishing lines in the water but who seemed to be accomplishing little but skipping rocks and horseplay.

"No more doubts," he told her firmly as they descended the shallow slope of the creek. He pointed at the water. "The fish can hear you, you know." He winked.

Just then, a hungry bluegill jumped out of the water, going after a horsefly that had hovered too close to the surface. Her heart leaped the same way.

His charming ways are a danger to me. What am I doing here, alone with a man I know I have no reason to trust? He was a drifter, a jack-of-all-trades, who'd stay in Simpson Creek until it suited him to be elsewhere. It would be foolish of her to depend on him, and she had never been a foolish girl.

She wouldn't let herself become accustomed to his presence, Ella resolved as he cut up the bait into smaller pieces and baited their hooks. Men never stayed. Still, she couldn't deny it was pleasant having nothing more to do for the next couple of hours than sit on the bank, appreciating the bright, clear day and watching the creek flow by, for Bohannan apparently held to the fisherman's dictum that one couldn't be chattering and expect to catch fish.

Just as well. She had been afraid that with no one else around, and nothing else to do but feel for a tug on his line, he would give vent to curiosity and ask her where she had come from, about her people, her home, her schooling. That was information she shared with no one, not even her friends in the Spinsters' Club. She was always vague when anyone inquired about these things. Why would she want to admit that she had no people and no home, and had been raised in an orphanage, with only the barest, catch-as-catch-can sort of education? Most of the Spinsters' Club members had been living in Simpson Creek all their lives, and had never had to make up stories about who their parents were because they had been loved and sheltered by them since birth.

But maybe Nate Bohannan had a past he wasn't proud of, too. Maybe, in addition to his shady medicine-show partnership, he'd been involved in things even worse, things that might have put his face on a wanted poster.

She stole a glance at him as she pondered these things. He seemed intent on watching the spot where his fishing line met the water, so for a moment she studied his high, angular cheekbones, his long, slightly aquiline nose, the way his lips tightened as he watched the water.

"Ella..." he murmured, not taking his eyes from the creek.

She yanked her gaze away from him, and pretended she had been studying the way the sun peeked through the cottonwoods and live oaks to dapple the shade at her feet.

"What?"

"I think you have a bite."

Chapter Nine

Ella gave a little shriek and yanked the pole upward as the line traveled out into the creek. He thought the fish might come off the line, but it had apparently swallowed the hook well, for in a moment the fish, flopping wildly, was hoisted free of the water.

"I caught a fish! My very first one!" she cried.

She was laughing and squealing at once, and he couldn't help grinning at her excitement as he helped her swing the pole toward them and land the big cat. He figured it had to be three pounds if it was an ounce.

"You've never caught a fish before?" he asked. "Well, it's a very big fish for your first catch. Must be beginner's luck that you caught one before I did," he teased. He saw that she looked away, shuddering, as the fish flopped on the bank, its gills flapping in and out. To spare her, he unhooked the fish and put it on the stringer, then resubmerged it in the creek after tying the other end to a bush.

"You didn't have any brothers or a papa who took you fishing?" he asked.

"No." Her one word sank between them like a heavy stone dropped straight down into water.

Even though she avoided his eyes, Nate knew by the way her lips tightened that he'd strayed on to dangerous ground.

"Well, now I have to catch up to you," he said, keeping his tone light. "My honor as an experienced fisherman is at stake."

He caught one within minutes, and by the time they left, they had a stringerful of catfish as well as four greedy bluegills. After her promising start, Ella had caught a fish for every two he reeled in, and she'd laughed and enjoyed herself more than he'd imagined her capable of. *Had no one ever shown her how to have fun?*

"Well, it looks as if I have my work cut out for me," she said, eyeing the day's catch as they reached the back of the saloon. "Goodness, I hope I can get them all ready to fry by the time I'm supposed to open for supper. The alley cats will have a feast tonight, as well as my customers. Thanks for taking me." She reached for the stringer. "I guess I'll see you later…"

Ella had been such a good sport all afternoon, throwing herself enthusiastically into the task of catching supper, but he hadn't missed the little shudder she'd just given as she eyed the fish.

"*Tsk-tsk,* Miss Ella, did you think I was going to leave you with such a nasty, smelly job after I had the fun of catching them with you? That'd hardly be fair." Nate told himself his offer to help clean the fish was mere chivalry and not the fact that he wanted to earn one more of her brilliant smiles and spend more time around her. It wasn't a privilege he deserved, or that he'd have for long, but he wanted to take advantage of it while he could.

She blinked, then gazed up at him as if he was some

sort of hero. "You'd do that for me?" she breathed, eyes wide and luminous.

Looking at her, he could hardly catch his breath. "Sure," he said, his voice sounding shaky to him. "By the time you have some breading mixed up—myself, I use flour, cornmeal and a little oregano, salt, pepper and garlic when I can get it, but you use what you like—I can have these fish ready for the pan," he boasted. He felt as though there wasn't much he couldn't do under the effect of her grateful smile.

"You've got a deal, Mr. Bo—"

"It's *Nate,* remember?" he interrupted her to say, thinking how much he'd like to kiss that upturned, smiling mouth of hers, then deciding he had surely lost his mind.

"Nate," she repeated.

It was one of the best suppers she had ever served at the little café. Ella had used Bohannan's breading recipe, and though she'd had to dash over to the boardinghouse to borrow some garlic from Mrs. Meyer, the result was well worth it.

"Piscine perfection," Mr. Avery, the banker, her first guest that evening, called it. Ella had to stifle a giggle at the description, but she glowed at his praise. Since the flow of customers was usually slower on Sunday nights, she took the money and did the serving while Bohannan kept an eye on the fish frying in the skillet. She darted a glance at him to see if he'd heard the compliment.

He had. He was smiling, and she couldn't help smiling back. For a moment they shared a triumph that echoed in her soul. She hadn't expected how much fun it would be to experience even such a small success together.

"Then you must have a second helping, sir, on the house," Ella said, and served it to him.

"That's right sweet of you, Miss Ella. I'll be sure and tell everyone I meet what a good meal it was," Mr. Avery said.

She took that promise with a grain of salt, for Main Street was nearly deserted on a Sunday evening, but she appreciated the spirit of it nonetheless. Then George Detwiler and his mother showed up, and she left the banker's table to greet them.

"Ella, I told George I was too tired to cook this evenin', and we'd see what you were fixin' up," the old lady announced. "Mmm, fried catfish! I haven't had that in a coon's age." Her gaze roamed the room, and Ella saw it light on Bohannan flipping fish in the skillet. "Got yourself a partner, I see."

It was plain from Mrs. Detwiler's broad grin that the older woman thought Ella and Nate had been cooking up something else between them, too. Ella felt herself flush. She was forgetting all her resolve. She had to get hold of herself. *But I don't want to,* a little voice inside her insisted.

"Evening, Mrs. Detwiler, George," Bohannan said from the stove, rescuing Ella from the need to respond. "Yep, I was kind of at loose ends this afternoon, what with the saloon and the mill bein' closed, so I decided it was a good day to go fishing. Miss Ella very kindly agreed to come along, and thanks to her beginner's luck—"

"Mr. Bohannan is exaggerating," Ella said, enjoying the moment in spite of her nervousness. "He caught twice as many as I did."

"But she caught the first," Nate said.

Then the mayor and his wife came in, saying it was their cook's night off. Ella knew they normally patronized the hotel restaurant on such nights—it had been Mrs. Powell's favorite boast—so their presence at her little café felt like a signal honor.

The evening continued, with new customers replacing the others at her three tables and a few others trickling in for fish sandwiches. Anticipating the end of the evening, she wondered if Nate would offer to help her with the dishes again, or even offer to walk her home. Did she even want him to?

Also, she began to hope that Zeke Carter had eaten elsewhere tonight. Since he'd been so unpleasant to Nate only this morning, she'd thought it only fair to warn Nate that the cantankerous old man usually came on Sunday evenings, but as her usual closing time drew near, she began to think they'd been spared.

Perhaps Carter had remembered she'd invited Nate to sit with Maude and her, and he would shun her café from now on. Well, she hated to lose a customer, but that was up to him.

Just as the last customer left, though, and she was moving toward the door to turn the open sign to closed, she saw the old man outside reaching for the door latch.

Her heart sank. But she pasted a welcoming smile on her face and opened the door for him. A customer was a customer, after all.

"Bet you thought I wasn't comin'," Zeke Carter said as he came in the door. "What's that I smell—fish? That'd be good for a change. You don't usually have it on the menu."

"Well, I hope you enjoy your meal," Ella said, gesturing toward a seat that faced the door. With any luck, he might not spot Nate at the stove, at least anytime soon. "The catfish were caught in the creek only this afternoon," she added, not mentioning who had done most of the catching. If Carter did notice Nate behind the counter at some point, she prayed he wouldn't renew his unfriendly behavior.

Carter became aware of Mayor and Mrs. Gilmore at the far table, finishing their meal, and after exchanging greetings with them, he began a loud, rambling soliloquy about the town council, which supposedly never performed up to his standards. The mayor listened politely enough, putting in a word now and then when he could, and Ella managed to get the freshly fried fish to the old codger's table without him noticing who had cooked it. When she had taken the plate full of fish and biscuits from Nate, he'd murmured, "Since he's your last customer, why don't I just slip into the saloon and wait. Maybe he'll never even realize I was here. You can let me know when he's gone." The wink he had given her had been conspiratorial and had sent her pulse rate skyrocketing. *He does want to wait for me.* She could hardly wait for Zeke Carter to leave!

The mayor was fidgeting and obviously wanted to get away from his loquacious constituent. Carter regularly ran against the mayor whenever Gilmore was up for reelection, but he never won more than a couple of votes—his own and Mrs. Powell's, probably. Maybe she could help the mayor at the same time as she was helping herself.

"Would you like some coffee, Mr. Carter? Maybe a slice of peach pie?" she asked.

"Sure. And you kin get me s'more of that fish. It's the best thing you've offered in a long time."

Ella wasn't sure how he had managed to taste it since

he'd been so busy talking. Well, if she wasn't getting the old man out the door as soon as she had wished, she had at least distracted him so the mayor and his wife could make their escape.

"Coming right up," she said, glad that Nate had left a last serving on the stove. The sooner she served it, the sooner she could bid Zeke goodbye.

Mayor Gilmore assisted his wife as she spread her shawl over her shoulders. Then, as they made their way to the door, Mrs. Gilmore called back, "Ella, dear, be sure and thank Mr. Bohannan for such a delicious catfish dinner. Was that breading his recipe? I'll have to have our cook ask him about the ingredients. Bye, now."

As the door closed behind the Gilmores, Carter let his fork fall to his plate with a clatter. His eyebrows shot up to his scalp line and his eyes bulged out as if someone was strangling him.

"*Bohannan* cooked this?" he demanded, jabbing a finger at the fresh plate she'd just set down in front of him. His face purpled as he jumped to his feet. "That snake-oil salesman? You let that charlatan cook my supper?"

He lurched past her and looked over the counter as if he expected to find Nate cringing beneath it, then rounded on Ella.

The injustice of his words sparked her own ire. "Yes, he cooked it, and your first helping, too, the one you called 'the best thing I've offered in a long time,'" she snapped. "He was cooking when you arrived. And he's not a 'snake-oil salesman' anymore, as you very well know. Do you want this second helping or not?"

"That I don't, missy," Carter snarled, throwing his napkin down. "Didn't know Bohannan was your fancy man, Miss Ella, but since you've taken up with him, I won't be back. You best care about your reputation, or ain't no one gonna eat at this place!" He stormed out the back door, slamming it behind him.

He'd gotten away without paying for his meal, Ella noticed absently as the tears began to fall, and he was no doubt heading for the hotel restaurant to give Mrs. Powell an earful.

He'd tell the cook, all right, and before noon tomorrow half the town would know that Miss Ella Justiss had a "fancy man," the same fellow who had helped bilk them of their money. And they too would begin to question whether they should patronize the café. After all, maybe this girl who'd blown into town like a tumbleweed from who-knew-where was no better than she should be.

From there it was easy to imagine the ladies of the Spinsters' Club, and even Reverend Chadwick and his wife, begin to avoid her. In no time flat, she would be a pariah.

In the midst of her sobbing, Ella must not have heard the door from the saloon open, or the footsteps coming toward her, because she was startled to feel a man's arm around her. Nate's arm around her.

"Miss Ella, what's wrong? I heard the door slam— what did that old coot say to you?"

For a moment she couldn't stop crying, couldn't deny herself the comfort of those warm, strong arms holding her as she wept. Then, gradually, she became aware that they were standing in front of the café window, the table lamps illuminating them for anyone who might be standing outside.

She wrenched away from him, feeling the chill on her arms now that she had abandoned that warm refuge. "You m-mustn't… S-someone could see…"

He shrugged, as if that hardly mattered. "You're crying. I wanted to help you. What did he say to you?" He looked from her to the door as if Zeke Carter might still be lurking outside.

"He found out you c-cooked his meal…" Ella said, her voice thick as she struggled to get the words out and control her tears. "And he called you my 'fancy man.' I can't… You'd better go," she said at last.

"Go?" he said as if it was a foreign word. "Because of an accusation from a cranky old fool? If I go, it will be to find him and make him apologize to you, Miss Ella. He can't talk to you that way."

"No! You can't do that! It'll only make things worse!" she cried. "Don't you see that I can't afford to lose my reputation, Mr. Bohannan?"

He blinked. "Lose your reputation? Why would anyone listen to the likes of him? Your customers know the kind of person you are."

Why didn't he understand this? Didn't he know how rumors worked? He'd experienced harsh treatment just this morning because of his previous job, but how could she explain that if a *woman* lost her reputation, it could be so much worse? She'd already had to leave Round Rock when someone had speculated that she was a soiled dove from some other town, looking to start over among honest folks.

"Please, just go," she said, weary from the force of the emotions that had swept through her.

"But the dishes—"

"I'll take care of them," she said. "It's always been up to me before."

"Let me walk you back to the boardinghouse when you're finished, at least. It'll be dark."

"Thank you, but I'll be fine. I've always done it." She didn't mention that on summer evenings, when she left the café at dusk, she avoided going right past the saloon to Main Street so as not to call attention to herself from the rowdy, liquored-up customers. This meant walking a ways down the road leading south, then passing the grounds of the mayor's house, but the journey was safer that way.

For a moment, Nate looked as if he was going to say something but thought better of it. Then he just stared at her, his blue eyes unreadable. At last, he turned on his heel and went out through the door into the saloon, and the next thing she heard was the sound of his steps on the stairs to the upper floor.

Fortunately, there was already hot water waiting on the stove for the dishes. *Bless Nate Bohannan for that little courtesy, at least.* She did the dishes in silent misery, tears trickling down her cheeks to splash in the warm water below. She left the dishes, cups and silverware drying on the counter. After thrilling the alley cats that habitually congregated at her back door at night with a bounty of fishy scraps, she walked around to Main Street.

Now that it was fall and growing dark earlier, usually the light from the moon and stars—and on other nights, from the saloon—was enough that she could cross the street without any other illumination. But tonight, wary because of her confrontation with Zeke Carter, and because the saloon was dark and the moon was new, she carried the lantern as she crossed Main Street diagonally to the hotel, then walked through the alley between the hotel and mercantile to Travis Street and the boardinghouse.

* * *

Bohannan watched her progress. He had been standing at the window of his dark room since he heard the back door of the café close, and now he watched the bobbing light of the lantern and the figure lit by it until they were swallowed by the alley.

Ella had been so full of joy this afternoon when she caught the first fish, and had seemed to take pleasure in their time together at the creek and in their preparing dinner together. Why had she let a bad-tempered old coot like Carter buffalo her as he had? Why was she so fearful of gossip? No one paid attention to tale-telling bullies like Carter and that cook from the hotel—they just considered the source and went on with their business. Yet the same Ella whom he'd been so close to kissing this afternoon had been cowed by an old man's empty threats.

Had something happened in her past to cause this overreaction? What was it?

In the space of an afternoon, he'd been so charmed by her he'd been contemplating abandoning his plan to go to California and join his cousin's elite circle of influential men. He'd been thinking, when he walked her home, of asking if he could court her, and maybe even kiss her. He'd take up roots in Simpson Creek and become a pillar of the community.

Now, of course, there was no point in making such a plan. Any attention paid to Ella Justiss would be as welcome as a rattlesnake in a prairie-dog town.

There was no point in contemplating staying and trying to help Ella overcome her fears. Here in Simpson Creek, he'd always be soiled by his association with Salali. In time they would forget about Salali's vandalism and only remember that Nate Bohannan had been peddling snake oil. He'd never gain their full respect. He should just stick to his original idea and leave this little town and the troubled Ella behind when his work was done. That would sure be a sight easier.

But he'd never taken the easy path in life.

Chapter Ten

"Ella, are you avoiding me?" Maude asked as she entered the café just as Ella finished cleaning up after serving breakfast. They were the only ones in the place. "You came in last night and went straight to your room before I could catch you in the hallway, and you were gone this morning at the crack of dawn. Mrs. Meyer said she didn't even see you. I'd ask if I did something to offend you, but I haven't seen you since church yesterday, so I don't see how I could have."

Ella faced her best friend with a guilty smile. "No, of course you didn't offend me, Maude. I'm sorry you thought that even for a second. I just didn't feel like talking when I came back from supper last night." She'd been afraid Maude would ask about the fishing expedition, and she hadn't wanted to talk about it—not after the way things had turned out. Instead she had crept into the boardinghouse by the back door, stealthy as a thief, and put her things away in the kitchen, not even pausing to gather what she'd need for the morning.

"Didn't the fishing go well?" Maude prodded. Her tone was warm and sympathetic, but Ella saw the speculative gleam in the other woman's eyes.

"It went fine. We caught plenty, and the customers raved about the fish," Ella said briskly, hoping Maude would leave it at that. It didn't feel right to be evasive with her friend, but how could she tell her about Zeke Carter's threat?

"I thought so. I ran into Mrs. Detwiler on the way here, and she said to tell you it was the best catfish she'd ever eaten. Did you and Mr. Bohannan have a fight afterward, then?"

She stared at Maude. "Of course not." Nor had she and Bohannan exchanged anything but the most commonplace pleasantries when he'd come in this morning for breakfast, but the café had been full. "Now, unless you're coming to the butcher shop with me while I place my order, I've got to get going."

Maude wrinkled her nose. "No, thanks. It's bad enough when Mrs. Meyer sends me out to the chicken house to select Sunday dinner."

Ella grinned. "It's not so bad. Mr. Flynn's already done the butchering. Though there is a smell…"

"That's what I mean. All right, I'll see you later," Maude said. "But remember, honey, if you want to talk—about Nate Bohannan or anything—I'll always listen."

"You're a good friend to have, Maude Harkey. Thanks." If only she *could* tell her everything, Ella thought as she walked west on Main Street to Flynn's Butcher Shop. Not only about Zeke Carter's nasty accusations but about her contradictory feelings for Nate Bohannan. But how could she, when she didn't understand them herself?

Yesterday, at the café and the creek, she'd had such a good time with Nate. She'd felt her guard slipping, that protective instinct that kept her from being hurt. It had felt good, as if she was shedding a rigid shell that no longer fit her. But then old Zeke had said the ugly things he had said, and she felt once more dirty and shamed.

It had something to do with the asylum, she knew. Something had happened there to make her feel damaged, somehow. Something her conscious mind couldn't grasp but that reached out clawing fingers for her in her dreams. Even then, she couldn't turn and identify who, or what, the clawing fingers belonged to. Before she could turn and identify who it was, she always woke up, screaming.

The nightmares were why, when she'd come to live at the boardinghouse, she'd requested the bedroom at the east end of the hallway upstairs. There was a storeroom next to her, and between her room and Maude's lay the three rooms Mrs. Meyer saved for travelers such as the drummers and the stagecoach driver. These were frequently empty, so no one was apt to hear her if she had one of her nightmares.

She knew Mrs. Meyer had been puzzled when a longtime boarder had left and she'd offered Ella the room next to Maude's, thinking Ella would want to be situated next to her friend, but Ella had declined. But the proprietress had respected Ella's wish to keep her isolated room, even if she wondered why.

No one but Ella knew how many times she checked to make sure her room was locked before she blew out her lamp at bedtime, and how she always kept the key under her pillow, where she could touch it during the night to reassure herself no one could break into her little sanctuary.

"Miss Ella, what kin I do for you today?" Mr. Flynn asked, opening the door of his shop, causing her to nearly jump out of her skin. "Whoa, easy there, ma'am!

Didn't mean to startle you, but you've been standing outside my window fer five minutes at least, just starin', but not like you were seein' anything…"

Goodness, she'd have to be careful, or rumors that she was a little "tetched in the head" could be added to Zeke Carter's nasty insinuations.

"Oh! I'm sorry, Mr. Flynn, I'm afraid I was lost in thought," she said, flustered that the butcher had seen her in such a state. "I—I was just wondering whether I ought to increase my order for this week. Business has been good lately."

"An' you've got that fellow who's repairin' George Detwiler's tables an' chairs to feed, too, I hear," Flynn said in his chatty fashion.

Ella winced inwardly. Did everyone in town know all her business, or had the butcher already heard Zeke Carter's gossip? But Flynn's expression held no slyness, so maybe she was just worrying too much. Still, she kept her voice casual. "Yes, Mr. Bohannan is taking his meals in the café. But that's only for a little while."

Saturday evening, Nate left the lumber mill well satisfied with his day's work. Once Detwiler had approved his first efforts on the table legs, Nate had decided to finish a complete set—a table and four chairs—at a time so that the saloonkeeper could remove a plank table for each set he completed. He'd finished the second group today and varnished both sets, leaving them to dry in Dayton's shed, away from the sawdust particles that always hung in the air inside the mill. The shed wasn't locked, so he could carry them back to the saloon Sunday afternoon when it was empty. At this rate he could be done with the saloon's tables and chairs in a week, then start on the café's furniture. There were only three table-and-chair sets to be done for Ella, but they'd each take longer since he planned to make them fancier than the plain ones in the saloon. He could be on his way to San Francisco again in a month, away from the woman whose image had begun to float through his mind like those persistent sawdust particles in the air of the mill workroom.

Once he left Simpson Creek, he'd never see Ella Justiss again. The thought wrenched his heart, but that was ridiculous. He'd known the girl for nine days. There was no reason that she should be anything more to him than a girl he'd passed a pleasant afternoon with, the one who'd cooked his meals. One of two people whose property Salali had damaged, for which Nate had atoned.

But he knew somehow the memory of her would haunt him the rest of his days if he didn't at least try to do something to better the situation between them. Since last Sunday night, she had been civil to him when he showed up for meals but no more so than she would have been to any stranger passing through. If there were others in the restaurant, she always seemed to check if they were watching before she replied, even though their conversations held nothing beyond the mundane. If they were alone, she looked out the window to see if anyone was about to come in. Was she watching for Zeke Carter, afraid of another verbal attack?

Always leave a place better than you found it, his pa used to say. Simpson Creek didn't need his help to make it a better place—it was already a pleasant little town populated by mostly well-meaning folks. He would certainly leave the saloon a better place than it was after Salali's destruction. But Ella…he wanted to help Ella somehow.

With any luck, he would be her last supper customer

of the evening, but even if he wasn't, he planned to bide his time till they were alone in the café.

An elderly gentleman and his wife were just leaving, praising the food as they left—"Tasty, and so much more economical than the fare served at the hotel"—when he entered through the saloon.

"Good evening, Miss Ella."

She looked up from wiping the table that had just been vacated. "Good evening, Mr. Bohannan. Did you have a productive day at the lumber mill?"

"I sure did. I should be able to finish Detwiler's and work on your pieces in a week."

"That will be good."

He hated such stilted conversation, and her formality in calling him "Mr. Bohannan." Not when there was so much he wanted to say to her—even if he hadn't figured it all out yet.

She'd made beefsteak with smothered onions that evening, with boiled potatoes, and apple pie for dessert, and he tucked into the meal with enthusiasm.

From the sounds filtering through the door, the saloon was doing a land-office business. Now and then a shriek of laughter or a hoarse guffaw penetrated the tinkling piano music. Evidently using crude plank tables hadn't dimmed Detwiler's customers' gusto for his establishment.

Nate took his time eating, watching out of the corner of his eye while Ella washed the dishes and dried them.

"That was a good meal, Miss Ella," he told her when she was finished.

"Thank you, Mr. Bohannan."

"I'll walk you home, if you're ready to lock up."

"It's not necessary, Mr. Bohannan."

"Nevertheless, I'd feel better about it if I did." The

sound of a glass breaking and a shout from within the saloon reached them just then, and Nate nodded meaningfully toward it.

"Very well then," Ella said, hanging up her apron.

He gestured for her to precede him through the door. She locked it behind them, and they walked in silence around to the front of the saloon, both pretending not to see the cowboy sprawled in the dirt by the horse trough.

After crossing Main Street, they entered the alley between the hotel and the mercantile, going single file of necessity, due to the narrowness of the passageway. When they emerged onto Travis Street, however, he stopped halfway between the boardinghouse and the Bishops' home and faced her in the gathering dusk.

"Miss Ella, has that old coot—that is, Mr. Carter— said anything further to you that he shouldn't have, after that incident last Sunday?"

Her eyes widened and he could tell it surprised her that he was bringing up the subject again.

"No, he hasn't. I haven't seen him. That one time was quite enough, though." She hunched her shoulders, as if remembering a blow.

"Has anyone else said anything, or treated you differently in the last few days, that would make you think he's been spreading tales about you?"

She blinked up at him. "No. What are you getting at, Mr. Bohannan?"

"Perhaps he's just an old bag of wind, a bully full of empty threats. It would be a shame to let him make you jump at shadows."

"How— I'm not jumping at shadows." She lifted her chin, but something in her expression, even in the failing light, told him she was aware of what he referred to.

"Aren't you? It seems to me you're letting the insinuations of a cranky old man rule your life. If Mr. Carter and that cook from the hotel had their druthers, you'd be reduced to what they want you to be, a joyless woman who just goes back and forth to her café every day and does nothing else for fear of their wagging tongues."

Then he heard how he must sound to her, a Johnny-come-lately expert in her life, when he knew so little of what had gone before.

"I'm sorry. I had no right to say that. I just—"

"No, you're right," Ella said, surprising him. "And if Mrs. Powell had *her* way, I'd still be working in the hotel restaurant with her bullying me. I wouldn't have my café. But you don't understand—"

Now it was his turn to interrupt. "I'd like to be your friend, Ella Justiss. Are you going to let a couple of miserable meddlers prevent that, for fear of what they *might* say?"

"Once they've said it, it's too late to wish they hadn't."

"But you have friends, don't you? Maude and the preacher's wife, and the ladies of that Spinsters' Club I've heard about? Friends who know you're an upright, good person all the time you've lived here, and who would stand up for you if those two started ugly rumors that anyone with a lick of sense would know wasn't true?"

"I…I suppose. But why would *you* want to be my friend, Mr. Bohannan?"

Because I'm charmed by your dark eyes, by your pluck and determination, your simple beauty... "Because I like you," he said.

His frankness seemed to take her aback, and he saw that old wariness wash over her again.

"But you're going to be leaving as soon as you're finished repairing all the furniture."

"Then I don't see what harm a friendship between us can do, Miss Ella," he said. One glance at her suspicious eyes told her he would have to go further. "I'm going to tell you right out, I don't have any nefarious plans for you, Miss Ella. I'd like to be your friend during the time I'm here, that's all."

Did those tense shoulders relax the least little bit?

"Why does it matter so much to you?" she asked, surprising him again. Her eyes never left his.

"I haven't stayed anywhere long enough to have a friend lately," he admitted. "It's always good to have a friend, don't you think? Someone you can confide in, be honest with? I think you need someone like that, too, Miss Ella."

Perhaps he'd gone too far with that last sentence, he thought as he saw her guard go up again. "Why would I confide in you, a man, and not Maude or some other female here in Simpson Creek, Mr. Bo—"

"Nate," he corrected gently. He noticed she didn't correct his assertion that she needed to confide in someone.

"Nate," she repeated. "Answer the question, please."

"It has nothing to do with me being a man, but because I won't be here long. Who better to confide in than someone who'll travel on and can never betray what you've told them? Besides, I've heard confession is good for the soul."

Ella stiffened. "I have nothing to confess, Mr. Bohannan," she said, her voice icy as a blue norther blowing into town. "I've done nothing wrong. I've been an upright citizen ever since I left the—" She broke off abruptly, clapping a hand over her mouth, her eyes stark with obvious dismay at what she'd almost said.

"I'm sorry, Miss Ella," he said quickly, wondering what she'd been about to say. *What place had she left that she couldn't even speak of it?* "I didn't mean to imply you needed to confess a wrong you'd done. I just meant something's eating at you, and maybe it would help you to talk about it, that's all."

She put her hands on her hips. "Have you been a preacher sometime, too, along with being a carpenter, a medicine-show assistant, a banjo player and who knows what all else?" Ella asked him, her tone sardonic. "You sound like one."

He couldn't help laughing at the notion. "A preacher? Me? No, I'm afraid not, Miss Ella." He thought about the simple, bedrock goodness of a man like the young reverend he'd heard preach last Sunday, and knew how unworthy he was of ever being a preacher.

"Evenin', Miss Ella," a man said, startling both of them. It was Sheriff Bishop. How had the man gotten so close without either of them hearing him coming? "Mr. Bohannan," he added, as Nate turned to face him. "I'm just out making my rounds. Everything all right, Miss Ella?"

"Evening, Sheriff," they said in unison, and Ella added, "Yes, everything's fine."

"I was just escorting Miss Ella back to the boarding-house," Nate said, "now that the café is closed for the night. There's a rowdy bunch at the saloon right now, and I didn't want anyone bothering her."

The sheriff studied him, his eyes betraying nothing. Just then, the sound of hooting and hollering reached their ears, coming from the direction of the saloon, followed by the sound of galloping hooves.

Nate tossed a see-what-I-mean look at the sheriff, and Bishop nodded. "Reckon I ought to mosey over to the saloon and make sure Detwiler's keeping his customers corralled." He turned and strode purposefully in that direction.

They watched him go, then turned toward the boardinghouse. He guessed Ella was glad their conversation had been interrupted, considering the topic.

Chapter Eleven

The preacher's wife laid a detaining hand on Ella's arm after the Sunday service was over. "Ella dear, I know you have to get to the café, but would it be all right if I paid you a call this afternoon? I have to fix my husband and his father their dinner, so it'll be after the noontime rush, of course. I have something to discuss with you."

What could Faith want to talk to her about? Had she heard gossip from Zeke Carter or Mrs. Powell? Had one of those two busybodies seen Bohannan walking her home the night before? Even though Faith and her husband had welcomed Bohannan to church, was Faith going to advise her not to associate with the man?

Something of Ella's apprehension must have showed on her face, for Faith said quickly, "Don't be alarmed, Ella. It's good news, I promise."

Ella tried to relax her features. "I'm always in the mood to hear *that*. I'll see you later." She left the church-yard and headed for the café, still wondering what was on Faith's mind.

Bohannan—*Nate,* she corrected herself—had come into the sanctuary with the Detwilers after she and Maude were already seated in their usual place. He'd given her a nod and a smile, then he and the Detwilers had settled in a pew a couple of rows down.

Ella had seen Maude eye her with surprise. "Why isn't he sitting with us? You said you didn't have a fight," she'd whispered.

"No, we didn't," Ella had whispered back, giving her friend a quelling look. "I'll explain more later." She'd guessed Nate was being careful since Mr. Carter and Mrs. Powell were present, but she hadn't been able to stifle a twinge of resentment that the two busybodies made such discretion necessary. Until that moment, she hadn't realized how much she'd been looking forward to Nate's company during the service.

Now, with church over, she resolved to put that subject from her mind, as well as her coming talk with the preacher's wife. She would concentrate on her cooking and her customers, and that was all.

But she couldn't stop the thoughts. Would she get any time to talk to Nate today? Would he come and help her with the customers, as he had last week? Since accepting his friendship had been a tacit agreement that she needed a friend to confide in, she found herself wanting to spend time with him. Only as a friend, of course.

Nate did come, and took the money while she served the customers as before, taking bites of his own dinner at intervals when he was not busy. He stayed behind to help her wash and dry the dishes, too. They were just finishing up when the bell over the door tinkled, announcing the arrival of Faith.

She'd told him the preacher's wife would be coming and that she didn't know what it was that Faith wanted to talk about, but he evidenced no curiosity about it.

"Reckon I'll see you at suppertime, Miss Ella," he said, hanging up the damp dish towel he'd used. He exited through the same door Faith had come in, and she saw him pass by the window. She couldn't help wondering where he was going. Out for a walk? Well, it was nothing to her, she reminded herself, and turned back to Faith.

"How nice that he was helping you, Ella. My, Mr. Bohannan seems to be settling right into life in town," Faith Chadwick remarked after the door closed behind him.

Ella shrugged, determined not to let on how much his helping her had pleased her. "Yes…well, he doesn't have anything else to do, I suppose. The lumber mill isn't open today, of course, so he can't work on his furniture repairs today."

"Oh, he didn't tell you he's going to start playing the piano for church?" Faith said. "Sarah's husband wants her to get some rest because of the baby that's coming, so Mr. Bohannan has kindly agreed to step in, as long as he's in town. I told him he was welcome to come in and practice this afternoon, and whenever he was free in the evenings. I suppose that's where he's headed now."

"He seems to be a veritable fount of hidden talents," Ella said wryly, knowing it was illogical to feel hurt that Nate hadn't told her of this first.

Faith laughed. "Yes, he does! Fortunately for the church, piano playing is one of them. He may not be in town forever, but it's nice of him to help us while he can. Now, Ella, about my reason for coming…"

"Let's sit down," Ella said, gesturing toward one of the empty tables, aware that she'd been remiss in not inviting Faith to do so sooner.

"Thank you," Faith said and settled herself on a chair. "Ella, as you know, the church has a fund for helping people who need it."

"I know. The Fund for the Deserving Poor, isn't that what you call it?"

"That's right. We've been able to help so many people in Simpson Creek through the generosity of those who donate."

What does this have to do with me? And then she was afraid she knew.

"Oh, Faith, I'm sorry. As much as I'd like to help, I'm afraid the business isn't doing well enough yet that I could afford to donate—"

"No, Ella! I should be the one to apologize," Faith said quickly. "I didn't make myself clear. I've spoken to the group that maintains the fund within the church, and we're agreed. We'd like to help *you*."

Ella looked blank. "Help me what? I'm not destitute, Faith." She made a sweeping gesture to encompass the tables and chairs, the counter and the cooking area behind it. "I have my own business. I have a place to live. I'm not exactly 'deserving poor.'"

Deserving was a description she'd never felt fit her. Poor—well, she'd always been uncomfortably close to that.

Faith's expression was crestfallen. "Oh, dear, I meant no offense. I've *told* them they needed to change the name of the fund to something more…I don't know… broad? I mean, we've helped a lot of those who truly *are* destitute and will continue to do that, but since God has blessed us with enough contributions, we also want to help those within the church who merely need a little hand in obtaining what they need to better their lives. I've discussed with them the problems you've experienced because of having your business at the back of the saloon, and, Ella, we'd like to help you build your café in another location."

Ella could hardly believe her ears. "That…that's very nice of you, but I don't own any land for such a place, nor do I have the funds yet to purchase it."

"But the church *does,* Ella dear. As a relative newcomer to Simpson Creek, maybe you're not aware that the original deed for the church land includes the meadow across the creek from it, on both sides of the road. We'd like to lease you a piece of it big enough to accommodate your café, and schedule a building day for the church men to construct the café for you. Like a barn raising," she concluded with a smile. "We'll make an event of it—the ladies will cook the midday meal, the men will build your café. All you have to do is accept, Ella dear."

Ella sat still in her chair, her heart pounding, wanting to accept and achieve her dream, but fearful, too. *What strings are attached to such a gift?* "I appreciate the offer, Faith, but I'm not destitute," she repeated. "I make my own way. I have a roof over my head. I'm sure there are many more worse-off folks than me—"

"Ella, the church is a body of believers who are supposed to help each other," Faith said patiently. "Don't let pride stand in your way. It might be years before you could afford to do this for yourself. Yes, we help people who are truly penniless, but before you came to town, we helped Milly Brookfield—Milly Matthews back then—rebuild her barn after the Comanches burned it down. Everyone had a glorious time. Please say yes, Ella."

Milly Brookfield, the founder of the Spinsters' Club, had once needed the town to raise a barn for her? Now she was married to an Englishman who was on the town council, their ranch was prospering, and the Brookfields were considered pillars of the community.

Charity girl. You ain't nothin' but a charity girl, the voice within her jeered. *What makes you think you got a right to anything? What makes you think you kin say no?*

Where had that voice come from? she wondered.

"Just think of it, Ella. It was nice that Mr. Detwiler could give you a start, but think of having a place of your own where you don't need to fend off drunken customers from the saloon. My husband and I would be nearby if you needed help, and it would be so handy for your Sunday after-church customers. I imagine your business could triple! You'd get all the travelers coming in from the East before they even saw the hotel restaurant."

Ella closed her eyes, picturing it. A café of her own, just as she'd dreamed of. All she had to do was agree to let them build it for her. She'd never have to be afraid of who was coming through the door from the saloon, or of walking back to the boardinghouse past a saloon full of rowdy customers... ELLA'S CAFÉ, the sign over the door would proclaim in neat lettering. Breakfast, Dinner and Supper—Reasonable Prices for Tasty Fare. She could expand her menu, maybe even hire help. Folks would come from all over the county...

Nothin' but a charity girl, accepting handouts. Don't you know there's always a price when you take charity? Now, just come sit on my lap, girl, and tell me how much you appreciate what I've done for you...

She tried to suppress a shudder as that haunting voice from the past faded, leaving her no more of a memory of the speaker than it ever had. And what would a *church* expect in return? Surely there could be no unpleasant obligations to a congregation of believers.

"I…I don't know, Faith. I appreciate the offer, but I'll have to think about it," she said.

"Don't just think—*pray* about it," the preacher's wife advised, rising. "You don't have to decide today, dear. We'd have to schedule a Saturday for it, of course. But it would be better to get it under way before cold weather comes."

"Of course. I—I'll let you know very soon. And, Faith," she called as the preacher's wife neared the door, "I want you to know I appreciate the offer, no matter what I decide."

After Faith left, she stood there for a long time, staring out the window without actually focusing on anything. What should she choose to do about the amazing gift she was being offered? Perhaps Faith was right— she should pray about it. *Lord, what should I do? Is it right to accept such a gift?*

No heavenly Voice answered her, but she couldn't think of anything in scripture that forbade accepting such charity.

What would Nate say about it? she wondered. He'd probably think her a fool to do anything but jump at the chance, she thought. But would he give her Godly counsel? She had no idea how he stood with the Lord. Maybe he wasn't even a believer. After all, it hadn't been that long since he was helping peddle a potion he knew to be useless at best—hardly the actions of a Christian.

She would wait on an answer from the Lord, Ella thought. In the meantime, however, she would talk it over with Maude, who was always a source of wisdom and common sense.

Ella needed to tell her why Nate had chosen not to sit with them at church this morning, too. She'd had an opportunity to ask him about it when they were doing the dishes, and she'd been right that he was being cautious in the presence of the gossips. Well, she'd better get going or she and Maude wouldn't have any time to talk before she had to return to fix supper.

"Are you still expecting Zeke Carter to come in?" Nate asked that evening after he had complimented her on his supper of ham, scalloped potatoes, black-eyed peas and peach cobbler.

Ella shrugged. "Who knows? I usually keep the café open for another hour or so," she said.

"Then perhaps we ought not to provoke him with my presence this time," Nate suggested. "I'll sit in the saloon until you're ready to put up the closed sign, then I'll come help you clean up."

"Perhaps that would be wise," she agreed as Nate pushed open the door that led to the saloon. *Oh, why can't the quarrelsome old man move to another town?* Well, even if she didn't have to defend Bohannan's presence to the graybeard tonight, she resolved that Carter would learn not to assume he could push her around.

The man trudged in right after she had completed the thought. He surveyed the room, squinting suspiciously behind the counter, then sat down and turned his gaze to her. "What's fer supper tonight?"

She told him. "And I'm sure you'll enjoy it," she said, then drew herself up and looked him right in the eye. "But before I can serve you, Mr. Carter, there's the matter of payment for last Sunday night's supper. I'm sure you just forgot," she added pleasantly. "It was four bits."

He glared at her. She returned his gaze steadily, though she held her breath, half expecting a verbal explosion. She was glad she currently had no other customers whose presence might make him even more apt to be belligerent.

"Consarned distrustful females," he grumbled, but pulled out the coins, fairly slapping them into her outstretched palm. "I was gonna pay you after I et my vittles tonight. Remembered I hadn't paid soon's I got home the other night."

Ella said nothing more, letting him save face.

She served several other customers after she'd brought out Carter's dinner, and the old man offered her no more difficulty. He didn't even seem to notice when the music began filtering through the door from the saloon, though Mayor Gilmore did.

"Hmm, George must be practicing," Ella heard him say to his wife. "I don't remember him playing that well before."

Ella smiled to herself and pretended she hadn't overheard. She wasn't about to inform the mayor that it was Nate Bohannan playing, not George Detwiler—not when Zeke Carter's ears were clearly tuned to everything that was said. Instead, she just enjoyed the music, especially the haunting tunes that had been popular during the War Between the States, such as "Tenting Tonight" and "Lorena."

As the tables began to empty, she washed each customer's dishes, so that by the time the last diner left and she'd locked the door, the dishes were all done. Hanging up the damp dish towel, she went to tell Bohannan she was all finished in the café.

He stopped playing and rose from the piano bench as she approached. "Is the troll gone?" he asked with mock fearfulness.

* * *

As he'd hoped, calling Carter a troll made her giggle, which transformed Ella's usually guarded features and did something funny to his heart.

She covered her mouth, then tried to assume a stern look. "Mr. Bohannan, I'm sure it's not right to call him a name," she said. Then, as if realizing her sternness was utterly unconvincing, she let herself grin back at him. "But it fits, unfortunately."

"You ready for some help cleaning up?"

"No, I'm all done, thank you," she said. "It was most pleasant listening to you play while I worked. My, my, you're quite the musician."

Her admiring tone caused a fullness in his chest that he was quite unused to. "Why, thank you, Miss Ella," he said, bowing to hide how good her words made him feel—good enough to stifle the regret he felt at knowing he'd never see that banjo again, thanks to Salali.

"Mayor Gilmore thought it was Detwiler playing," she added with a conspiratorial chuckle. "I'd have enlightened him, but the 'troll' was still there."

"I'm glad you didn't," he said. Should he offer to walk her home now? he wondered. But he didn't want to end this moment. She might not be so relaxed with him once they were outside where anyone might see them.

"Faith—Mrs. Chadwick, that is—tells me you're going to be playing at the Sunday services for a while," she said. "From what I heard tonight, I can see the congregation won't suffer in Sarah's absence."

He ducked his head and rubbed his neck to hide his pleasure at yet another compliment. "I'm happy to help out," he said, and refrained from adding, *while I can*. He didn't want to remind her of his temporariness in Simpson Creek.

"I was surprised when you didn't agree to play for Detwiler in the saloon," she said suddenly.

He shrugged. "I really didn't want to spend my evenings surrounded by cigar smoke and whiskey. I'm glad he was able to get someone else."

She looked at the door then, and he knew she was thinking of leaving. *Not yet,* his heart pleaded. Then he got an idea. "Before I came to Simpson Creek, it'd been a long time since I'd been a regular churchgoer, Miss Ella. My pa and I used to go, in some of the small towns we lived in… And Miss Sarah left a list of hymns for next Sunday as a suggestion, but the truth is, I don't remember how fast or slow some of them should be played. Before I walk you home, could I play the hymns for you, and maybe you could let me know if I'm playing them right?"

"I…I suppose so," she said, and looked as if she would sit down in a nearby chair—one of the ones he had repaired. He wanted her closer, he realized.

"Could you… I mean, would you be willing to sing them as I play, so I can tell if I'm getting the tempo right? Especially this song, 'O Day of Rest and Gladness.'"

Ella looked doubtful. "I—I've never sung by myself before… You should get Maude to practice with you—she has a lovely singing voice. She's sung solos at church before."

"I heard you sing when you were next to me in church, and you have a very pleasant voice, Miss Ella. Besides, it's just the two of us. No one else will hear," he coaxed. "Come and stand right here close to me so I can hear you," he said, pointing to a spot on the plank floor near him but not so near she would get uneasy and refuse. It felt like luring a wild creature. He turned back to the piano and began to play the introductory bars of the hymn.

She missed her cue the first time. Without looking up, he began again and nodded his head when she was to begin.

This time, Ella began to sing, shyly at first, but then as he played on, her voice gained confidence and rose in a lovely soprano above the piano chords.

"I think *you* should be singing some solos, too, Miss Ella," he praised after the song was done.

"Oh, no, I wouldn't like that," she insisted. "You mustn't suggest it to anyone." But he could tell she enjoyed the compliment.

"I'm sure you know the next one," he said, and launched into "Holy, Holy, Holy." This time, after she'd sung a couple of lines, he joined her, fitting his tenor voice to hers. Their two voices fit perfectly together. Ella faltered in surprise at first, but since he kept playing, she kept singing along. The closing hymn would be "Abide with Me," but after they sang and he played that one, Nate was loath to stop. He began "Lorena," one of the songs he'd played while she was still working, and together they sang the hauntingly beautiful lines.

Was he imagining it, or had she stepped a little closer while he'd played?

"You're much too modest, Nate," she told him. "You played those songs perfectly."

Well, he had made it a point to attend church when he could—at least until he had fallen in with Salali.

Enjoying himself, he might have started another tune, but she said, "It's getting late. Besides, I want to ask your opinion on something as we walk."

She threw her shawl around her before he could assist her, and they walked out to the café again and out the back door.

Darkness closed around them as they walked around the side of the saloon and emerged onto Main Street at the front of the building. Here and there lamps gleamed from windows—in the hotel across the street, behind the wrought-iron fence in the mayor's grand house—but for the most part, their only illumination consisted of the silvery light emanating from the all-but-full moon above.

"You wanted my opinion?" he prompted.

"Yes. I told you Faith was coming to talk to me about something, remember? I've asked Maude what she thinks about what Faith said, but I thought it would be useful to ask more than one friend."

"I'm honored that you number me among your friends, and my opinion worthy of consideration, Miss Ella." He kept his tone light. "Go on."

"The church is offering to build my café, on ground it owns, with funds it collects for the 'deserving poor.' It would be located on the other side of the road from that meadow across the creek."

He waited, but he didn't hear a question in what she had said. "That's wonderful news, Miss Ella," he said as they went single file through the alley. "Just what you'd been hoping for, wasn't it, getting away from the saloon? And so much sooner than you thought possible."

Emerging onto Travis Street, she turned to him. "But it doesn't seem right to take money intended for the destitute."

"They're offering it to you, Miss Ella. The church must want you to have it. I don't see a catch in your accepting such a gift, do you? Are you hesitating because you think there are strings attached?"

She twisted her hands together, her dark eyes searching his face. "No, I can't think what the 'strings' could be. Faith says they're expanding the goals of the fund to include folks like me—not destitute but who just need some additional help—but I don't know…that's an awfully big gift…"

"What did Miss Maude say?"

"That I should take it."

"There, you see? I agree." He'd have liked to tease her by adding "unless you'll miss the drunken cowboys," but of course that wouldn't be a laughing matter to a woman alone like Ella. "When would they build it?"

"In a couple of weeks, if I agree. They'd set a day when everyone could help—like a barn raising, she said."

"I think you ought to tell Miss Faith yes, before she changes her mind," he said with a chuckle. "I can't think of one good reason to turn down a deal like that." He wondered why Ella would object. Had someone once convinced her she didn't deserve good things?

Ella's eyes remained troubled. "She said to pray about it. I guess I should."

A couple of older men were sitting on the porch of the boardinghouse, whittling and talking, so by tacit agreement, Ella and Nate detoured around to the back door where they could not be overheard.

"I reckon praying's always good advice, Miss Ella." She looked so pretty in the moonlight. If he'd known her longer, he would have kissed her. Too bad he'd be riding on before he could know her that long.

She studied him again. "I enjoyed the singing. I'd better go inside."

"I enjoyed it, too." He wanted to prolong the moment just a bit longer. "You know, the preacher told me

I could come in and play the church piano anytime I wanted. Maybe we could do that some evening."

Ella blinked. "Perhaps. Good night, Nate."

"Good night, Miss Ella. See you in the morning."

He walked back to the saloon, hoping Ella wouldn't let pride interfere with her accepting a wonderful gift. Those church folks were nice people, and he was glad they wanted to help Ella. She deserved something good happening to her.

It would be nice to see her in her new place, he thought wistfully, but unless they set the date for the café raising soon, he'd probably be gone before it happened. There'd be no more reason to stay once he'd finished her furniture.

Or was there? Her new place was apt to be a bit bigger than the little room behind the saloon. Ella might be needing more tables and chairs than she'd had before...

Chapter Twelve

Three days later, after she closed the café for the night, Ella told Nate she'd been praying about it and had decided she would accept the church's offer to build her café. She'd given Faith her answer that very morning. "And thanks to the fund, everything's included, from the foundation to the tin roof," she told him. "And it's going to be a little bigger than this place! Isn't that wonderful?"

"I thought you looked like you had a happy secret," he said, grinning. "I'm right glad for you, Miss Ella. Did you tell Detwiler? What did he say? Bet he's going to miss your meals."

She nodded. "Yes, but he was glad for me," she told him. "He said it was better for a lady's place of business not to be attached to a saloon, and I told him he could come eat three meals a day if he wanted, on the house. And he told me I could take the stove with me 'cause he wasn't going to use it. Wasn't that nice of him?"

"George is a generous fellow," he agreed. "Got a heart as soft as summer butter, as my pa used to say."

Ella would have liked to ask more about his father,

but before she could form a question, Nate asked, "So when's this café raising going to take place?"

"Two weeks from Saturday." She willed her expression not to change, not to betray the only cloud hanging over her joy, which was that the café raising could not take place as soon as she had hoped. Reverend Chadwick would be away for several days at a meeting of San Saba County preachers. He had wanted to be present, not only to bless the new building but to help erect it, too.

But Nate Bohannan would be gone by then. He'd said he would be done with Detwiler's tables and chairs by the end of this week, and that it would only take him a week to repair and rebuild the ones from her café.

"It's going to be a big event," she went on, aware that she was chattering so he wouldn't see that she wasn't as completely happy as she ought to be. "All the men from church will help build it, and the women will cook the food for the noon meal. Of course, it will take me a couple of days after that to get everything set up and ready to go. I plan to have a grand opening…"

She waited, but Bohannan said nothing more. His eyes got that unfocused look that made her think his mind was hundreds of miles away from Simpson Creek.

Well, she couldn't let his absence on her big day matter. She'd known from the start that Nate Bohannan's time in Simpson Creek was temporary. Having her own café was the fulfillment of a dream, one that would benefit her long after Bohannan was only a memory. She would enjoy his friendship while he was here, and when he had gone, she would go on with her life—just as he would.

"Want to go down to the church and help me practice, like we talked about?" he suggested.

Why not? Perhaps singing with him would lift her mood. And maybe she could get him to raise the mysterious curtain on his past life a little. It was a pleasant night for a walk—warm, but with just a hint of fall in the air.

They had just reached Main Street, however, when a broad figure came bustling out of the gloom as if she had been waiting for them—or at least, for Ella.

"You must think you're the queen of Simpson Creek now," Mrs. Powell snarled, advancing on them like a hen whose position at the top of the pecking order had been threatened. "Havin' 'em build you your own restaurant like you was somethin' special."

Out of the corner of her eye, Ella saw Nate take a step forward as if to place himself between her and the cook, and she was touched by his protectiveness. But she laid a restraining hand on his arm and murmured, "I don't feel special, Mrs. Powell, just very fortunate. And blessed."

"Don't suppose you even care that your fancy café might put the hotel restaurant outta business," Mrs. Powell huffed. "The hotel proprietor said if we don't stop losin' customers to your café, we might have to close. Don't 'spose you worry about that one little bit, you selfish girl! You don't have one ounce a' gratitude for all I taught you."

Ella could have retorted that she'd learned nothing from her about cooking *flavorful* food, but she couldn't bring herself to stoop to this woman's level. "I think there's plenty of room for two restaurants in Simpson Creek, Mrs. Powell. If anything, your restaurant's business might be helped by mine being across the creek. I doubt those staying at the hotel are going to search out my café when the hotel restaurant is right in the lobby."

"But you'll get all the folks ridin' into town from the east, not t' mention all the folks from church!" Mrs. Powell wailed, then clamped her jaws shut as if she thought she'd said too much. "Well, you'll be sorry if you build that café, missy, you just wait and see."

Now Nate did interpose himself between the two women. "You're not threatening Miss Ella, are you, Mrs. Powell?"

"Never you mind, Mr. Snake-Oil Salesman!" the woman screeched at him, backing away. "It ain't none a' your concern, noways!"

Nate sighed as the woman scuttled away, reminding him of a great hulking spider retreating into the shadows of her web. He supposed if he were to stay in Simpson Creek, he'd still be "that snake-oil salesman" not only to Mrs. Powell and Zeke Carter, but to anyone in Simpson Creek with a memory

It didn't matter what they thought, he decided.

"Let's keep walking," he whispered to Ella, offering her his arm. She took it.

He felt her trembling, but her mouth was set in a firm line and her back was as erect as if she had a ruler for a spine. The moon hung overhead, a few days past full, and it was enough to illuminate the silent tears snaking down her cheeks.

He didn't mention the tears, knowing how difficult it was for Ella to hold on to her composure. Nor did he say a kind word to her. If he did so now, she'd shatter like fine crystal.

They sat down on the church steps. He had a feeling they wouldn't be making music tonight, but he didn't care. He'd only suggested it as an excuse to spend time with her.

"I was real proud of you back there, Miss Ella. You could have been mean right back to that woman, but you responded like a lady, one with grace and dignity."

"But she's right!" she cried, giving way to the sobs he'd known were multiplying within her. "What gives *me* the right to be given something as wonderful as that? I don't deserve such a thing! What if my café *does* put the hotel restaurant out of business and her out of a job? What will happen to her? And what will folks think of me then?"

You could always offer her a job scrubbing your dirty pots, he wanted to suggest, but he knew she wouldn't find the image amusing. Instead, he pulled her into his arms, smoothing her hair back, soothing her the way one would a child. For several long moments she sobbed against his chest.

He wasn't even conscious of lowering his lips to kiss the top of Ella's head, but he felt her stiffen, and realized what he'd done.

She drew back.

"I'm sorry," he murmured, hoping she wouldn't flee now like a frightened deer. "I didn't even think…"

She *was* going to run, he decided, or slap him—he wasn't sure which. If he was going to keep her here, he knew he'd better distract her with a question, and quick. "Miss Ella, who was it that made you think you don't deserve anything nice?"

She blinked, then swiped a hand over a wet cheek. He wished he'd had a handkerchief to hand her.

"Wh-what makes you think someone d-did that?" she asked in a quavering voice.

She wasn't outright denying it, he noticed. "Because you keep saying you don't 'deserve' this," he said. "If any one of us *deserves* something nice to happen to them, it's you," he said gently. "Was it your mother or father who made you feel that way?" His father had never done that, and his mother had died before he could remember her, but it was a logical place to start with Ella.

She looked startled, as if that was the very last thing she expected him to say. "It couldn't have been Mama," she said quickly.

"Why is that?"

She hesitated like one being ordered to jump into an icy stream. "Because she died when I was about five," she said. She looked him right in the eye, and then she looked away, as if she dreaded the questions that must follow.

"So your father raised you, then?" he probed.

She shook her head, more tears escaping from tightly clenched lids.

"H-he was having trouble taking care of me and making a living, too, so he put me in the c-county asylum. He said he was c-coming back…b-but he never did," she stammered in a voice so soft he could hardly hear it.

He stared at her, hardly able to believe his ears. "Your father left you in an *asylum?*" he echoed. Had there been no aunts, uncles, grandparents? No neighbor who'd take in a motherless girl while her father found his footing? Then the full implication of "county asylum" hit him. "There were *adults* in that place, too?"

She nodded. "All ages of people, from babies to elderly folks…some of them merely destitute, some—" she took a deep breath and shuddered "—not in their right minds."

"Lord have mercy," he breathed. *She had been a little girl growing up in the company of lunatics.* He'd heard of such places, a single institution in a county taking in everyone who had nowhere to go, no one to care if they lived or died. All of them living together in crowded rooms… Those who were able were forced to work to repay what it cost to feed them.

He'd thought *he'd* had it tough, losing his mother early on, and being raised by an itinerant father who never put down roots for long, but clearly he'd had no idea what true misery was. He would have wept tears of repentance, but he was afraid doing so would frighten her. He felt as if he could barely breathe.

"You…you won't t-tell anyone, will you?" Ella asked, halting over the words. "No one in Simpson Creek knows….that I came from such a place." She faced him again, eyes glittering in the moonlight, brimming with unshed tears. "I've never told anyone. I—I made up something about who raised me…"

She'd never told anyone she'd been raised in an asylum because everyone knew what kind of people inhabited such places, and it would be assumed that after growing up with the insane, Ella herself might not be too sound of mind.

And she'd told him because, as he'd pointed out, he was safe to confide in, because he'd soon be gone.

"I won't tell a soul," he promised her. "Your secret is safe with me, Ella."

It was as if the floodgates had been opened, and now she couldn't stem the rush of words. "I was there so long no one could remember where my father had moved to, after he left me there. They didn't keep the best records, and if he ever contacted them about me, they didn't say."

"Did you have some sort of schooling there?" he asked. Ella always used good grammar, and he'd seen her read the words from the hymnal. And she had to be able to do some ciphering, didn't she, to add up costs and amounts of ingredients in recipes?

"Yes, when we weren't needed to do work, like tending the superintendent's wife's garden. I was luckier than most—I worked in the kitchen, so I always had something to eat." Her gaze grew distant then, as if she was lost in remembrance.

So that was how she had learned to cook—probably taught by another tyrant like Mrs. Powell.

"When did you leave there?" he asked, keeping his voice even and matter-of-fact, as if what she had been saying hadn't horrified him. "Did they help those who had grown up to gain employment and a place to stay?" He was afraid he would not like her answer.

Ella's laugh was bitter. "The girls, yes—but rumors reached those of us still there as to what sort of employment it was, and I wanted no part of it. So I escaped one night…and walked until I came to a town." She avoided looking at him then, and Nate was sure there was much more that she wasn't saying.

For a moment he could say nothing, so lost was he in sorrow for the horror she had experienced because of a father who hadn't lived up to his responsibility. No wonder Ella never thought she deserved anything. She and every one of the other children at that place had probably been made to feel like a charity case, an object of pious scorn or, at best, condescending pity. How far Ella Justiss had come from that, though. She'd made her own way, asking only for a chance. What a fighter she was!

"I think you're a remarkable woman," he murmured, taking Ella's hand. "Don't you think you could trust Maude with a secret like this? She seems like a good friend to you." Most young ladies had confidantes, a sister or a best friend, didn't they? He didn't like to think that when he left, Ella would be back to having no one who really knew her.

She shrugged. "Maybe, but I'd already told her a made-up story when I first met her. She'd be angry that I lied to her."

"Not if you told her what you told me," he said, but he guessed from the defiant, proud lift of her chin that she didn't want anyone, not even a friend, to pity her, either. "But of course that's up to you," he added. "At least promise me you won't let bullies like Mrs. Powell push you around now that you're a successful businesswoman about to have her own independent establishment. You know that woman's just jealous 'cause you're young and doing this all on your own."

Ella gave him a watery smile. "Perhaps you're right," she said.

"That's m—" he began, then hastily amended it to "that's the spirit." He'd been about to say, "that's my girl," which of course were words he had no right to utter.

"It's getting late. I'd better be going home now."

He stood up and held out a hand to her to help her rise.

"Come here, charity girl...let me show you the secret ingredients that make Mister Antoine's biscuits the flakiest in all the South. Why, I once served them to Beauregard himself..." the Cajun-accented voice purred. "The superintendent and his wife will be quite pleased when I bring them to the table at supper. But I will save the best ones for you, my sweet little girl..."

Then she felt that familiar heated, fleshy touch of his hands on her shoulder...

She woke to a pounding on her door, and heard a man calling, "Miss Ella! Miss Ella! You all right?" Then the sound changed direction, as if the man had turned to call down the hall. "Mrs. Meyer, Miss Ella's screamin' somethin' fierce. You reckon some Comanche's climbed in her winder, or one a' them drunken drummers? Reckon I oughta fetch that shotgun."

"Don't be silly, Delbert." Then Ella heard the proprietress's calmer, no-nonsense voice against the door. "Miss Ella? Open the door if you're all right, otherwise I'm going to use my key..."

Heart pounding, Ella stared at the knob rattling in the door, conscious of the chill of a cold sweat beading her arms, shoulders and neck, and the hair that clung damply to her forehead.

"I—I'm all right, Mrs. Meyer," she called out. "J-just had a nightmare, that's all. Sorry I disturbed you." She tried to sound as if she was merely embarrassed and laughing at herself, but while the vestiges of the dream still clung to her with icy tentacles, it was hard to even formulate the words, let alone convince anyone, especially herself.

"What in tarnation—?" she heard another male voice inquire from down the hall, and heavy footsteps coming closer.

Good heavens, she must have awakened the whole house. Waves of humiliation swept over her. She heard the floorboards creak as if the bodies outside shifted position.

"Ella, it's me, Maude. I'm going to warm some milk and bring it up to you. Let me in when I come back, okay?"

She heard murmuring and footsteps as the inhabitants of the boardinghouse dispersed from their post outside her room.

It had been foolish to think that discussing her dreadful childhood with Bohannan wouldn't resurrect her familiar nightmare, Ella thought as she waited for Maude to return. Should she confide in Maude, as Bohannan had urged? Maude would be willing to listen, she knew.

Ella had only skimmed the surface of what she could have told Bohannan. The hour had been growing late, and she hadn't wanted to risk seeing pity in those blue eyes. If she told Maude about her past, and went into more detail, would it be like shining the light on vermin, sending those remembrances fleeing into the darker, deeper recesses of her brain? Or would it bring those memories that she couldn't quite recall to the surface, memories so horrible that they would destroy her if she fully remembered them?

Chapter Thirteen

Ella was just mounting the steps to the boardinghouse the next day when Maude came bustling out.

"Did you come back so we could walk to the meeting together? That's nice."

Meeting?

At Ella's blank look, Maude crowed, "You forgot, didn't you, silly goose? Don't say you're not going to the Spinsters' Club meeting."

"I...I didn't remember," Ella admitted. "I suppose I can go, but I can't stay very long, as usual." It would be fun to go and tell the other ladies about the café raising, for she hadn't seen any of them since she'd decided to go ahead with the plan.

Maude chuckled. "Somebody's a little distracted these days, and I think I know why," she said in a sing-song voice.

"Well, sure I am," Ella replied. "I keep changing my mind about the layout of the café, where I want the windows, whether to expand the menu—you know the sort of thing."

"It's not what, but *who* that's distracting you," Maude

retorted. "I think a certain tall handsome fellow with twinkling blue eyes is to blame."

"Maude Harkey, I wish you would stop teasing me about Bohannan," Ella snapped. "He and I are friends, but I have no intention of losing my heart to a man who doesn't mean to stay in Simpson Creek a minute longer than he has to."

"Peace!" Maude said, holding up a hand. "I didn't mean to get you all riled up." It was clear she wasn't daunted by her friend's vehemence. "So he's still planning on leaving when he finishes the furniture?" she asked as they made their way down Main Street toward the church social hall where the Spinsters' Club meetings were held. "Once he started playing piano for the church, I rather thought he might decide to stay. Did he say where he's going?"

"To California," Ella said, pretending great interest in the display of fabric and notions in the window of the mercantile so her voice wouldn't betray that she cared one way or the other. "San Francisco, to be exact."

"Why there?"

"A business opportunity, he told me the other night," Ella said, remembering the conversation they'd had on the way back from practicing his music. "His cousin is apparently a man of some wealth and influence there, and he's offered Nate a partnership in a hotel, as well as introductions to his powerful friends."

Maude wrinkled her nose. "He didn't strike me as the sort of person who'd be interested in that kind of life," she murmured. "A man who's good at working with his hands, who likes to play music…"

Ella shrugged. "To each his own, I guess. It doesn't matter to me, anyway. He said he thought he'd be done repairing my three tables and the chairs that go with them at the end of this week, and tomorrow is Friday, so I'll imagine he'll leave the next morning." No matter how much he'd encouraged her to accept the church's gift of the café, she thought, he apparently didn't care enough to stay and see it built.

Maude gave her a look that said Ella hadn't convinced *her* of that, even if she'd managed to fool herself. "Ella Justiss, all you'd have to do is crook your little finger and that man would stay."

"Oh, you think so, do you?" Ella retorted, lowering her voice because they'd reached the churchyard by then, and a trio of ladies were just entering the social hall ahead of them. "I don't, and I think you're a great deal more interested in Mr. Bohannan than I am. Why don't you go flutter your eyelashes at him, if you find him so fascinating? See if he'll stay for *you*."

She had her hand on the door and would have flounced on into the social hall ahead of Maude, but her friend placed a gentle hand on her shoulder, detaining her. "Ella, I didn't say *I* was interested in Mr. Bohannan," she said calmly. "I'm not."

Ella realized how she had lashed out at her friend, and how defensive she had sounded. "I'm sorry, Maude. I didn't mean to be so cross."

"It's all right. And just between me and you, I've about resigned myself to being an old maid."

That stopped Ella short. "Horsefeathers, Maude. You won't be an old maid. You just haven't made the right match yet."

It was Maude's turn to shrug. "The Spinsters' Club's been in existence for four years now. If the Lord wants me to have a husband, He'll find me one. If not...well, I intend to find out what else He wants me to do with my life." She sighed. "We'd better go on in. It wouldn't do for the president to be late, would it?"

Ella followed her friend inside, wishing she had a share of Maude's equanimity. She herself longed to be cherished by a strong, protective man—and yet there was something fearful about that, too, something buried deeply in her brain that she couldn't identify, the same something that visited her in her nightmares. *Mustn't think about that now...*

Maude banged the gavel, calling the meeting to order, and Ella soon discovered that the other Spinsters had already caught wind of the coming café raising and planned to play a major role in it. They had taken it upon themselves to make a list of what dish all the ladies of the town, both married and single, were bringing for the noon meal, to assure the menu would be varied. Ella was not to bring anything, Maude told her—her job was to relax and enjoy directing the workmen.

"Thank you," Ella breathed, touched at their thoughtfulness. "You're all so organized. I didn't even know anyone knew about the event. Did you tell them all, Maude?"

Her friend nodded, eyes sparkling. "With a bit of help from Faith," she said, nodding toward the preacher's wife, who was also present. "We're all so pleased for you, Ella honey, and we wanted to make sure it's a special day."

Tears stung Ella's eyes. "Y'all have thought of everything!" she cried. "I don't know how to thank you."

Maude made a carefree gesture. "We're all there for each other, aren't we? I'm glad we've grown beyond a group of women only out to make marriages—though that's still important, of course."

Ella was a relative newcomer to Simpson Creek, but

she'd heard tales of the way the Spinsters had rallied to nurse the victims of the flu epidemic, and she'd seen the way they'd provided emotional support for each other, brought over meals when there was illness and helped with new babies.

After refreshments and the latest news had been enjoyed, the meeting broke up.

"Are you stopping back at the boardinghouse, Ella?" Maude asked.

"No, I need to get back to the café to start working on supper. I'll see you later." She left Maude talking to some of the other members.

Nate gazed with satisfaction at the four sets of newly repaired tables and chairs he had just varnished for Ella—her three sets, plus an additional one he had built.

He'd wanted to make the furniture with lots of decorative features like scrolled tops on the top rail of the chairs, caned seats, a midrail with an oval wood medallion with E carved into it, as well as fancy spindle legs for both table and chairs. But that would have been the work of months, not weeks, and her new café would need furniture before that. So he'd been forced to be practical, but the end result had been much nicer than the serviceable pieces she'd had in her café that had been no better than what was in the saloon. He'd varnished the new pieces a darker shade, too, that he thought she would like.

He could still picture making furniture with those fancy touches on them for her, though, perhaps for a bedroom dressing table and bench, where she would sit and comb out that thick, dark hair...

Thinking like that was a waste of time. He'd be hundreds of miles away long before Ella ever had more than just a room at the boardinghouse

"You do beautiful work," said a female voice, startling him. "Are those for Ella?"

He whirled around. It was Ella's friend Maude Harkey from the boardinghouse.

"Miss Harkey," he said, wondering why she had come. "Thank you. Yes, those are for Ella's—*Miss* Ella's—café," he corrected himself. "What may I do for you?"

The red-headed woman hadn't come to flirt with him, he thought, judging by the no-nonsense way she met his gaze. That was a relief. Maude Harkey was certainly an attractive woman, and she would be a credit to any man, but she wasn't the one who tempted him to throw his dreams of San Francisco to the wind.

The woman replied, "You know I'm a good friend of Ella's, right?"

"Yes, she's told me that." He wondered where this was leading.

Maude seemed to hesitate, her gaze wavering, then she drew herself up straight again.

"I don't want anything to hurt my friend," she said, looking him in the eye again.

He waited, but that was all she seemed to want to say.

"Why are you telling me this?"

Again, Maude Harkey seemed to waver. "Are you planning on leaving town as soon as you deliver those tables and chairs to her?" she asked, nodding toward them where they stood drying in the lumberyard shed.

He was sure as blazes *not* going to discuss his plans with this woman, not when he hadn't finished debating with himself on that very subject. *What business is it of hers?*

"That was the deal we agreed upon, George Detwiler, Miss Ella and I," he said. It was the truth—that *was* the original deal. "Room and board in exchange for repairing and rebuilding the furniture for the saloon and the café."

"You don't look like a fool," Maude said.

He blinked. Even for a redhead, it was a bold thing to say.

"No? And what would make me a fool, Miss Harkey?"

"Thinking that the grass is greener in San Francisco, Mr. Bohannan," she said crisply.

"I'm not sure what you're saying, Miss Harkey." He was determined to make this woman say exactly what she meant and stop talking in riddles.

"Like I said, I care about my friend Ella and don't want to see her hurt."

"That makes two of us, Miss Harkey. But what does it have to do with me?"

His words seemed to encourage her a little, but she was still diffident.

"I—I've only known Ella Justiss since she came to Simpson Creek a couple of years ago—not always, like the rest of my friends—but I…think she's had a hard life. I know her parents are dead and she's been alone for a while, but other than that, she's pretty closemouthed. I think somewhere along the line, she was hurt."

You don't know the half of it, Nate thought, remembering what Ella had told him about the asylum. He felt humbled anew that Ella had chosen to confide in him when she hadn't told her close female friend.

She did it because she knows I'm not staying, Nate reminded himself. Yet Maude seemed to be hinting that Ella would be hurt if he left.

Did Ella really care about him as much as that?

But how badly would she be hurt if he declared he was staying, then started feeling confined by small-town life, and left later?

He rubbed the back of his neck. "I haven't made up my mind to anything, Miss Harkey," he said.

The lack of a clear answer seemed to flummox her. "Pray about it," she said. "Don't be blind *and* a fool. Good day to you, Mr. Bohannan." Then turned on her heel and fled.

He stood staring in the direction Maude had gone long after she was out of sight.

It had to have been difficult for Ella's friend to come face him like that. He had to admire the strength of the two women's friendship that she would take such a thing upon herself. He knew with certainty that Ella not only hadn't put her up to it but had no knowledge of her friend's action.

It was a little early yet for supper, but he couldn't accomplish anything more today. After putting his tools away, he shut the door of the shed and headed back up the road toward the café.

He hadn't noticed the tiny telegraph office until he'd passed it this morning, and it had gotten him thinking. He needed to let his cousin Russell know where he was and what had happened to delay him, and that he was still planning to join him in San Francisco. A letter would take weeks, and by the time his cousin answered, Nate would be on the way. But now he could send a telegram, and hopefully get an answer in a day or so.

He pictured the message arriving in the telegraph office in bustling, prosperous San Francisco, and a messenger delivering it to Russell Blake's grand hotel situated on the bay. From Russell's letters, he knew it was a city built on steep hills, bustling with commerce, the air salty and filled with a dozen languages and the scent of many ethnic cuisines. He pictured the rolling fogs and chilly temperatures—hard to imagine in Texas, when the days could still be hot as blue blazes in late September and usually would be so until November.

San Francisco—what a change it would be from Simpson Creek, with one main street, one hotel, one church, with Ella's café being only the second eating establishment. Though the town was nestled in the central Texas Hill Country, the only hills in sight were at a distance, and the only scent that reached his nostrils was that of the horses tied here and there to hitching rails.

He'd be a stranger when he arrived in San Francisco, a greenhorn. He was used to being a newcomer—his life had been a series of new places where he and his father would live until Cal Bohannan got an itch to find a newer place. Nate was tired of always being on the move, always being new. San Francisco would be his final destination, he'd promised himself.

He'd settle down and raise a family there. Russell had told him that many of his powerful friends had lovely sisters and daughters, and as Russell Blake's cousin and partner, he could have his pick to be his wife and the mother of his children.

He'd only been in Simpson Creek a short time, but he was already known to everyone, and he'd gone quite a ways in learning all their names, too. They no longer counted him a stranger. He hadn't had an auspicious introduction here, thanks to Salali, but most days it seemed like everyone but Zeke Carter and Mrs. Powell had resolved to let bygones be bygones.

His stomach rumbled, reminding Nate it had been a long time since the noon meal. He'd better get that telegram sent and get on down to Ella's café. He pushed the door of the little telegraph office open.

Simpson Creek would always be a source of fond memories to him. He'd tell his children someday about the time he'd been an assistant in a medicine show, an occupant of the jail for half a day, then the man who repaired furniture and played piano for Sunday services at the church. But when he tried to picture the refined lady who was his future wife, the only woman whose image came to mind was Ella Justiss.

Chapter Fourteen

"Will you still be done with the tables and chairs for the café tomorrow?" Ella asked as she finished putting away the last of the supper dishes. She'd closed early tonight, for after a few early customers, it seemed as if everyone else had chosen to take supper elsewhere, and she didn't feel inclined to wait around on the off chance someone would arrive at the café just before seven.

Ella hoped her question didn't make her sound apprehensive, but surely it was better to know when Nate was leaving than to continue in ignorance. She knew she would miss his presence at meals and his compliments on her cooking, as well as the time they spent together most evenings. Even with the prospect of the soon-to-be-built new café to cheer her, it felt as if her life would return to its former humdrum state after he was gone.

Nate looked up from the *Simpson Creek Intelligencer* he'd been perusing. "I thought you might like to stroll down to the lumberyard this evening and have a look at what I've done. You can let me know if you like them," he said. "I've been keeping them in the shed while the varnish dries."

What's he going to do if I say I don't like them, she

thought with a crossness born of her uncertainty, *stay on and make entirely new sets?*

"All right, we can do that," she murmured, realizing he hadn't answered her unspoken question as to when her furniture would be done—and when he would be leaving. "But I'm sure they'll be fine. After seeing your repairs to George's tables and chairs, I'm sure I'll be happy with mine."

Detwiler had been so pleased with the tables and chairs Nate had repaired for him, in fact, that he'd given Nate an unexpected double-eagle tip and declared to the occupants of the saloon that the drinks were on the house. Twenty dollars would go a long way on Nate's travels if he was careful, Ella thought.

"You like cooking for folks, don't you?" he asked after she'd locked the café and they walked away from it.

She looked at him, but his shadowed face revealed nothing. "I suppose I do." She *did* like it, she realized. She felt valuable when people ate everything on their plates and went away with satisfied looks on their faces.

"Do you ever wonder why you like doing that?" he asked. "I mean, why that, and not something else?"

She shrugged. A man wouldn't understand that it wasn't as if there were that many things for a single female to do—honest things, that is, she thought as she heard one of the saloon girls utter a shrill laugh as they passed the front of the saloon.

"I learned to cook at the asylum," she reminded him.

"Did you choose that? Or were you assigned to do it?"

"I jumped at the chance," she told him honestly. "Cook's helper was the only one who could be sure of getting enough to eat."

He glanced at her, then back at the boardwalk in front of them.

"Did you like doing it—beyond getting enough to eat, I mean? Did it make you feel accomplished? Important?"

"Hardly," she said with a chuckle. "The superintendent and his wife had a way of taking any sense of accomplishment away from an orphan, even the one who helped prepare their much tastier, fancier foods. But then Franny came along…"

"Franny?"

She hadn't thought of Franny in years, Ella realized. "Franny Gaines. She was one of the younger girls—very frail and sickly. Any exertion made her short of breath. Cook said she had a bad heart, that she wouldn't live to make old bones." She shivered involuntarily as she remembered the girl's wan, pasty face, the hopeless eyes. "By the time she got to the lineup for meals, she was always last, and some of the bigger kids often stole her food. I made it my business to give her extra bread and meat that I tucked away in my apron. Stole sweets for her from the superintendent's table, too. She always smiled at me like I hung the moon."

"Whatever happened to Franny?"

Ella shrugged. "I woke one morning and her bed was empty. They said she'd died during the night." She blinked to stop the involuntary tears that sprang to her eyes, all these years later, when she remembered how devastated she'd felt.

"I'm sorry. I didn't mean to make you sad," he said softly.

She glanced at him. "It was a long time ago. And I know I made her happy while I could. The night before she died I'd given her a big piece of chocolate cake, and she could hardly stop smiling long enough to eat it. I always felt good about making her smile like that, with what I'd cooked."

They proceeded in silence for a ways after that. It was the farthest she'd ever walked with him, she mused as they turned right at the church and strolled down Fannin Street past the parsonage, a couple of houses and the school. The street paralleled the course of Simpson Creek, which ran fairly straight for a mile or two before it turned northeast and joined the San Saba River.

She supposed a proper miss would not go even this far away from town with a man, even though the lumber mill lay just beyond the school. But she felt as if she had no reason not to trust him—she felt *safe* with Nate Bohannan. Besides, there was no one to see them, unless one counted the owl who had hooted at them from the branches of a cottonwood as they walked past in the fading light. It was the opposite end of town from the hotel and the saloon, the only place that saw any activity in the evenings. Nate carried her lantern, and the light bounced over the short path that led down off Fannin Street to the lumber mill, which loomed over the creek.

"Did Mr. Dayton leave you a key?" she asked, for everything looked closed and dark in the mill.

Nate chuckled. "I don't think Dayton trusts anyone so far as that," he said. "But he doesn't lock his shed, and I put the pieces in here to keep them away from the dust while the varnish was drying." He led her around the side of the large building to a small shed. He'd given her his arm before, but now he let her go, saying, "Now close your eyes. I don't want you to open them till I've lit the bigger lantern inside."

Obediently, she did as he asked, and listened as he pushed open the door. She heard a soft thud as he set his lantern down. She heard him strike a match, and then a brighter light glowed against her closed lids.

"You may open your eyes now, Miss Ella."

As her eyes adjusted to the light, she saw table-and-chair sets grouped together, with spaces in between, as if they already graced the floor of her café. With a cry of admiration, she rushed forward, extending a hand and running it appreciatively over the surface of the closest table. She could feel the grain of wood, sanded so smooth that it felt like glass, and yet the grain of the pecan wood still felt alive beneath the pads of her fingers. She moved on to a chair. He'd used some sort of oil on the pieces, so that her touch glided over each glossy surface, and the lantern made them gleam with reflected brilliance.

"They're *wonderful,* Nate," she breathed, unable to believe any part of this same wood had been present when Robert Salali had wreaked his havoc on the café and saloon. Not a scar or gash remained. "I like the darker color." She closed her eyes and sighed with pleasure, then opened them again as her fingers explored the top rail of one of the chairs. "They're *perfect,*" she told him, and was surprised to see that his gaze was trained upon his boots. "What's wrong?"

"Nothing, Miss Ella. I'm glad you like them." He'd forced himself to look away, unable to watch any longer as her expression changed from surprised, to pleased, to utter bliss as she closed her eyes and let her fingers stroke the surfaces he'd sanded for endless hours. It was all he could do not to take her in his arms and kiss her until she knew what true bliss really was.

But he could never do that and still leave her in the not-too-distant future, he knew.

"You're quite the craftsman. Thank you so much," Ella went on, and then was silent for so long that he was forced to look up again.

She was staring at the tables and chairs, and even in profile, he could see the confusion furrowing her lovely brow. He watched her point a shaking index finger at each piece as she counted it.

"But…but there's a whole additional set of tables and chairs here," she said, turning back to him. "You made more than I originally had."

Her dark eyes were shining up at him, and once again, he had to rein himself in. He let himself grin, though he still tried to make it sound as if it was not such a tremendous feat. "Well, you'd said your café's going to be bigger than the one you have now, so I thought you'd need more tables and chairs. Actually, I thought of making one more set."

He'd had to spend some of the money Detwiler had given him as a tip for the additional furniture, though the lumberman had tried to talk him into a barter deal—another table-and-chairs set for his missus instead. But he'd been reluctant to make any deal that would keep him longer in Simpson Creek, until he made up his mind to go or stay.

Her brow furrowed again, then her eyebrows rose. "Then you're not…l-leaving tomorrow or the next day?" she asked. Her eyes held a wariness, as if she wanted to give way to joy but was afraid to.

He gave an elaborate shrug. "A fellow would have to be a pure fool to ride away from a feast like I hear there'll be at the café raising," he said. "Figured I might as well keep busy building another table and chairs, meanwhile….unless you're sick of feeding me, that is."

"You'll stay through next Saturday?" she cried.

"You'll be there building my café along with the rest of the men?"

"Reckon I will," he said, letting his grin broaden.

"I suppose you're an expert café builder, too?" she asked dryly.

"As a matter of fact, no, I've never built anything big like that," he admitted, "but I figured I might as well add it to my repertoire of skills. I'm sure some of the other men can teach me about how to frame a building and lay a floor and such, but I have an idea or two about how your counter ought to look, and you'll be needing cabinets for your supplies and dishes like the ones you have now..."

She clapped her hands together and gave a little jump. "Nate, I'm so glad you'll be here that day!" Then she astonished him by leaning up and kissing him on the cheek.

No man could have resisted her then, he told himself later.

Don't forget your plan, a voice inside him clamored. *You're going to San Francisco to be a rich tycoon. You're going to marry an heiress.*

He told that voice to shut up, and put his arms around her and lowered his lips to hers, groaning inwardly as he tasted their sweetness. *I'll never be able to leave now...*

Then he felt her pushing against his chest—no, that was too mild a word. She was struggling against him like a wild bird in a tiny cage, uttering strangled, terrified little moans. Instantly, he released her.

"Ella—Ella! What's wrong?"

She looked dazed, like someone waking from a nightmare—as if she didn't even know him.

"Ella, it's me, Nate," he said, keeping his voice soft and soothing. He longed to hold her, to stroke her hair and calm her, but he knew he must not even touch her. "I'm sorry…" he murmured. "I—I didn't mean to frighten you. I shouldn't have done that…"

He saw it as she must see it—he'd taken advantage of their isolation here to do something he would have never dared to do otherwise.

Her dark eyes were troubled, but at least he could tell she recognized him now. "I—I don't know what came over me just then. It—your kiss—felt good, honest it did. Then something came over me, something I don't understand…and I got scared."

"Probably just an attack of common sense," he said wryly, keeping his voice light, not revealing how disappointed he was that the moment had gone so wrong. For a few seconds there, he had been flying, full of hope and optimism and—had it been *love?*

Now he wondered even more what had happened to her in that asylum that tormented her.

"I suppose we'd better get you back to the boardinghouse before your friend Maude sends out a search party."

"Yes. Yes, you're right," she said, and they walked back, not touching, with at least a foot between them.

Waving a sheet of paper, Mr. Jewett, the telegraph operator, flagged Nate down the next morning as he headed down Main Street toward the lumber mill. "Got an answer for ya from Californy, Mr. Bohannan!"

Suddenly his breakfast bacon wasn't sitting too well. He hadn't expected his cousin to reply so quickly, and the fact that he had could be either good or bad. Striding over to where the wiry older man stood outside his office, he took the paper from him, but before he could read it, Jewett said, "Sounds like he wants you out t' San Francisco awful bad. You gonna go?"

Nate shrugged. He didn't take the time to be offended that the telegrapher felt free to comment on the message's contents; telegraph operators seemed to feel they had a right to be nosy since they were the ones who translated the mysterious Morse code dots and dashes into meaningful communication. But even if Nate had been inclined to confide in the man, he couldn't very well tell Jewett something he didn't even know himself. He'd lain awake much of the night after seeing Ella home and he still didn't know what his course should be.

"Thanks," he said, handing Jewett a dime as a tip, then kept walking.

He didn't pause to unfold the message until he was safely ensconced in what he had come to think of as "his" workroom in the mill. It read:

Nate cease dallying in one-horse town and get out here {stop}

Opportunity knocks but once {stop}

Wine women & song for the asking {stop}

Advise when you are on way {stop}

Nate groaned and crumpled the paper into a ball, throwing it into a corner. Then, thinking Dayton might find it, he got up and stuffed the ball into his pocket. Before last night, he'd hoped Russell had already given up on Nate coming and had taken someone else into partnership. Now he just didn't know what he wanted to do, not after Ella had pushed him away as she had. He cared for her—loved her, if he was honest with himself. But what if there was something in her past, some fear that had too strong a hold on her? What if she never got over it?

Russell still wanted him to come, and he sensed impatience in his cousin's deprecatory labeling of Simpson Creek as a "one-horse town." The siren song of San Francisco and all that Russell had promised washed over him. Wine, women and song, money and power. A wealthy, beautiful wife, compliant in nature, free of the kind of shadows that hung over Ella...

But what if, as a wealthy old man in San Francisco, he realized he'd left the real prize in Texas?

How could he make the right decision without knowing what would happen? No one could know the future—God wasn't about to strike him with a lightning bolt on the way back from the lumber mill and reveal his new course, as He had struck Paul en route to Damascus, Nate thought, remembering Reverend Chadwick's sermon last Sunday.

He should pray about it, Nate knew. But he wanted an answer *now,* while he stood at this fork in the road of his life, before he chose the wrong path.

He was struck by a sudden wish to open the pages of a Bible at random and seek guidance that way. He'd seen his father do that. What was that story he'd told him about—something about a man named Gideon, in the Old Testament, and the laying out of a sheepskin as a means of having the Lord show him His will? He wished he knew his scriptures better.

"Don't hear no work gettin' done in here at my lathe," Dayton grumbled, startling Nate out of his daydream. "Don't reckon all this time you been usin' it, you thought about me havin' to use it again one day. If you ain't gonna make me a table an' chairs for my missus, I'm a-gonna have to be sittin' in front a' that lathe again one a' these days. Not that I could make anythin' near like what you can do."

He'd been so lost in his thoughts that he hadn't heard

the big man lumber into the room. "Sorry," Nate said. "You're right. I need to finish this set before the end of the week when Miss Ella's café goes up, so I'll get back to work."

Satisfied, the other man trudged out of the workroom, and Nate set the table leg he'd been about to work on into the vise.

He could go and visit the preacher and ask him about that story of Gideon and the sheepskin. Reverend Gil could show him where it was in the Bible, too, and let him read it.

Dayton was right, though. He needed to finish Ella's furniture so it would be ready for the opening. Ella had sent his noon meal wrapped up in brown paper so he wouldn't have to take more time going back to the café to eat. Maybe if he set to work with a will, he could make up for the time he'd lost daydreaming. Then he could justify leaving a few minutes earlier than usual to stop at the preacher's before he went to Ella's café for supper.

He prayed Reverend Gil would be able to help him find the answer he needed.

Chapter Fifteen

"You gonna bring me my meal, girl, or just stand there lettin' it get cold?" Zeke Carter groused, snapping Ella out of her thoughts like a bucketful of cold water on a lit match. She realized she'd picked up his plateful of food from the stove and had been about to take it out to the irascible old man when she'd started thinking about last night. *That kiss*...

"Sorry, Mr. Carter, didn't mean to make you wait," she said, keeping her tone even. Why did he keep coming here, she thought, if all he did was complain?

"'Bout time," he retorted as she set his plate of roast beef hash in front of him. "You think I'm gonna walk that extra distance to get bad service like this when you move t'other side of the creek, you better think again, missy."

"It's totally up to you where you eat, of course." Why was he taking his dinner here today, anyway? He usually didn't come to plague her until Sunday night. "Is your daughter away?" she asked, determined to be pleasant.

"Yeah, not that it's any a' your bidness. She don't care if her old father has a decent meal any more'n you do, but goes gallivantin' off to visit her sister in Austin. She'll probably come back after I starve t'death," he concluded gloomily.

"Oh, I'm sure between Mrs. Powell and me, we can keep that from happening," she told him. She couldn't help hoping it would be mostly the other woman who would keep him fed.

Carter stopped with his fork halfway to his mouth. "You bein' pert, missy?"

She shook her head. "Just concerned for your welfare, Mr. Carter."

A cowboy seeking a sandwich for the trail came in then, saving her from further conversation with the old man, and she was soon able to go back to her contemplation.

The kiss had been her own fault. What red-blooded man wouldn't kiss a girl if she threw herself at him as she had, especially given their isolated surroundings? Of course, Nate had turned her impetuous kiss on his cheek into a real kiss!

She'd started to enjoy the kiss, she admitted to herself, every bit as much as he seemed to, until alarm bells within her had begun to clang. He'd kindly called her pushing him away "common sense," and maybe it was, but there'd been some element of fear within her, too.

A fear that had triggered another of her nightmares last night. This time she'd managed to awaken herself and stifle her scream with the pillow before anyone pounded on her door.

What had Nate thought of the kiss? Not much, apparently, for he had apologized, which was hardly flattering. But he was probably just being gentlemanly, Ella protested to herself. He'd assumed the fault for taking advantage of a thank-you peck on the cheek.

He hadn't given her much of a clue as to his thoughts this morning when he'd come for breakfast, either. She'd caught his gaze resting on her once, but his eyes had been unreadable. He hadn't winked at her, or grinned. He was probably thinking what a strange, prudish girl she was—to initiate a kiss then act as if he'd attacked her.

There wasn't anything in his look to make her think he cared for her—not enough to stay in Simpson Creek after her café was completed, anyway.

Had the kiss been just a thing born of the moment? How could she tell either way?

Now she wished she had paid more attention when the Spinsters' Club ladies chattered and giggled about the ways of men, for she couldn't go to Kate Patterson, for example, and ask her how she'd first known Gabe Bryant, who was now her fiancé, loved her. Ella wouldn't want to answer Kate's natural question as to what had prompted her questions, or take the chance that Kate might mention it to other friends, or worse yet, her aunt. That would have been the same as standing in the middle of Main Street on a Saturday morning and shouting it at the top of her lungs.

Maude would be discreet about her questions, Ella thought—but Maude had never had a serious beau, so how could she know how to advise Ella about what Nate Bohannan might be thinking? And she couldn't bear the thought of Maude's look of pity if Nate rode away the day after he'd finished the cafe furnishings and made a fool out of Ella for hoping.

"The story of Gideon and the sheepskin…" For a moment Gil Chadwick looked blank as he sat across from Nate in the parsonage parlor. A few seconds passed while he stared off quietly, then: "Oh! You mean the time Gideon laid the *fleece* out, to get the Lord to show him a sign."

Sheepskin? Fleece? It was the same thing, wasn't it?

The preacher seized a well-worn Bible from his nearby desk and began to thumb through it. "Yes, that's in the book of Judges, in the Old Testament. Chapter six, to be exact." He stopped turning pages and smiled. "Yes, that was certainly an illustration of God's patience with His people as we seek His will," he added with a chuckle, and began to read: "'Behold, I will put a fleece of wool in the floor, and if the dew be on the fleece only, and it be dry upon all the earth beside...'"

Nate listened patiently as the young preacher explained that Gideon had insisted that God not only prove He would save Israel by making the fleece wet when the ground was dry, but also the reverse. In His infinite patience, God had done so, and Israel was saved from its enemies.

"May I ask why you're inquiring about this?" Gil asked.

Nate rubbed his jaw. "Well, Preacher, I...uh...need to make a decision. And it needs to be the right one. My pa told me this story about Gideon once, a long time ago. I wasn't sure I remembered it right."

He couldn't very well tell Gil how he was going to lay this particular fleece—that he would look for guidance from the preacher's sermon this Sunday as to whether he should go or stay—for fear that it would influence the preacher's sermon topic.

"I see..."

Nate feared the preacher, who studied him now with perceptive hazel eyes, could indeed see, somehow, what was on his mind. "Papa also used to open up the pages of the Bible at random, when he needed Heavenly guidance," he said, trying to distract Chadwick.

Gil Chadwick chuckled. "That's an approach a lot of folks use, but sometimes it works better than others. One time when I was younger, I was rather disheartened about something, and I tried that. My finger fell on the verse about the apostle Judas leaving the temple and hanging himself. I'm very sure the Lord didn't intend me to do that!"

Nate laughed, too.

"But you know, Nate," the preacher went on, "the easiest way of all is just to pray about your decision. The Lord wants us to talk to Him as friend to friend."

"I…I have trouble hearing His answers that way, Preacher. Guess I'm not much good at praying." He'd never stolen, or murdered, or committed any of the other major sins, but he hadn't stayed on the straight-and-narrow path all his life. Sometimes he knew he just didn't *listen* for what the Lord might be saying.

"It's hard to be quiet and listen for that 'still, small Voice,' isn't it?" the preacher agreed. "But don't be too hard on yourself, Nate. This town saw you make the right choice to stay and help, when you could have left George Detwiler and Miss Ella in the midst of the destruction your former employer wreaked. And you've helped the church by playing piano so Sarah Walker can prepare for her coming baby."

"I appreciate your saying that." Nate was glad he had come. Reverend Gil was an easy man to talk to, even if he did tend to give a fellow too much credit.

A door opened down the hall, and a savory scent reached his nostrils. Nate stood as Mrs. Chadwick entered the parlor and laid an affectionate hand on her husband's shoulder. The reverend smiled up at his wife.

"Hello, Mr. Bohannan," she said. "It's good to see you. We certainly enjoyed hearing you play the piano last Sunday."

"Thank you, ma'am."

"Would you like to have supper with us? There's plenty, and you're more than welcome."

"Thanks," he said again, "but I know Miss Ella's expecting me at the café. I'd best be leaving. Reverend Chadwick, I appreciate your time."

"I'll be praying for you, Nate," Chadwick said as he extended his hand.

Nate headed for the café, feeling lighter of heart than when he'd arrived at the parsonage. It was clear the young preacher and his wife shared a deep love. Nate wanted that for himself—a wife he loved, who loved him back.

Will it be Ella, if I can find out what frightened her the night before—or some as-yet-faceless lady in San Francisco?

He'd try praying, for sure. But he couldn't help wondering what the sermon would be about on Sunday, and whether it would shine any light on his decision.

Meanwhile, perhaps he should watch for a sign—one might appear even before next Sunday.

Nate had never listened as hard as he listened to the sermon that Sunday. Reverend Chadwick spoke about how the apostle Peter had walked on water in the Sea of Galilee just like Jesus, but then Peter had gotten scared and would have sunk like a stone if Jesus hadn't taken hold of him.

If there was some sort of clue in the discourse about what choice Nate should make, he hadn't heard it. Then again, maybe fleece-laying was only for holy men, he thought, and he sure wasn't one of those. But hadn't God promised to answer any believer's prayer one way or another? Perhaps he just had to be open to the Lord's leading.

The preacher concluded his sermon, reminded everyone to come and help out at the café raising the following Saturday, then gave the benediction. Nate sighed a lot more gustily than he'd meant to, but he felt as much in the dark as ever.

Was it merely that the Lord couldn't be told when to give a sign? Maybe it had been sort of presumptuous of him to expect that the sign would appear right in the middle of church as he'd asked for it to, as if the Creator of the world was his to command.

"What's wrong?" Ella asked him softly as everyone stood to leave.

He hoped his grin looked genuine. "Not a thing, as long as you save me a couple or three fried-chicken legs for dinner, and some of your mashed potatoes and gravy," he said.

He was guiltily aware that Ella was puzzled at his behavior. She had to be wondering why he'd kissed her a couple of nights before, then acted as if the kiss had never happened. He'd been as friendly as always, but no more than that, and had not suggested she join him when he'd gone to the church to practice the hymns after supper.

He hated thinking he might've given her the impression that the kiss was a mistake. Especially when he'd like nothing more than to kiss her again. But now that he'd asked the Lord for a sign, he was afraid of "muddying the waters," so to speak. He only hoped God wouldn't wait too long. Wasn't there some scrip-

ture verse about a thousand years being but as yesterday when it was past? He didn't have that long to wait!

"What's wrong?" Maude asked, startling Ella, who
hadn't realized her friend had followed her away from
church.

She was panting a little after having run to catch up
with Ella, and was clearly unaware that Ella had just
asked the same question of Nate.

"Nothing," Ella said. "I'm just in a hurry as usual
to get Sunday dinner started. Are you going to eat at
the café?"

"I'd like to, but I'd better not—Mrs. Meyer made a
point of telling me she was fixing pot roast, my favorite. But I thought I'd walk with you and ask why you
and Nate are acting so strange with each other. You
keep saying you haven't had a fight, but first he looks
at you when you're not looking, then you do the same
when he's not."

Ella stopped stock-still in the alley between the jail
and the mercantile and faced her friend, after taking a
wary glance over her shoulder to see if anyone else was
nearby. "Maude, when are you going to get it through
your head that a person wouldn't bother to fight with
someone with whom she has no more than a temporary
friendship? He won't be staying forever."

"Maybe *you're* convinced about that, but you haven't
convinced me," Maude retorted. "Isn't it time to be honest with *yourself?*"

Ella stared at her, and all of a sudden her long-held
resolve crumbled. She needed to talk to someone, she
realized—someone who might be able to shed some
light on Bohannan's on-again, off-again manner with
her. He hadn't stolen a glance at her once during the

sermon. Instead, he'd seemed to listen so intently it was as if he was trying to memorize it. And he'd seemed disappointed when it was over. Why?

"All right, let's suppose I *do* care," Ella said. "But can we talk about it back at the boardinghouse? The church diners will be descending on the café all too soon—including Nate himself—and this is a chat that's going to take a while."

Maude flashed her a triumphant look, as if satisfied that Ella had finally given in. "All right, that makes sense," she said. "I'll meet you there right after dinner—unless Bohannan wants to take you fishing."

"Little chilly for that, I think," Ella said, pulling her shawl around her more closely, for there was a nip of fall in the air today. But perhaps "chilly" also referred to the state of affairs between herself and Bohannan, for reasons she could only guess at.

Chapter Sixteen

Telling Maude all she had held inside for so long left Ella feeling limp as a fallen cake. She told her everything that had passed between her and Nate Bohannan, from the first spark of attraction she had felt toward the stranger who had saved her from the drunken drifter, through the development of her feelings for him and the way he seemed to care for her, seeing the furniture he'd repaired and the new pieces he'd made for her, and hearing he was going to stay at least through the café raising. Then that kiss…

The tears had begun to flow when she tried to explain the unexplained fear that had caused her to push away from Nate right in the middle of the kiss. Maude pressed a handkerchief into Ella's hand, and calmly waited until Ella went on.

"I lied to you, Maude. I lied to you all—about where I came from," Ella said, her voice thick with tears.

Maude's eyes widened.

"I didn't live in San Antonio with an aunt until she died like I told you. The truth is, I came here from Llano, where the last café I worked at was. Before that, I worked in Boerne and Round Rock—always cooking jobs, never anything dishonest. I'm sorry, Maude," Ella murmured through her tears. "All y'all were so nice and welcoming when I came to Simpson Creek... But you'd all grown up here, and had normal lives—at least before the war. Who was I? An orphan, a runaway 'charity girl' from an asylum—" she pronounced the despised label bitterly "—who'd lived among insane people. Why would you believe I wasn't one of the crazy ones? I didn't know anything about my parents, except the name they'd given me."

Maude began, "Ella, that wouldn't have mattered—"

Ella held up a hand. "That's what Nate said, too. He said I should tell you about it, just as I told him."

She saw Maude blink in surprise. "You told Nate about this?"

Ella nodded. "I'd never told anyone in the other towns about coming from an asylum. At first I was always looking over my shoulder, afraid they'd find me— the asylum officials. They'd gone after one of the little boys who ran away, you see—they brought him back and paraded him in front of us, his hands still tied, as a warning to the rest of us."

A tear streaked down Maude's cheek at this point, but she just wiped it away. "Go on," she urged.

"I left Boerne because I saw a man who looked like Mr. Antoine, the one who'd taught me how to cook at the asylum. It couldn't have been him, of course—I know that now. But after that, I ran whenever anyone started asking questions..."

Maude stroked a damp curl back off her forehead. "You poor dear. No wonder you wake up with nightmares. I wish you'd told me this earlier. There was no need to carry this burden around all by yourself— I would have understood, and so would any of your friends in the Spinsters' Club. As for anyone else, well, there's no shame in being an orphan, but it isn't anyone's business where you came from."

Ella smiled wanly at her friend. "I don't know what I ever did to deserve a friend like you."

Maude grinned back at her. "You've been a blessing to me, too, you know. It's been good to have another female my own age here at the boardinghouse." She waited a moment, then when Ella said nothing else, she asked, "But may we return to the subject of Nate Bohannan? You said he kissed you, down at the lumber mill," she prompted. "What happened after that that frightened you? Did Nate…take liberties?"

Something in Maude's face warned her that the consequences would be dire for Mr. Bohannan if Ella's answer was yes.

"No, it was nothing like that," Ella said quickly. "It was…just as I started to enjoy the kiss, I got scared, too. I can't explain it, Maude. I don't really understand it myself. I know it's got something to do with the asylum, and my nightmares…but I always wake up before I can see who it is…"

Maude's brow furrowed. "Who it is?" she echoed.

"Someone's reaching out to grab me," Ella explained. "But I don't know who."

Maude pondered that, then asked, "Do you think Nate started acting different because you stopped the kiss?"

Ella shook her head. "I don't think so… He escorted me back here, and everything seemed fine." She shrugged. "Who knows? There's no use worrying about it, Maude. He's always said he wasn't staying in Simpson Creek—in fact, he said it was all right to confide in him *because* he wasn't staying."

Fatigue began to wash over Ella now like waves rushing to shore. "I'm just glad he decided to wait to leave till after my café is built…" Her voice trailed off and she smothered a yawn, more tired than she could ever remember feeling, now that she had unburdened her soul.

"You look sleepy. Why don't you take a little nap, Ella," Maude suggested.

"Oh, no, I can't," Ella protested. She'd been lying on her bed against the pillows, and now she struggled to rise. "It's nearly time to go start supper at the café."

Maude pushed gently at her shoulder. "You've got an hour," she told her. "Plenty of time for a little catnap. Close your eyes. It'll do you a world of good."

Ella let her eyes drift shut. She just needed a few minutes…

Nate went to the café for supper as usual, hoping it wouldn't be as busy as it had been at dinnertime. He'd barely exchanged a glance with Ella then, for she had been continually in motion, as if she was trying to be in three places at once. Hopefully they would get a chance to exchange a few words, and he could assure himself Ella was all right.

Instead of seeing light coming from the window, however, he found the café dark, and a handwritten note showing in the door window—*Café closed due to illness of Miss Ella. Meals will resume tomorrow.*

What could be wrong with her? It must be something serious, because the note was written *about* Miss Ella, not *by* her. If it had been something minor, like a headache, hardworking Ella would have come anyway and soldiered through it.

Without another thought, he turned on his heel and ran to the boardinghouse, fear gripping his heart.

Maude didn't look at all surprised when she came to the kitchen door of the boardinghouse and saw Nate through the window, breathing hard, his hand poised to rap at the door again. She opened it before his knuckles connected with the wood.

"What's wrong with El—Miss Ella, that is?" he demanded. "I saw the sign…it—it's nothing serious, is it?" He held his breath while he awaited her answer.

"Shh," she said. "I don't want to wake her. Good evening to you, too, Mr. Bohannan," she said. "No, it's nothing but a sick headache, and since she was still fast asleep when it came time to wake her, I decided she needed the sleep more than she needed to go cook. Why? Are you afraid you'll miss a meal?"

He felt himself tense at her tart words. "I know you don't have any reason to think well of me, Miss Maude, but I care about Miss Ella. I was worried about her," he said.

"Yet you're still planning on leaving after her café is built."

He decided she was being deliberately provocative, but he dared not lose his temper at Maude when he needed information from her. He took a deep breath and forced himself to relax. "I…I don't know," he admitted. "Haven't you ever been unsure about something, Miss Maude? Trying to decide whether the course you wanted to take was the right one?"

Her expression softened. "I'm sorry, Mr. Bohannan. I didn't mean to be harsh. I'm sure she'll feel better tomorrow. I'll tell her you inquired."

He turned to go, but then he heard her say, "Wait a moment."

Without telling him what she was going to do, Maude fixed him a sandwich from the leftover ham from the boardinghouse supper. "Ella will fret that you went hungry when she wakes. Let me fix you something—we have plenty of ham left over from our supper here."

He stared at her for a moment. "Thank you, Miss Maude. You'll…let me know, won't you? If Ella needs anything?"

After promising she would, Maude bid him goodnight in a lot more kindly manner than she'd used when she'd let him come in.

When Ella finally awoke, she was frantic when she found out she'd slept right through the supper hour.

"How could you have let me sleep so long, Maude?" she cried after pelting down the stairs and checking the grandfather clock that sat by the front door. "You knew I had to fix supper! What about my customers? What about Nate?"

Maude put firm hands on Ella's shoulders. "I put a sign up that you were ill. It wasn't far from the truth, you know—you were completely tuckered out after telling me all that, and you could very well have fallen ill if you'd tried to carry on as if nothing had happened. It won't hurt your customers to learn you're human like the rest of us—and look at it this way, you didn't have to put up with Zeke Carter tonight."

A chuckle escaped Ella. "I'm sure he ambled over to the hotel restaurant instead, and grumbled about the higher prices." But worry still clawed at her.

"Mr. Bohannan called to inquire," Maude said, looking like the proverbial cat that swallowed the canary.

"He *did?*" She couldn't quite suppress how much pleasure the idea gave her.

Maude appeared pleased at the excited note in Ella's voice. "He did, and I told him you had a sick headache. You did have one, didn't you?"

Slowly, Ella nodded. "It's gone, now that I've slept."

"Good. And don't fret that he'll go hungry tonight. I sent him off with a sandwich."

Nate had lain awake half the night worrying that Maude had underestimated the severity of Ella's indisposition. What if Ella had taken a turn for the worse, he worried, and expired all alone in her boardinghouse room? But when he saw her in the café the next morning, there was nothing to suggest that her illness had been anything more than Maude had claimed. Only violet shadows underneath her eyes suggested she'd been as restless as he had been last night.

"Perfectly fine," she said when he asked how she was feeling. "Maude says you came to the boardinghouse to check on me—that was kind of you."

"I was worried," he admitted, glad there was no one else in the café to interrupt their conversation.

"I…took your advice," she murmured.

For a moment he was confused. He'd given her advice? What right had he to be advising anyone about anything? "You did?"

"I did. And you were right. It was good to get it off my—" She floundered now, and her cheeks grew pink. "To unburden myself. And Maude understood, just as you said she would. She's a good listener."

"Good." He didn't know what else to say about that. "I've just got one chair left to make," he said when he couldn't think of anything else.

"Good," she said, and looked as lost as he was in this conversation. Fortunately, the mayor and the bank president came in then, and spared Nate the effort of continuing.

"So this is your café's last week behind the saloon, isn't it, Miss Ella?" Mayor Gilmore called out as Ella brought Nate his eggs, bacon and griddle cakes. "Are you getting excited about the new place?"

"I certainly am, sir," she responded, smiling.

"Any idea when you'll be up and running after that?" the bank president asked. "I confess, the day just doesn't go right if I don't start it with your coffee."

"You're very kind, Mr. Avery. I expect early next week. It depends on when the interior work is completed. Mr. Bohannan, here, will be working on that."

The bank president turned and nodded at Nate. "Then it should look just fine. Dayton says you do good work."

Nate nearly choked on a bite of bacon, and took a sip of coffee to hide his surprise. The sour-faced mill owner didn't seem the type to sing anyone's praises.

"He sure does, Mr. Avery. I'm very pleased with what he's shown me so far," Ella chimed in, giving him a smile.

The warmth Nate felt within him now had nothing to do with the hot coffee. Bemused, he finished his breakfast and headed for the lumber mill.

He'd miss the good people of this town when—if— he left, he thought as he walked down Main Street. Salt of the earth, they were. He'd make friends in San Francisco, he thought, but his cousin's moneyed, powerful associates would be nothing like the citizens of Simpson Creek.

But what was here for him, though, once he finished Ella's furniture, if nothing changed between himself and Ella? He liked the people of Simpson Creek, but if he stayed, she would be the reason. But he had no real place in the life of the town, no job. He didn't even have a place to live.

He'd repaired the saloon's and the café's furniture, and atoned for what Salali had done. Even his volunteer position as the piano player at church was temporary. Once the doctor's wife gave birth, she would probably want to resume playing for the Sunday service. No, he'd better stick to his original plan and go to San Francisco. And ignore the aching hole he knew he would have in his heart.

Perhaps he could go to California, make his fortune and come back for Ella? But that might take years, and it was an arduous, dangerous journey. In the meantime, they would have lost the best years of their lives, and why should she wait on the strength of a mere promise from him that he would return someday?

"I just saw Mr. Avery," Nate told Dayton when he got to the lumber mill, "and he passed along your compliment. I appreciate what you said."

"It's only the truth," Dayton said. "I've been out to the shed lookin' over what you made," the mill owner said. "You do real fine work. I was thinkin'…you could make furniture as a business here, Bohannan. We ain't got no furniture maker here in Simpson Creek, y' know. Folks use what they've had in the family for years, and the new pieces they knock together, well, they're crude, an' not much t' look at, as a rule. But you, you're a craftsman. You an' me, we could be partners—me supplyin' the lumber, you makin' the furniture. You could keep workin' right here," he said, indicating the lathe that Nate had spent so much time with.

If Dayton had grown wings and a tail, Nate wouldn't

have been more surprised. "I thought you couldn't wait to have your lathe back," he said.

Dayton looked sheepish. "I said that, all right, but I got t' thinkin'. I could expand, if I had a partner. I could add on a room t'show the pieces you built for sale. What d'ya think?"

Taken by surprise, Nate stared at him. "I—I hadn't figured on staying," he said, reluctant to let this man know about his ambivalent feelings. "I only stayed to fix the tables and chairs that Salali wrecked. There's a partner waiting for me in San Francisco. I won't have to work with my hands there," he said, holding out his hands, callused and rough from so much time spent sanding and planing wood. "I'll be a businessman. My cousin's making money hand over fist there."

Dayton wrinkled his nose. "Well, if ya want t' go be a swell, I guess there ain't nothin' here in little ol' Simpson Creek t' keep ya." His face took on a shrewd cast. "But I reckon there ain't no Miss Ella Justiss out in Californy."

Nate stiffened as the jab hit home. What could this grumpy fellow, who never came to church, never came to Ella's café, know about his feelings for Ella Justiss? Did everyone know what he should do—but him?

"Sorry, Bohannan," Dayton mumbled. "I reckon it ain't none of my business—Miss Ella an' you, I mean. But you think about my offer, all right? You could do a lot worse, believe me."

"I'll think about it." He was glad Dayton's apology had forestalled the temptation to tell the man to mind his own concerns.

A cynical voice inside him said the smartest thing for him to do would be to finish Ella's tables and chairs, sell his watch and buy a horse quiet-like, keeping the rest of the money for his journey and light out for California in the middle of the night.

Ella will get over it, won't she?

There would be no feeling that everybody's business was everybody's business where he was going. But apart from Cousin Russell, no one in San Francisco would care whether he lived or died, either—unless he was able to establish himself as his cousin had done. Maybe not even then.

Dayton left the room and Nate tried to immerse himself in his work, but he kept finding himself staring straight into space, pondering what he should do. Then he got his hand too close to the drive center while turning the lathe, and it sliced the side of his index finger.

Smothering a spate of nasty words, he told himself that was what he deserved for daydreaming when he should be paying attention. Grabbing a nearby rag to stem the flow of blood, he went to find Dayton to ask if he had a clean cloth he could use for a bandage.

"Nope," the man said. "You better go see Doc Walker, get him t' clean it up proper."

"I don't have time for that. It's not that big a cut. I need to finish the piece I'm working on."

Dayton made shooing motions. "Go on, now. You don't wanna get lockjaw from that there cut. That chair leg'll keep till you get back."

Who'd have ever thought Dayton would suddenly turn into a solicitous fussbudget? Surely the next thing he'd see were pigs flying through the air over Simpson Creek.

He didn't want to go see Dr. Walker; he wanted to go see Ella. Surely she'd have a clean handkerchief, or something, and could bind his wound as easily as a sawbones would. And it wouldn't cost any of his dwindling cash. But then he remembered Ella had mentioned something about having to go to the butcher and the mercantile this morning. He didn't want to spend a lot of time looking for her, and delay her when she was busy, so he obediently turned in at the doctor's office across from the church.

To his surprise, he found Reverend Gil sitting in the doctor's waiting room, an open Bible in his lap.

"Hello, Nate," the preacher said, a smile creasing the face that had looked so studious before he'd looked up. He pointed to the bloody rag Nate held pressed to his finger. "Got a cut, have you?"

"Yes, I'm afraid the lathe bit me," Nate admitted ruefully. "I hope Mrs. Chadwick hasn't taken ill?" he asked, glancing at the doctor's closed examination room door.

"No, nothing like that, thankfully. My father, the old reverend, is in there. Dr. Walker likes to look him over from time to time. He had an apoplexy a while back before you came, and he's going on seventy now, so Walker keeps a close eye on him. He's a good man, our doctor."

Nate hadn't known what ailed the elderly preacher, just that he was always in a wheeled chair at Sunday services, and his speech was garbled and hesitant.

"I imagine the doc will be done with his inspection in a few minutes," Reverend Gil said. "Then he can see to your finger."

"That's fine, I'm not in a big hurry," Nate said, though a moment ago, he had been. He looked down at the open Bible on the preacher's lap. "Are you working on your Sunday sermon?"

Chadwick smiled. "I was, as a matter of fact. But

there's plenty of time before Sunday," he said, an obvious invitation to talk, if Nate wanted to.

Nate suddenly remembered the "fleece" he'd been trying to lay out. Last week's sermon hadn't seemed to point in any particular way. Was seeing the preacher here a heaven-sent opportunity, so he didn't have to wait till next Sunday?

"What Bible verse are you using for your sermon this week?" Nate said, hoping he didn't sound desperately eager for the answer. He wanted it to seem as if he was just making conversation while they waited.

Reverend Chadwick beamed at the question. It probably wasn't often one of his congregation showed an advance interest in his sermons.

"I'll be citing a couple of passages in the New Testament," he said. "One in Luke, chapter twelve, about the 'rich fool.' Maybe you're familiar with that story? The one where the rich man has so many possessions he decides to build new barns to hold it all, and thinks he's going to live for many years, so he can eat, drink and be merry?"

Nate had to admit he wasn't familiar with it.

"Well, he wasn't taking into account that no one is promised tomorrow in this life, and he died that night. And then what good did all his possessions do him?"

It was a sobering thought. "And the other text?"

The answer came promptly. "Mark, chapter eight, where it talks about denying oneself, taking up one's cross and following Jesus. Verse thirty-four always resonates so deeply—'For what shall it profit a man, if he shall gain the whole world, and lose his own soul?'"

The hairs at the back of Nate's neck prickled and stood on end. "Th-that'll be a real powerful sermon, Reverend," he managed to say. *Has the Lord been look-*

ing into my very soul? That was *him* the scriptures were
describing, wasn't it? Or at least, the man he was aim-
ing to be in California. He'd been planning to gain what
he saw as his share of "the whole world," hadn't he?

"Thank you, Nate. I hope so. I don't know why, but
the Lord seemed to keep bringing those verses to my
notice the last few days."

Gil Chadwick might not know why, but *he* knew,
Nate thought. He'd never expected the answer to be
so clear.

"By the way, how are you coming on that decision
you need to make?" the preacher asked him.

Nate searched the other man's face, but there was no
knowing look in his eyes, just honest interest. "It…it's
getting clearer all the time, Reverend."

Chapter Seventeen

"Excellent, Nate, excellent," Chadwick said, looking genuinely pleased.

Just then, the door to the exam room opened, and the old preacher came out in his wheeled chair, pushed by the doctor.

"He seems fit as a fiddle for a man his age, Reverend," Dr. Walker said. Then, as both preachers murmured their thanks, the doctor's gaze lit on Nate and his bloody rag-covered finger.

"What'd you do to yourself, Bohannan?"

By the time Dr. Walker was done cleaning and stitching his finger wound, it was past the time Ella stopped serving the midday meal, but Nate thought it likely Ella would still be at her café cleaning up and would have something put by for him. That might even be better—if they were alone, they might finally have a chance to discuss what had happened the other night when he kissed her.

He'd just stepped out into the street, however, when someone hailed him from behind. Looking around, he saw Sheriff Bishop trotting toward him on his horse.

"Dayton told me I'd find you at the doctor's, Bohannan." He nodded at Nate's bandaged finger. "Has he got you all fixed up?"

Nate nodded, wondering why the sheriff was looking for him. "What can I do for you, Sheriff?"

"We're forming a posse, and I want you to take part. Come on over to the jail and I'll explain everything." Without waiting for an answer, he turned his horse and headed for the jail himself.

Now Nate saw the unusual number of horses tied up at the hitching rail in front of and near the jail. With all these men, why did Bishop want him in the posse?

When he entered the office, he saw a handful of men gathered around Bishop, who was sitting on top of his desk.

"Ah, Bohannan. Join us," Bishop said, gesturing him in. "Now we're all here."

The others—Deputy Menendez, Jack Collier and Nick Brookfield, as well as a couple of others he didn't know—parted to let him into the circle, murmuring greetings.

"What's this about a posse?" Nate asked Bishop. "I don't even have a horse. And why did you say you wanted me, particularly?"

Bishop's face was grim. "I want you to come along because it's your old *compadre* Robert Salali we're after."

Nate stiffened. "I told you the morning after he wrecked the saloon he wasn't my *compadre,*" he said, irritated that the scoundrel was causing him trouble again, weeks after he'd fled town, leaving Nate to face the consequences. "Just my boss—and one I was about to leave, anyway."

"Sorry, I knew that," Bishop said, waving a hand as

if to dismiss Nate's objections. "But this time he's killed someone, and I need you to help us track him down."

"Killed someone?" Nate echoed.

"That's correct. Got word from Sheriff Teague this morning, over in Lampasas. I'd already warned him to look out for Salali, so when he showed up with his medicine-show wagon there, Teague was quick to send him packing—but not before he'd sold a bottle to a well-to-do widow he'd made eyes at. Teague thought he'd left town, but when no one saw the widow for a few days, he went to check and found her dead, her throat cut and a couple of empty bottles of the elixir he'd been peddling on the table. The house had been ransacked, and everything valuable had been taken. Then he was sighted heading southwest."

Nate closed his eyes as the sheriff's words sank in. So Salali had gone from being a scoundrel prone to rages to being a murderer. He should have known it could come to this. Men like Salali, unless checked, eventually became like rabid dogs that had to be put down for the good of society. Nate sighed.

He rubbed a hand over his forehead and eyes. "I don't suppose there's any doubt Salali killed her?"

"The woman reportedly didn't have an enemy in the world. Salali will get a trial in Lampasas," Bishop promised, his face as somber as his tone. "But first he's got to be caught. Teague's out after him, and I promised we'd do our part, too. That's where you come in," he said, leveling his gaze at Nate.

Nate waited, fairly certain of what was coming.

"My deputy was never able to find that hideout you said he had in the hills of southwest Mason County, so now I need you to show us to it, if you can. You think you can find it?"

Nate raked a hand through his hair as he thought. Being the secretive sort, the one time Salali had gone back to his hideout to make more elixir since Nate had begun to work for him, he'd left Nate at the base of the winding trail up a hill a score of miles north of the Llano River.

"Yeah, I think I can find it, though there's no guarantee that's his only hidey-hole, you understand. But I don't—"

"—have a horse. I know. I've taken care of that," Bishop said. "That buckskin out at the hitching post is for your use, and my wife's packed some sandwiches for you in the saddlebag. There's a bedroll tied in back of the saddle for you, too." He took a Winchester off the rack behind him and handed it to Nate, along with a pistol he pulled out of a drawer.

"Seems like you've thought of everything," Nate commented. *Except giving me a choice.* He felt he was still expected to atone for Salali's vandalism, if not his chicanery in selling the worthless elixir. And it would never stop if he stayed in Simpson Creek. Someone would always remember the wreckage of the saloon and café, and that he had been somehow associated with it.

But then he dismissed his resentment. There was never a convenient time to stop a lawbreaker, and Bishop and these other men were laying aside things they would rather be doing, too. Of all the men present, he was the only one with a real chance of finding the hideout.

"Consider yourself deputized. All right, men, mount up."

He wanted to ask how long they expected to be gone but realized there was no way Bishop could answer the question yet. It all depended on Salali.

"The sooner we get going, the sooner we can capture that skunk and be back in Simpson Creek," the sheriff said, as if guessing what Nate had been thinking.

"I—I need to let a couple of people know what I'm doing—Miss Ella and Detwiler," Nate said. He couldn't just disappear without telling Ella—Detwiler, too, for that matter, since he was using a room above the saloon. He wished he'd been able to finish that last chair before today—now it looked as if he'd be gone at least until the café raising, if not more. He hoped Ella wouldn't be too disappointed at having one less chair—and probably several fewer workers at the café raising, for that matter. It was very likely they wouldn't make it back in time.

Bishop narrowed his eyes. "Run ahead and let them know. We'll follow and be waiting outside the saloon, since we're heading down the south road out of Simpson Creek, anyway. You'll have to be quick, Bohannan."

"I will be."

Heading around to the back entrance, Nate was dismayed to find the closed sign already hanging in the door window. He took a quick look into the dim interior, but he could see that she wasn't still within washing up.

Frustrated that he wouldn't get to see her personally, and would have to leave a message with Detwiler, he jogged around to the front and pushed through the batwing doors of the saloon.

The only person inside was Dolly, who stood behind the bar, washing glasses.

"Hey there, Nate," she said with a lazy smile. "You get all them chairs an' tables fixed up for Miss Ella?"

"Almost," he said, smiling at her in a friendly but noncommittal way. Dolly had always been a little forward toward him, though he supposed once he would have welcomed her attention. "Where's Detwiler?"

"Gone home to have dinner with his mother," she said with a grin. "Anything *I* kin do for you meanwhile?" Her tone was rich with innuendo.

He gave her a short, cool smile. "No, unless you know where there's some paper and a pencil so I can leave him a note?"

Dolly rummaged underneath the bar but came up empty. "I'm sure he has some upstairs in his office…" She nodded toward the stairway and gave him another of her sultry smiles. "Come with me, and I'm sure we can get you…what you need."

"Thanks, but I'm sure I can find them," he said, and thanked God under his breath when two cowboys ambled in right then and demanded drinks.

Sure enough, once he'd climbed the stairs and entered the office, he found plenty of paper and pencils, and he wrote Detwiler a quick note explaining that he'd be out of town with the posse, and to please let Ella know he'd be back as soon as he possibly could. When he finished, he descended the stairs again and handed Dolly the note.

"Would you see that your boss gets this, please? It's very important," he said, giving her what he hoped was a winning smile along with the folded note.

"You bet I will, Nate," she cooed, giving him a look that would've melted a block of ice, if there'd been one in Simpson Creek.

"Thanks, Dolly," he said, and saw through the dusty window that the posse was already outside waiting on him.

"Did you see Nate go upstairs?" Ella asked Detwiler that evening, when Nate had failed to show up for supper, even after she had purposely dawdled at washing the dishes and wiping down the tables.

"Nope, I haven't," Detwiler said. "I ain't laid eyes on him since this morning when he left for the mill."

Dolly stepped forward then, a knowing smile on her painted face. "I saw him early this afternoon. He came here looking for George, then I saw him riding out with the sheriff and some other men. Heard tell they'd formed a posse to go after some desperado. You mean he didn't tell *you* he was leaving, Ella?"

"Nate's part of a posse? Why? He's not a lawman," Ella protested, visions of Nate wounded—Nate killed— in a shoot-out with some outlaw tormenting her.

"That's what a posse is made up of," Detwiler explained, his tone kind. "Armed citizens riding with the sheriff to catch a criminal."

"You wouldn't want your Nate to shirk his civic duty, would you?" Dolly mocked.

Ella had had enough of Dolly's sneering. "He's not 'my Nate,'" she snapped. "I was merely inquiring whether I needed to save his supper or not." Turning on her heel, she retreated to the sanctuary of her café.

Detwiler came in a few minutes later. "Sorry about Dolly's rudeness," he said carefully. "After you left, she told me she'd put a note from Nate in my office. He says they're after a crook who killed some poor lady in Lampasas. So I figure that's why y—Nate," he said, obviously correcting himself before calling him *your Nate,* "was invited along. Bishop must think he'll give them an advantage in tracking down that no-good. He asked me to tell you he'd be back as soon as he could."

"I—I see," she said. So he had thought to ask Detwiler to let her know. *But he could as easily have left you the note and asked you to tell Detwiler,* a petty voice within her insisted. "Well, like I said, it's no concern of mine what Nate Bohannan chooses to do with his time."

But Detwiler saw through her cross words. "He'll be all right, Ella. Nate Bohannan knows how to handle himself."

Ella shrugged as if it didn't matter to her. "You want an extra helping of ham and mashed potatoes, George?" she said, nodding toward the plate she'd kept covered and warm on top of the stove.

"Thanks. Don't mind if I do."

When he had gone, Ella stood there for a moment, staring unseeing out the back window.

Her first reaction had been concern—yes, and fear—for Nate's safety, but now Dolly's mocking words came back to taunt her. *You mean he didn't tell* you *he was leaving, Ella?*

Men, she scoffed. There was no use caring about one, because when the next exciting thing came along, they flitted away without a thought.

As they rode southwest, the hills came more frequently and the gently rolling landscape gave way to steeper climbs and deeper valleys.

Because of their late start, they'd pushed the horses hard that day and the only time there'd been any talk was when they stopped to water their mounts. Nate learned that the other two men on the posse were Hank Parker, whose ranch lay north of Simpson Creek, and one of his cowhands, Owen Sawyer. The other two men he knew from church, the Englishman Nick Brookfield, and Jack Collier, both ranchers and both married to ladies who had been in the Spinsters' Club that Ella belonged to.

The sun was setting by the time Bishop gave the order to halt and make camp. Collier made a fire with some dried mesquite, and before long there was fresh Arbuckle's coffee brewed.

The buckskin Nate had been loaned had carried him well that day, but he was more tired than he could remember being in a long time. It seemed everyone felt the same, for there was only mumbled conversation as they ate what they had packed in their saddlebags.

"We'll get an early start tomorrow," Bishop told them. "You think we can make it to that hideout of Salali's by late afternoon tomorrow?"

"Possibly," Nate said. He'd seen clouds off to the southwest before the sun had set, but often they blew away without dropping any rain. "But you don't want to take Salali on at the end of a day's ride—we'll need to be fresh."

"Of course not. Do you take me for a greenhorn?" Bishop snapped, then rubbed the back of his neck, fatigue evident in his movements. "Sorry. Didn't mean to bite your head off, Bohannan. I feel like I've been run over by a freight wagon."

"Don't give it another thought," Nate said. They'd covered a lot of ground since afternoon, and he knew Bishop wanted to bring Salali in to help his fellow sheriff—and to ensure no more innocent folks were victimized by the murdering charlatan. Nate wanted him captured for the same reasons. He only hoped that when he led them to Salali's hideout, they didn't come up empty.

Bishop flashed him a grateful look. "All right then," he said to all of them. "We'll aim to ride as close as we can to where the hideout is tomorrow, and make a cold camp so Salali doesn't get wind that we're on his tail. Eat up, men, then let's get some shut-eye."

Within minutes, everyone was curled up in their bedrolls around the fire. Soon, snores alternated with occasional crackles from the campfire, but Nate lay wakeful, thinking about both Ella and Salali.

He knew he could count on Detwiler to tell her where he had gone, but how would she react if he didn't make it back in time for the café raising? Tomorrow was Tuesday, and it would be at least Wednesday morning before they could attempt to capture the wily criminal. If they were successful, they'd have to escort him to Lampasas to stand trial.

Perhaps Bishop would let him head straight back to Simpson Creek. The remaining men should be enough to assure Salali got to Lampasas—if they all survived.

It was entirely possible that they might scale the hill and find him gone. But if Salali *was* there, he'd have the advantage, for the path to his cabin was steep and winding and only wide enough to allow one horseman at a time. Salali could easily pick them off as they rode upward, one by one. They might end up having to surround the hill and wait him out—which could take days.

Nate knew another way up to the hideout, but it was a path only a man on foot could take—and only if he was as agile as a mountain goat. He prayed he wouldn't have to use it, for Salali probably knew of it, too, and he might be covering it as well as the narrow horse path.

There was no guarantee their quarry would be alone. As much as Salali hated sharing, if it made him feel safer, he might have picked up a dangerous partner or two.

He hoped Ella would understand that he felt a deep obligation to help Bishop do this. He wouldn't have been able to respect himself if he'd refused and stayed safe in town.

But once this was over, he was going to do whatever it took to win the heart of his dark-eyed beauty back in Simpson Creek, and if he succeeded, he'd never leave her side again.

Chapter Eighteen

Tuesday, Wednesday, Thursday—the three days were endless for Ella since she knew nothing of what was happening with Nate.

She encountered Milly Brookfield at the mercantile Tuesday, and learned that the desperado the posse pursued was none other than Robert Salali himself, the same mischief-maker who'd wrecked the saloon and her café. But Salali had gone far past mischief and mayhem and had graduated to murder, Milly told her, for he had killed a woman in Lampasas.

Now Ella understood why Nate had felt obligated to join the posse. As illogical as it was to her, it seemed Nate still felt guilty by association for being in Salali's company when he'd first arrived in Simpson Creek. He'd long since atoned for that, Ella thought indignantly, by repairing and remaking the furniture that had been damaged, yet it seemed to her that the sheriff had shamelessly exploited Nate's guilt to draft him into the posse. The idea made her so cross it was hard to be civil to Bishop's wife, Prissy, when she passed her in the street later that day.

Wednesday evening, Ella fretted aloud to Maude in

the boardinghouse. "What if there's gunplay, and Nate's wounded, or worse yet, killed by Salali? What if Salali ambushes them and the entire posse is killed? And why are Simpson Creek men chasing after Salali anyway? Didn't the crime take place in Lampasas?"

"Easy, Ella," Maude soothed. "Sheriff Bishop knows what he's doing, and he won't let the men go blindly into danger. Besides, it's far more likely they won't see hide nor hair of that slimy scoundrel anyway. He's probably across the Rio Grande into Mexico by now. Sheriff Teague's backed up our sheriff before—I suppose Sheriff Bishop wanted to return the favor."

"I know what you're saying makes sense," Ella admitted, "but I feel so helpless. There's nothing I can do."

"Nonsense," Maude said. "You can pray, can't you?"

Of course, her friend was right, and Ella was ashamed that she hadn't thought of it. But she had prayed before—back in the asylum—and heard only silence from heaven. Who knew if prayer would help this time?

It couldn't hurt to try. *Lord, please protect Nate! And the rest of the posse,* she added quickly. They had wives and families who worried about them, too.

By Friday morning she was beside herself. The posse hadn't returned or sent word, but it seemed there would be enough men to build Ella's café without them. The ladies of the town, many of whom were Spinsters' Club members, had planned the menu for the noon meal with the same enthusiasm they always exhibited, whether the event was a matchmaking one or not. Mrs. Detwiler had promised to bake several of her famous chocolate cakes, and George Detwiler would furnish bottles of sarsaparilla for the kids.

Milly Brookfield and Caroline Collier had come in via buckboard and were staying with Milly's sister, Sarah, the doctor's wife. If either of them were anxious about their husbands' continuing absence, they concealed it well.

Hank Dayton came into the café to report that he'd delivered the lumber to the site, all ready to be used tomorrow. "Finest hardwood my mill ever produced," he boasted, proud as if he'd grown the trees from saplings himself. Then he just stood there as if he was waiting for something.

"How about a piece of pie and a cup of coffee?" she asked finally.

"On the house?"

"Of course." Worry over Nate had quite robbed her of her manners.

"Don't mind if I do," he said, then set about gobbling down the pecan pie as if it might evaporate if not consumed quickly. "Did your friend Nate tell you afore he left that I offered to go into business with him?" he asked, watching her with a knowing look in his eye.

Ella wondered how many times she'd uttered the phrase "He's not 'my' friend Nate." She certainly wasn't going to explain the nature of her friendship with Nate to the likes of Dayton, who'd never bothered to speak to her before.

"Mr. Bohannan and I didn't discuss his plans," she said coolly, trying to appear as disinterested as possible, though she wanted desperately to know that Nate had made a plan to stay.

"Yeah, did my best to interest him in selling his furniture outta my shop," Dayton said.

Ella shrugged, hoping it looked to the lumberman that what Nate did mattered not in the least to her.

"Sounds like he's still got itchy feet to go out to California, though."

Her heart sank at the remark. If Nate Bohannan returned with the posse, he still wouldn't be staying.

By the time Ella served the last midday meal behind the saloon Friday, she felt ready to explode if one more well-meaning customer asked her if she was excited about having her café built tomorrow or when it would be open for business.

That evening, after serving the last supper she would make there, she was crossing the street when she heard the sound of hoofbeats coming from the south road. She changed course and started walking in that direction. Could it be the posse at last?

It grew dark early now that September was drawing to a close, and she could not make out the identities of the horsemen, but eventually they drew near enough. Sheriff Bishop rode in the lead, with Nick Brookfield and Jack Collier flanking him and Hank Parker and Owen Sawyer bringing up the rear. They looked dusty, tired and travel-weary, but satisfied.

Where is Nate?

Before she even made a conscious decision, she found herself running across the road, waving her hands, calling, "Sheriff Bishop! Sheriff Bishop!"

The men drew rein as they spotted her and exchanged glances. She saw the sheriff straighten in the saddle as if girding himself for an unpleasant duty. Her heart suddenly felt heavy in her chest.

"Where's Nate Bohannan?" she demanded as her limbs started to shake. "Why isn't he with you? Was he— Did he—" She couldn't finish the sentence, for it would make the worst news real and final.

Bishop seemed to pick a place somewhere above her

head to focus before he spoke. "Bohannan had to...to take care of some business in Lampasas, Miss Ella. He'll be along as soon as he can."

They weren't telling her everything, she was sure of that.

"What aren't you saying? Why won't you tell me?" Her hands flew to her throat. "Is he dead?"

The final question seemed to loosen the sheriff's tongue at last. "No, ma'am, he's not dead, don't you worry. We captured Salali, and since Bohannan was w— That is, there's going to be a trial, and...well, he's going to have to stay in Lampasas awhile...hopefully not for very long..."

Ella narrowed her eyes at him. Sam Bishop's speech had always been direct and to the point, and now he seemed to be anything but.

"But don't you worry, Miss Ella," Jack Collier said, "Nick and I are going to be there bright and early tomorrow to help build your café."

Brookfield said cheerfully, "Since our wives are in town, we're taking a room at the hotel so we won't have to ride in from our ranches in the morning. Sheriff Bishop will be there, too, won't you, Sam?"

Bishop nodded, looking less guarded now that the subject had changed.

"That's...that's nice, gentlemen," Ella said, determined to remember her manners even though she was sure these men weren't telling her everything. "I appreciate it, especially as tired as you must be now."

"Nonsense. After a good night's sleep at the hotel, we'll be raring to go, Miss Ella," Nick Brookfield insisted. "See you in the morning."

"Yes," she managed to say. "Good night, gentlemen. Get some rest."

Ella supposed a normally curious individual would have inquired about Salali's capture, but there'd be time to hear about it later. She didn't want to detain the men further, for surely they were eager to get washed up and rest. It was sure to be the most popular subject talked about at the café raising tomorrow, and Faith's father would make sure every facet of the expedition was covered in the Simpson Creek newspaper.

She wished Lampasas wasn't at least thirty-five miles or more away or she would have set out to see for herself why Nate Bohannan hadn't returned with the rest of the posse.

By the time she reached the boardinghouse, she was sure what they weren't telling her was that Nate had decided to ride on to California as soon as they had placed Salali in the Lampasas sheriff's custody.

Why not? It would be easier than coming back and working on her café, then parting with her. Men always did what was easiest for them, didn't they? If caring about a female became a burden, they just dropped it and moved on.

Nate had very few belongings in his room over the saloon—perhaps a change of clothes or two—certainly nothing worth coming back for if he decided it was easier to go without telling her goodbye. What man wouldn't avoid the disappointment in a woman's eyes if he could?

He had done all he had promised to originally—even more than what he had promised to, truth be told—and if the cabinets and countertops for her new café were left undone, she hardly had a right to complain.

"That's just nonsense," Maude told her when Ella confided her fears to her friend back at the boarding-house. "If Bishop told you Nate had to remain behind for a good reason, it's the truth. He'll be back as soon as he's able."

"And you've known Nate for how long?" Ella retorted. "A few weeks?"

"I think I know a trustworthy man when I see him," Maude said with a stubborn edge to her voice. "You need to have more faith in Nate, Ella Justiss. Besides, Nate rode out on a borrowed horse, right? Unless Bishop just decided to give him that mount, which I doubt, he doesn't have a horse to leave on."

Her last sentence was said triumphantly, as if Maude's assertion defeated any further argument Ella could have made. "Now, stop being a nervous Nellie and take a look at this pie I made for tomorrow. I think it's the prettiest piecrust I've ever made."

Ella sighed. She wanted to believe Maude was right. Oh, how she wanted to believe it. But every time her gut had warned her about someone, it had turned out to be reliable, and she didn't think it'd be different this time.

Nate settled back on the cot in the Lampasas doctor's spare room and wondered if he'd done the right thing. He knew Bishop wasn't comfortable with not telling Ella that he'd been wounded, and that was why he hadn't returned with the rest of them to Simpson Creek, but Nate had insisted, sure that the truth would have her imagining him at death's door, or actually dead, instead of merely wounded in the leg and recuperating at the local sawbones' office overnight.

All he had to do was humor the crusty old fellow— who smelled faintly of whiskey and had none of Dr. Walker's kind manner, dry Yankee humor or professional skill—by staying overnight in this spartan spare room that smelled of bleach, and he could leave by sunrise tomorrow. With any luck he'd make it back to Simpson Creek in time to help finish the café. There'd be a trial, but Sheriff Teague had no idea when the circuit judge would arrive. When he did, Nate would be notified and would return to testify.

Now, though, Nate was becoming uncomfortably sure he should've allowed Bishop to tell Ella what had really happened, not just that he "had business to finish" in the matter of Salali's capture and trial. A lie of omission was just as much a lie as any other kind, wasn't it?

He'd had the best of intentions in not telling Ella he'd been shot. There wasn't any reason for her to spend one moment imagining his wound any worse than it was. The bullet had gone in the right side of his calf and right back out again—the optimum sort of wound, the old doctor had opined, because there was no pesky bit of lead to dig out.

But good intentions didn't excuse him, Nate realized now, for the more he thought about it, the more he realized that in sparing her one source of worry, he'd given her another—the fear that he wasn't coming back to Simpson Creek and had taken this opportunity to leave without going through a painful parting with her.

A woman who had grown up normally, with loving parents, would have believed Bishop's assurances that Nate's wound was minor, but Ella's childhood had been the stuff of nightmares and she had difficulty trusting.

He'd known that—so why had he thought for one minute it would be better to have Bishop tell her only part of the truth? She'd grown to believe in Nate over the past few weeks, but when she found out that he had actually been wounded and that Sheriff Bishop hadn't told her at his request, she'd never trust Nate again. No claim of good intentions would excuse him in Ella's eyes.

He'd been a fool. There was nothing he could do about it tonight, though. He'd just have to hope she'd forgive him when he returned and explained his reasons for doing as he had.

His mind drifted to Salali. With the advantage of only one narrow way into his hideout, the man had held the posse off with a seemingly inexhaustible amount of ammunition. He could have picked them off easily, one by one, if the posse had attempted to take the narrow-climbing deer track, since there was only room on the path for one horseman at a time. Bishop had naturally not wanted to make a foolhardy move that could have cost the lives of his entire posse. In the end, it had been necessary for Nate to use the secret second way into the stronghold, the one that had required him to clamber up the rocks behind Salali's crude cabin and get the drop on him.

Salali had pretended to surrender, even laying his rifle down until Nate descended to put the come-alongs on his wrists. Then, vicious as any cornered animal because he knew that a date with the gallows awaited him in Lampasas, he'd pulled pistols out of his back waistband and charged at Nate, guns blazing. It was deliberately suicidal, of course—he knew gunfire would bring the posse charging up into his hideout, but Salali preferred to force Nate to shoot him so he wouldn't have to die dancing at the end of a rope.

It would have been easy to grant Salali his wish to die here and now, for Nate was as competent with a pistol as he was with woodworking tools, but he had no desire to give the murderer the easy death he wanted or burden his own conscience by being Salali's executioner.

Salali was no gunfighter, and his shots mostly went wide of the mark. But one bullet had found its way to

Nate's right leg before Nate managed to knock him out with the butt of his rifle. Salali had awakened to find himself trussed up and loaded on the back of the horse they'd brought for the purpose.

"Good job, Bohannan," Bishop said, ignoring Salali as the captured murderer alternately threatened the posse and tried to bribe them into letting him go. "If I ever need a new deputy, you're the man I'm calling on first."

Nate knew the sheriff didn't hand out praise lightly. "Thanks, but I think young Menendez will stick with you till it's time for him to take over your job."

Bishop snorted and rolled his eyes. "Bite your tongue, Bohannan."

The pain in his leg brought him out of his reverie. Nate supposed he ought to try to get some sleep so he'd be fit to ride out of here in the morning. But his wounded right leg had commenced to thumping like thunder, and hurting worse than blue blazes. He should have let the old sawbones—what was his name, Gibson? Gilbert?—dose him with laudanum as he'd suggested, but Nate had taken laudanum once and he hated the weird dreams that came with the drug.

His leg hadn't hurt this bad earlier. The doc had said to ring the bell on his bedside table if he needed anything, but by Nate's reckoning, it was after midnight. If he took laudanum now he'd probably oversleep in the morning, and he needed to get going early. The old codger was probably deeply asleep, anyway. If Nate could just drift into sleep, he'd be better by morning.

It hadn't been chilly when he lay down, but all at once it seemed like a blue norther had blown in. He pulled up the scratchy old wool blanket. But it wasn't enough.

He felt sleep claiming him then, even as his teeth began to chatter.

Chapter Nineteen

Nate's leg was *not* better by morning.

He was vaguely aware of someone probing at his wound at some point, sending pain racing up his leg. Involuntarily, he groaned and swiped at the intrusive hand.

"Easy, now, son, you've got a fever, and this leg doesn't look at all good. I could fry an egg on it, it's so hot."

"I thought you said it was an easy, entrance-and-exit pair of wounds, the best kind of gunshot wounds to have," he retorted, but even to his own ears his resentful words came out like gibberish.

"Gonna hafta flush this out with whiskey, I reckon, after I give it a good scrub with lye soap," he heard the old man mutter.

From the fellow's tone, it sounded as if he regretted the waste of good whiskey. Then Nate drifted off and didn't know anything more until he felt something like a thousand stinging scorpions on his leg. He tried to swing his fists at whoever had let the vicious little critters loose on him, only to feel a pair or more of strong arms holding him down.

"That's right, hold him, boys, till I get done. I sure don't want to have to amputate this fellow's limb."

Those words sent Nate into a frenzy of struggling. He wasn't about to lie here and let someone cut off a part of him!

Ella, fetch Dr. Walker and get this quack doctor off of me!

One of his captors suggested using a hot branding iron against the wound. "That's what Pardee said he had to do with one of his hands on a trail drive when he got all gashed up. He's got a big ol' scar, but at least the wounds stopped bleeding."

"In the medical field we call that cautery, gentlemen," the doctor said, "and I sincerely hope we don't have to resort to it. But I may have to consider it if this leg doesn't get better."

Like thunder you will, Nate thought, but he couldn't seem to utter the sentiment as a coherent thought. He felt as if he'd been left staked out in the midst of a desert at high noon. Couldn't the fool see he needed a drink of water?

All at once the scorpions stopped stinging and he was left to float in oblivion for a while.

"I don't think we could have asked for better weather for our building day," Maude said to Ella as they each carried a basket full of fried chicken they'd cooked early that morning at the boardinghouse.

She didn't seem to require an answer, so Ella kept walking, but what Maude had said was true. It was as perfect as only an early fall day in the Hill Country could be—not a cloud in the sky, crisp and with a hint of a chill that heralded cooler weather to come, but that would burn off quickly as the sun rose.

It seemed as if the entire population of the town had gathered in the grassy field across Simpson Creek to build Ella's café. Nick Brookfield, Jack Collier and Sheriff Sam Bishop, looking much improved for a good night's sleep, were already wielding hammers and saws by the time Ella and the other Spinsters' Club members crossed the bridge over the creek carrying hampers and baskets full of food. Ella spotted Raleigh Masterson and Reverend Gil—the latter looking most unreverend-like in an old shirt and denim pants—and George Detwiler and Luis Menendez, all carrying boards, sawing them and nailing them in place. Faith's father, Mr. Bennett, stood in the shade of a live oak, taking notes on the scene before them, obviously intending to make the new café a front-page story in his newspaper. Mayor Gilmore was there, too, along with a fellow setting up a camera on a tripod. He had told her he would have pictures made to hang in the social hall that would record the event for posterity.

"Quite a big day for Simpson Creek, as well as for yourself, Miss Ella," Mayor Gilmore crowed. "Just think, we'll be a legitimate *two*-restaurant town now. Before long they'll be calling this a city not a town."

The Spinsters started to carry the long benches and tables borrowed from the church across the bridge themselves, but a number of young boys gallantly took over the job. Mrs. Detwiler stood there in all her glory, directing how they should be placed, and when that had been done, took over laying out each covered dish, basket of food, and jug of cold tea and lemonade.

All these people had assembled to make Ella's dream become a reality today. It was very humbling, and Ella knew she should be happy as a colt in clover. And she would have been, too—if Nate Bohannan had been working with the rest of the men.

Where is Nate, really? Fool, to base your happiness on what a man does or doesn't do, she lectured herself. *Never again.*

Her café would be square, thirty feet by thirty feet, and use the stone foundation of the old house that had stood there before, since it was still perfectly sound. As she watched the men hammer the floor joists into place, she pictured the café's interior with the tables and chairs in the front two-thirds, her work area in the rear. Perhaps in time, if her business prospered, she could put a table or two outside under the live oak trees for those spring and fall days when it was pleasant enough to dine outside.

"Mrs. Masterson, it looks like marriage agrees with you," Maude said, turning to greet a newcomer.

Ella looked up to see an approaching tall blonde woman carrying a covered dish—Violet Masterson, the most recent Spinsters' Club member, and also the newest bride, having married rancher Raleigh Masterson late last year.

"Indeed it does," Violet said in her charming English accent, color pinkening her cheeks. She was Nick Brookfield's sister and had met her husband when she'd come from England to visit her brother and his family on their ranch. "Hello, Ella. How exciting that you will soon have your own café! I'm so happy for you."

"Thanks, Violet. It's good to see you," Ella said, and meant it. She was glad to be distracted from her bitter, anxious thoughts, as well as genuinely pleased to see the Englishwoman. She hadn't liked Violet when they'd first met, due to Ella's misunderstanding a chance remark she'd overheard Violet make, but Violet had made the effort to bridge the gap between them. They'd been friends ever since, though now that Violet and Raleigh had moved to their ranch, Ella didn't see her as often.

"Violet, you look as if you're feeling better," Sarah Walker, Milly's sister and the doctor's wife, commented as she joined the group. "No more trouble with sickness in the mornings?"

Ella was startled, and looked closer. Was Violet with child?

Sarah must have noticed Ella's surprise, for she said quickly, "Oh, I'm sorry, Violet. Forgive my foolish chattering, please, if you weren't ready to make an announcement. Not exactly a discreet physician's wife, am I?"

Violet blushed again like the perfect English rose—transplanted to Texas—that she was. "Oh, it's quite all right, Sarah. I was actually just about to tell Ella myself. Raleigh and I are expecting a blessed event next spring, Ella. And yes, thanks for asking, Sarah, I *am* feeling quite well now."

"It's my turn to be happy for *you*, Violet," Ella said. "You'll make wonderful parents, you and Raleigh." She wondered which one of them the baby would look like, Violet with her blond hair and blue eyes, or her handsome husband, Raleigh, who was as dark-haired and dark-eyed as his wife was fair. She firmly squelched the wistful voice within her that doubted *she* would ever be a mother.

"Thank you. I'll just put my dish over there with the rest. I made tarts with the strawberries I put up in the spring." There was a touch of pride in her voice.

"Mmm. So you've become very domestic," Ella teased as she followed her to the long bench under the trees, recalling that Violet had come from English nobility. The daughter of an earl, she'd never done any cooking until coming to Texas.

"Quite, though not all of my attempts in the kitchen have come out so well," Violet said, giving a rueful laugh. "I had no idea how much work it was, keeping a house, even such a little one as we have now."

By the time the sun was high overhead and the men broke off working to enjoy the potluck dinner, they had a puncheon floor installed over the joists, the four frames for the walls built and the first two in place and joined together. Ella and the ladies served the men first, keeping them supplied with drinks and biscuits while the platters heaped with fried chicken, cold ham and beef were passed up and down the long tables.

The photographer the mayor had hired had taken pictures of the men at work, and once the men were done eating, he took a group picture of those participating in the café raising.

Once the men were back at work, the ladies took their turn eating, their laughter and talk punctuated by the rhythmic hammering nearby. After they ate and cleared away the dishes, some took out needlework, while others soothed children into naps on quilts in the shade. Mrs. Detwiler volunteered to go check on old Reverend Chadwick, Gil's father, at the parsonage. The chatting continued, though once the boards had been nailed over the frame and the men turned to hammering down sheets of tin over the rafters, they had to raise their voices to be heard over the racket. It seemed impossible that the babies and young children would continue to sleep, but they did, lulled by their full stomachs and the drowsy buzz of insects that their mothers fanned away from them.

It was a peaceful scene, but Ella's heart was not at

rest. Despite her resolve not to let an absent man ruin a happy day, in her mind's eye she kept picturing Nate among the workmen. From time to time, her gaze would involuntarily stray to the road east, hoping against hope she would see Nate trotting toward her. But of course that didn't happen.

If he was truly gone, who would build the cabinets that would hold her dishes, silverware, cooking pots and dry ingredients? There was no one in Simpson Creek that she knew of who did that kind of carpentry. Having to pay to have them made would put her in debt from the start—something she'd resolved to avoid. But she might not have a choice.

"Does anyone know a good carpenter?" she asked when there was a pause in the conversation. "For my cabinets," she added when she saw confused looks from those sitting nearest.

"But I thought Nate was building your cabinets," Maude said.

Ella shrugged. "That was the plan, but…" She forced herself to say the worst of it. "What if he doesn't come back?"

Maude's eyes widened in surprise. "You don't believe what he promised? Ella, honey, if that man told you he was going to build your cabinets, he *will* come back and build your cabinets."

Ella darted a glance at the other women, but their expressions were carefully blank, their eyes unreadable. *You know he's not coming back, don't you?*

She shrugged. "All right, I'll assume he's going to do that. But what if he doesn't? Does anyone know of a man who does that sort of work?"

Milly cleared her throat. "Prissy, wasn't Frederick

Von Hesse a carpenter? You know, the German fellow from Fredericksburg who married our Hannah."

Prissy, whom Ella thought had been looking a bit nervous, brightened. "Yes, I'd forgotten about him. But I'm sure Nate will be back, Ella."

She knew they didn't want to be the ones to confirm her certainty that Nate was gone forever. No doubt they thought it was best to let her get used to the idea gradually, as the days went by and Nate didn't come back to town. Then they wouldn't have to witness her pain, and she wouldn't be embarrassed because they had seen it.

Nate came awake to the poking of blunt fingers in his leg wound. Big, clumsy fingers that sent pain lancing up to his hip and down to his toes.

"Hurts!" he protested. "Stop!"

"Yes, I'm sorry, young feller, but your leg's worse. I'm afraid I'm going to have to cauterize it after all."

"No!" Nate cried. "Take me back to Simpson Creek. Dr. Walker'll know what to do," he added. What was wrong with his tongue? It was still so thick, and he couldn't make anything but gibberish sounds.

"Yes, it's either that or I'll have to amputate it," the man said grimly.

Now Nate began to thrash in earnest. He had to get away from this incompetent quack, had to get to Doc Walker! He couldn't face Ella without both his legs.

His struggles sent agony rocketing through him, but he kept fighting.

"Now, you settle down, Bohannan, I'm trying to save your life!" the sawbones shouted in his ear, pressing down firmly on his shoulders so that Nate, weakened as he was, couldn't sit up. "Junior, hold his mouth open so's I can pour some more laudanum down him," he said.

"I'm outta whiskey, and what I'm gonna do is bound to hurt. We'll let it take effect while I build a fire to heat that cleaver, then I'll use the flat of that to cauterize."

Junior? So this quack had a son he was training to be just as hopelessly incompetent as he was? He tried ineffectually to bite the fingers that pinched his cheeks open, then kept them open with something wooden— a spoon handle, maybe—until he tasted the foul brew that would send him into nightmare land again. He tried to fight against the drug's effects, but he knew it was a losing battle.

Lord, let me die if he can't save my leg...

Chapter Twenty

By late afternoon the last sheet of tin had been hammered in place and the stove from Ella's old café had been moved inside. The sawdust had been swept, the outer and inner walls whitewashed.

The photographer herded them all together for one last group picture in front of the finished café.

"You should be sitting in the front of the group, Ella," Maude urged her when she would have joined the other ladies in the front row. "After all, it's your new café."

Ella allowed herself to be pushed forward. She'd enjoyed watching her little building being built, but now that it was over and Nate had not appeared, she was ready to be alone with her thoughts.

After she'd settled into her position, she spotted a figure walking across the bridge toward them. It certainly wasn't Nate, but an old woman with a much-stained apron—Mrs. Powell, Ella recognized with a start. The old woman shambled slowly toward them, leaning on a cane, which Ella hadn't seen her use before. She stopped a few feet behind the photographer, staring at the new building.

"What's she doing here?" Maude hissed from behind Ella.

"I don't know," Ella whispered back. Mrs. Powell was staring at them, unblinking, mouth slightly agape. Had she come to denounce the project that threatened her livelihood?

Intent on taking this last picture, the photographer seemed unaware of the newcomer. "Quiet now, and be still, all of you, so there won't be a blur in the picture," he cautioned them from under his hood. "We have to hurry or we'll lose the light. Miss Ella, please stop looking to the side and face the lens," he added.

Obediently, Ella stopped her wary watching of Mrs. Powell. The flash of the powder in the photographer's tray dazzled her eyes and she blinked until she could focus without spots in front of her vision.

When she could see again, she noticed the old woman trudging back over the bridge, her shoulders hunched.

"Guess she came to see what the competition was going to look like," Jane Jeffries muttered. "Did you see that blank look in her eyes? Creepy, if you ask me."

"Poor old thing," Milly Brookfield murmured.

It couldn't have been easy for the hotel cook to see Ella's brand-new café, all new and freshly painted, Ella thought, feeling a rush of compassion for the old woman, despite the way Mrs. Powell had bullied her in the past. *Lord, please make sure there's enough business for both of us, so she doesn't lose her position.*

The photographer, meanwhile, had folded his tripod and loaded it and the camera onto the curious hooded wagon that functioned as his darkroom in the field. Men gathered their tools, while the women collected their children and loaded their baskets with the dishes and silverware they'd brought.

Ella had thanked the builders and the ladies individually during the afternoon, but now she felt compelled to do it again. "Thank you, thank you, everyone," she called, seeing that folks were beginning to leave.

"You're welcome, Miss Ella," George Detwiler said, apparently speaking for everyone, but then he added for himself, "I'll miss having your fine cooking handy in back of the saloon, but you let me know when you're ready to open, and Ma and I will be your first customers." With a wave, he turned and walked back toward town.

Ella stepped inside her new café so she wouldn't have to watch everyone leave. "That is the question, isn't it? When will I be ready to open?" she asked aloud in the empty interior. Dust motes danced in the fading sunlight let in by the west-facing window. *When will I be ready to open, if Nate never returns?*

"Talking to yourself?" Maude asked with a chuckle, startling her.

"Oh! I—I thought you'd gone," Ella said. "I...I was just standing here picturing where everything would go."

She knew from the skeptical expression on her friend's face that she wasn't fooled.

"I didn't want to leave you alone out here, not with that addled old woman prowling around," Maude said.

"Oh, I don't think Mrs. Powell will be back. I imagine she's busy making supper at the hotel by now."

"So, what will you do about the cabinets you need?" Maude asked her. "Not that I think Nate won't return, of course," she added quickly—too quickly.

Ella shrugged. "I suppose I'll wait a few days and see if he comes back. Then I'll have to borrow the hutch and trunks I was offered, at least until I can contact Mr. Von Hesse, I suppose."

"All right then," Maude said brightly. "Let's go back to the boardinghouse and rest up from our busy day. Tomorrow's Sunday—let's think up something fun to do after church. Maybe we could walk outside town to where that big pecan grove is and gather some up to make pralines."

"All right." She was grateful for her friend's presence and her loyal support. Gathering pecans and making pralines would at least be better than sitting in her room, imagining Nate on a train to California.

"But I can't discharge you today," Dr. Gibson protested the following Thursday when Nate informed him he was leaving. "Young man, you still had a fever only yesterday, and the day before that I still thought I'd have to amputate that leg. You go jostling your wound over the road between here and Simpson Creek, and you're liable to undo all the good I've tried to do."

Without asking permission, he whisked the sheet off and squinted at Nate's wounded leg without speaking.

"It's mending," Nate concluded for him. *No thanks to you and that red-hot whatever-it-was that you branded me with like a calf at roundup time.* "I can't spend any more time here. I need to be back in Simpson Creek." *With Ella.* "Now, hand over my clothes, or I promise you I'm going to ride out of Lampasas in this nightshirt!"

Gibson was still sputtering when a familiar voice said from the doorway, "Easy there, Bohannan."

Nate looked past the doctor to see Sheriff Bishop standing there.

"You giving the doc trouble?" Bishop asked with

a grin. "Thought it was time I'd better check on you again. Looks like I'm just in time."

Nate was pretty sure Bishop had heard him shouting at the sawbones all the way down the street. "Sheriff, tell him I'd be perfectly able to ride back to Simpson Creek if he'd just hand over my clothes."

"Consarned ungrateful patients," the doctor muttered. "If he leaves now, he's apt to get that leg infected again. I came mighty near to havin' t' cut it off, as it was."

Nate saw Bishop glance at the still-uncovered wound and blanch at the blackened scar where the entrance wound had been cauterized. The sheriff quickly looked away and swallowed.

"Dr. Gibson, if you think it'd be better, I can rent a buckboard and take him back in that," Bishop said. "I'll have our physician in Simpson Creek keep an eye on that," he said, nodding at the wound. "If that's all right with you, I'll settle up with you about his bill."

"You don't have to pay for me," Nate protested, though he didn't know how he'd pay for himself.

"You were serving on a posse, remember?" Bishop retorted. "The town can pay for your care."

Nate wanted to say the citizens of Simpson Creek shouldn't have to reward this quack for nearly killing him, but he figured he could keep that sentiment to himself until they were out of Lampasas. "Fine," he said. "But I can ride—"

"If the doc here says you're better off going in a buckboard, you'll go in a buckboard," Bishop said in a voice that brooked no argument. "The horse I loaned you can pull it. I'll tie my mount to the back. Now, stop jawin' and get dressed."

Nate wanted to get out of Lampasas badly enough

that he complied, and moments later, he followed Bishop out of the office. He was surprised at how weak he felt, taking those first few steps. The fever had really sapped his strength.

Suddenly he remembered something Bishop had said when he arrived. "You said you thought it was time you checked on me 'again.' Does that mean you'd been here before today?"

"When you didn't show up back in town by Sunday morning, I thought I'd better come see what had become of you," Bishop remarked as they made their way down the boardwalk. "I rode over here Sunday afternoon, and I could see for myself you weren't in any shape to leave yet. You were talkin' out of your head. Dr. Gibson said to check again today, unless he sent word otherwise, so I did."

"You should have seen Sunday that the old quack was trying his best to kill me, and hauled me out of there. I don't remember much from when I was feverish, but I do recall he and that son of his were awfully eager to cut off my leg. Simpson Creek's lucky to have a good doc like Nolan Walker."

"That's a fact," agreed Bishop. "Now, if you can wait a few more minutes before we start back, I'd like to stop in here and say a quick howdy to Sheriff Teague."

Nate hadn't been paying much attention to where they were walking, but he saw now that they were approaching the Lampasas jail. He was surprised—even a little touched—that Bishop had come to see about him before checking in with his fellow lawman.

Bishop hesitated at the door. "You can wait outside if you'd rather not see Salali—he's in one of the cells."

Nate found he wasn't opposed to the idea. The next time he'd face the man, it would be across a courtroom during the trial, when he was called to testify. But he'd never gotten to say his piece about what the charlatan medicine man had done to him. "It won't bother me," he said, and gestured for Bishop to precede him inside.

"Mornin', Wade," Bishop said as they entered. "Just wanted to let you know I'm taking Nate, here, back to Simpson Creek to finish healing up."

Wade Teague, a stocky man in his late thirties, said, "That's fine. You feelin' better, Bohannan? As I said the other day, I'm much obliged to you for capturing Salali."

"Right as rain, thanks," Nate said, though in truth his branded leg was beginning to throb. He felt Salali's gaze before he looked over to the left cell behind Teague's desk, and straightened. He didn't want to show any sign of weakness.

As the two sheriffs began comparing notes about their respective jurisdictions, he met Salali's eyes. The other man motioned him closer.

Curious as to what Salali wanted to say, Nate stepped behind the desk and looked at the man behind the bars. Was he about to be cursed by a man bound for the gallows?

But Robert Salali surprised him. "You know, I underestimated you, Nate Bohannan," he said in a low tone. Clearly, he didn't want his words to carry past Nate, but he needn't have worried. The two lawmen were thoroughly engrossed in their conversation.

"Oh? How's that?" Nate asked. "Are you saying that because I had a harder skull than you figured when you whacked me over the head with that skillet and left, not caring if I was dead or alive?" He shut his mouth, wishing he hadn't let that bitterness slip out.

Salali had the grace to look the slightest bit ashamed. "Not just that," he admitted with a wry twist of his fleshy lips. "I just never figured you'd have the sand to come after me and be the one who brought me down. There's more to you than I thought. I've had some time to think since I was brought in here—" he gestured at the small enclosed space "—and I want to say I'm sorry I stole from you."

The words put Nate on his guard. Why would Salali say that? What did he want?

"You know, you didn't get everything that day," Nate said. "You missed the good watch in my front vest pocket." He'd left it under the floorboard of his room in the saloon, and now he wished he could dangle it in front of his former employer.

Salali groaned. "Yeah, I remembered that later," he admitted. "Too bad for me. It would've fetched a pretty penny—more than your banjo did, for sure. Good for you, Bohannan. Listen," he said, motioning Nate closer, "I've got a proposition for you."

The idea that this man had the gall to think there was anything he could offer him lit a spark of anger. "What? You're going to offer to give me the recipe for that worthless swill you sold as Cherokee medicine so the secret doesn't go to the grave with you?" he taunted. "No, thanks. I'm ashamed I helped you sell even one bottle."

As soon as he said the words, he felt like a hypocrite. He'd known the truth of the Gospel since boyhood, yet he hadn't even begun to live like a Christian till he'd come to Simpson Creek and seen how real Christians lived. And he was still in his infancy as far as living his faith went.

"Bohannan, look, if you break me out of here, we'll be partners," Salali whispered, urgency creasing his oily face. "Fifty-fifty. I'll even let you call the shots."

The man's skin had taken on a pasty tinge. He was afraid to die, and willing to offer anything for a chance to escape the noose, Nate realized.

"Not interested, Salali," Nate said, then made his tone kinder. "If I were you, I'd be thinking about making things right with the Lord. You can't bargain with Him, but you can be forgiven."

But the only spark in the prisoner's eyes was that of malice. "Found religion, did you?" he sneered. "You weren't so righteous when you were helping me sell that 'worthless swill,' as you call it."

"I'm not righteous, Salali. Only the Lord is. But I *am* forgiven," Nate said. "You can be, too, even after murdering that woman."

But he could see he was getting nowhere. Salali's face remained hard and set.

"Think about it," he said to the prisoner, and turned on his heel. "I'll be waiting outside," he told Bishop, and found a bench outside the jail where he said a prayer for Robert Salali. As soon as he finished it, he was overwhelmed with the desire to see Ella again.

Within half an hour they had rented a buckboard, harnessed Nate's borrowed horse to pull it, with Bishop's mount tied by a rope to the back, and were headed west to Simpson Creek.

The first few miles passed in silence. Bishop probably had his own matters to think of, but finally Nate could stand it no longer. "Did…did the building get done all right for Miss Ella's café?" Nate asked, carefully keeping his tone offhand, as if he was merely making conversation. He couldn't ask what he wanted to—if Ella had missed him being there, and if she worried when he didn't return with the rest of the posse.

He could feel Bishop's gaze on him. "It did," the sheriff said, and maddeningly let it go at that.

Which left Nate in something of a dilemma. He could either ask more questions and betray his interest, or let it go and be tormented by not knowing until he could talk to Ella. Maybe Bishop had no idea about such matters, anyway. Men didn't pry into other men's romantic interests, so perhaps Bishop didn't even know of the feelings Nate had for Ella Justiss.

Something about the sheriff's manner made Nate suspect Sam Bishop was all too aware of Nate's feelings, but whatever the truth of it was, Nate wasn't about to show his hand to this man.

"It'll be good for Simpson Creek to have a nice café, right near the church," Nate said, giving no more than he'd gotten.

Bishop grunted a noncommittal reply. Silence resumed, broken only by the clip-clopping of the horses' hooves as they trotted back toward Simpson Creek.

It didn't matter, Nate told himself. He didn't need the sheriff to tell him what he'd learn for himself soon enough. After all, the road into Simpson Creek led right past the café site. With any luck, Ella would be there—doing what, he didn't know, for surely she wouldn't have opened for business yet—and he could tell her the truth about what had happened to prevent his return. She'd understand why he'd asked Bishop to give her that vague excuse about why he'd remained in Lampasas.

"Don't ever ask me to cover up the truth for you again," Bishop said suddenly, as if the words had been pent up behind his lips for too long and couldn't be contained any longer. "I shouldn't have agreed not to tell Miss Ella you were wounded. None of us should. You shouldn't have asked us to."

"I—I didn't want her to worry about me," Nate protested, though he'd already come to the same conclusion as Bishop. "She would have, you know that." It sounded like a lame excuse even to him.

"You sayin' she didn't have a *right* to worry?" Bishop almost shouted the question. "I reckon it was her right to fret about you if she chose to—or would her worry have been a burden to you 'cause you don't care enough? If that's the case, I can turn this wagon around and we can head back to Lampasas. Once the trial's done, you can light out for anywhere you like but back to my town. None of us will stand for you breakin' Miss Ella's heart."

For half a mile Nate could only stare at the hard, set face of the man next to him who'd turned his gaze back to the road ahead.

"I don't have any intention of breaking Ella's heart," Nate said. "In fact, I'd like you to drop me right at the café when we get back to town. If she's there, I'll talk to her about what happened as soon as I lay eyes on her. If she's not at the café, I'll go to the boardinghouse and find her."

"I ought to refuse to drop you anyplace but at Dr. Walker's so he can check you over, but it's likely to be suppertime before we get there and I don't want to call Nolan away from his meal. I expect that'll keep till morning," he said, nodding at Nate's wounded leg.

"I'll have him check it first thing in the morning," Nate promised, wishing he could sprout wings in order to get back to Ella sooner.

Chapter Twenty-One

Ella wandered listlessly around the café, running a feather duster over the tables and chairs, although there'd hardly been time for them to gather dust since they'd been moved into the new building. She kept her back to the mismatched hodgepodge of furniture behind her—Faith's hutch, the rough-hewn pair of tables others had offered that held her cooking utensils, pots and skillets, the steamer trunks that held her flour, meal and condiments.

The loaners had brought their items of furniture at various times through the day, and Ella had spent her time arranging her equipment and supplies in them so she could open the café for business tomorrow. She was grateful that the townspeople had been so generous in loaning them, of course, but the total effect looked so... so *haphazard,* she thought, and detracted from the neat new perfection of the rest of the café, with its matched tables and chairs.

Stop being so prideful about unimportant details, Ella Justiss. What you have here will have to do until Mr. Von Hesse can come and build your cabinets. As

*long as the food is delicious, that's all your customers
will care about.*

The letter she'd written to the German cabinetmaker
who lived in Fredericksburg lay, ready to mail, on one
of the tables. She had written it while waiting for the de-
liveries of the borrowed furniture, and she would mail it
at the post office on the way back to the boardinghouse.

Glancing out the window, she saw that the light was
fading. Time to return to the boardinghouse and have
supper. She hoped Maude had saved her a plateful of
whatever Mrs. Meyer was serving that day, for the male
inhabitants of the boardinghouse would cheerfully con-
sume every last bite in the crockery bowls and platters
without a thought for her.

She heard the sound of hoofbeats and the creak of
a wagon approaching from the east, and readied herself to explain to yet another would-be customer that
the café wasn't open until tomorrow, but supper could
be purchased at the hotel. She'd had several inquiries
throughout the day from folks passing through Simpson Creek—the townspeople already knew the grand
opening was tomorrow, of course. It was gratifying to
think that customers were so eager to patronize her
new establishment.

If only she could regain the joy she had once felt
about the prospect of having her own café, separate
from the saloon.

She heard two men's voices outside in the wagon, and
then heard the wagon move on. Maybe they'd figured
out for themselves that the place wasn't open.

She was just moving toward the door, intent on
reaching for her shawl where it hung on a hook, when
the door opened, and she stood face-to-face with Nate
Bohannan.

For a heartbeat she thought she had called up his image from the dreams that had plagued her ever since the posse had returned without him.

"Hello, Ella." He pulled his hat off.

The voice sounded real enough. And the twinkling blue eyes and light brown hair with its tendency to curl were certainly his, as was the caressing Southern drawl.

"You…you're not here," she murmured in confusion. "You're on the way to California."

Now *he* looked confused. "No, I'm not. I'm right here, Ella, and I need to explain what happened, why I didn't come to the café raising. It looks real nice, by the way," he said, gesturing around him.

Despite the joy she felt at realizing it truly was him and not some figment of her imagination, her irritation at the hodgepodge of furnishings washed over her again.

"*This* looks nice," she said, waving a hand at the tables and chairs he'd made. *"That—"* she gestured at the borrowed furniture behind her with her pots and pans stacked on the long table and her cooking supplies overflowing from the trunk "—looks like a real sow's nest." She raised her chin. "Regardless, I shall open tomorrow with what I have, until a carpenter can come from Fredericksburg to build what I need."

He blinked. "From Fredericksburg? But *I'm* going to build your cabinets, Ella. I said I would, didn't I?"

"You did. But how was I supposed to know what had happened to you, when you didn't come back with the others? As I said, I figured you had gone on to California. I waited, Nate—and during that time, I haven't been able to conduct my business because everything had been moved here, including the stove—so it wasn't as if I could just keep serving meals behind the saloon until you decided to waltz back into town." Her words had erupted from her in a bitter flood, but she couldn't have halted them, even though she saw anger kindling in his eyes.

"'Waltz back into town?'" he repeated in disbelief. "I don't think I'll be 'waltzing' anytime soon."

They glared at one another, and then he surprised her by saying, "I need to sit down for a minute." He pointed to the nearest chair.

"Why not? You built them, after all," she retorted waspishly. As he did so, a last shaft of western sunlight illuminated his face, and she saw the tinge of paleness under his tan and the faint sheen of sweat on his forehead.

"Nate…" she began, uneasily aware that something was wrong. "Are you all right?"

"No, but I will be," he said. "Now, I hope I don't offend your maidenly sensibilities, Ella, but I want you to see why I didn't come 'waltzing back into town' in time for your café raising, despite my promise." He pulled his right boot off, then pushed his denim trouser leg up until his calf was visible—with a hideous red-rimmed blackened scar right along the side of it.

Ella gave a shriek and looked away, then sank into the chair opposite him, her face covered with her hands lest she see the terrifying sight again. "Nate, what on earth—"

"You can open your eyes, I've covered it again," he growled.

She saw that he'd shoved his pants leg back down again and was pulling his boot back on.

"I took a bullet in the course of helping to capture Salali," he said. "I've spent the last few days at the doctor's in Lampasas, fighting to keep my leg. The doc finally laid a red-hot knife blade to it to kill the infection.

I was out of my head a good bit of the time, so that's why I didn't send word."

Ella trembled as she raised her gaze to his, and shivered as she saw the chill in his eyes. "I—I'm sorry, Nate. I had no idea," she said. "Wh-why didn't Bishop tell me? I would've come to Lampasas and nursed you myself."

"He told you what I asked him to, Ella."

"Why?"

Ella shut her mouth as the sudden sickening realization hit her. "You didn't want me there," she murmured as a tear trickled down her cheek. Agitated, she swiped at her eyes to prevent the other tears that stung her eyes and threatened to spill over and join the first one. "That's the truth of it, isn't it? You didn't want me coming to Lampasas fussing over you, worrying about you… You didn't want to be bothered with me."

He rubbed his eyes wearily, and then focused on her again. "The only lick of truth in what you just said, Ella Justiss, is that I didn't want you worried about me, or to miss your café raising because you came to Lampasas to nurse me. Yes, I should've had them tell you the truth, I know that now, but at the time we all thought it would be a simple matter of having my wound cleaned by the sawbones there. I thought I might even make it back in time to help finish the building."

She didn't dare look at him, so she kept her eyes downcast. "I knew they were acting funny," she murmured. "Sam, Nick and Jack, I mean. They wouldn't look me in the eye. I should've kept after them till they told me the truth."

"What you *should've* done was trust me," he said, that frosty edge still in his voice. "But you didn't. You jumped to the first conclusion you always jump to, that you're being abandoned."

"That's not fair," Ella protested as his words ricocheted around her soul. "I…"

She had been about to snap, *I've certainly got reason not to trust, haven't I?* But she was as tired of that excuse as he apparently was, from what he'd said. "Nate, I—"

"I am probably going to have to testify," he said, interrupting her without apology, "but it'll likely be a while till they can get the circuit judge to Lampasas. In the meantime, I'm going to build your cabinets and countertop, Miss Ella."

It was the second time he'd resorted to the formality of calling her "Miss" Ella, and it didn't bode well, despite the fact that he was going to do as he'd promised.

"Thank you," she began, knowing this would mean a certain amount of pounding and sawing in the background while she served her customers, but that was a temporary inconvenience. She could feed him at noon and at suppertime, and surely that and spending time with each other again would help erase the chill from his tone. He was just tired from the trip back, and probably that dreadful wound still smarted considerably and was making him cross. "I—"

"Don't worry that I'll be underfoot and bothering your customers with the noise and mess, Miss Ella. I intend to work at night, after you've closed up. It'll only take a few days, and you'll never have to lay eyes on me. And then you'll have your cabinets and countertop." He was still watching her, but his eyes hadn't warmed one little bit.

"And then we…" She wasn't even sure how she was going to finish her sentence, but he didn't give her a chance to figure it out.

"And then I'll be leaving," he said, finality vibrating

in the air between them. "I said I should've had them tell you the truth, but *my* truth is I didn't want you to have to worry. But it's obvious you don't trust me, and you never will. So once I'm done here—" he waved a hand at the back of the restaurant, where he'd build her cabinets "—I'll be gone, and you can tell yourself you were right about me all along."

He stood up, which cost him some pain, she saw, and clapped the hat back on his head.

Ella whirled away from him, unwilling to let him see the tears streaming down her face. He was not a man to be moved by tears, and she was not about to beg.

He kept on moving and let the door slam behind him. He was disgusted with her, she realized.

Nate was disgusted with himself. He had no idea why the quack doctor in Lampasas had thought riding in the buckboard would be any easier on his still-painful wound than riding a horse. It had been last night since the doctor had dosed him with laudanum, and now his leg pained him like a herd of red ants hid inside it.

And now, because the pain had made him cranky, he'd lashed out at Ella, when all he'd wanted to do on the way back from Lampasas was to take her in his arms and tell her he'd never leave her again. Instead, he'd reacted to her understandable irritation at being lied to and verbally painted himself into a corner. Now he'd have no choice but to leave after he'd built her cabinets and countertop, for that's what he'd said he was going to do. She wouldn't beg him to stay, not after the way he'd talked to her.

He well deserved the lonely years that lay ahead for him.

Had he expected her to fall at his feet, kissing his

boots when he entered her café, after not having any real idea where he'd been? How had he gotten the tomfool notion that it was better to leave her in ignorance, unable to do the very thing that earned her own food and lodging?

If he'd let Bishop tell her what had happened, she could have postponed moving the stove and her supplies into the new building and left the café open behind the saloon till he could come back. What a selfish idiot he'd been!

And now she must hate him, he thought, remembering his last sight of her rigid back. How he wished he could erase the past few minutes and start over.

What was done was done, he thought, climbing into the buckboard. He'd told Bishop he would take care of leaving the buckboard and the loaned horse at the livery until someone could return the wagon to Lampasas so that the sheriff could go on home to his family.

He sat on the driver's seat for a moment, irresolute. He wanted to go back into the café and try to apologize, but he was afraid of the scorn Ella would heap on his head. He wanted to go to Dr. Walker's and ask for some willow-bark tea to take the edge off of his pain.

But perhaps the pain was his just deserts for the way he'd talked to Ella. He'd endure his punishment, he thought. He clucked to the horse and headed for the livery. Once he'd turned the horse and wagon over to Calhoun at the livery, he'd go tell Detwiler he'd only be using the room above the saloon for a few more days, then climb the stairs and go to bed.

Everyone in Simpson Creek made a point of stopping in at the café the next day, whether they stayed for a full meal or merely stopped for a cup of coffee while they congratulated Ella on her grand opening. Her tables were continually occupied, and folks insisted that her chicken fricassee tasted even better in her brand-new building with the birds chirping in the trees outside and the sound of the creek babbling on the breeze.

Nate Bohannan did not come in, however. Maude mentioned that she'd seen him limping into the doctor's when she'd gone to the post office.

"Good. That means he's letting Doc Walker check his leg as he's supposed to," Ella said. The sheriff had told her of the Lampasas doctor's instructions.

"It's early yet," Maude said in her cheerful way. "Surely he'll come in for supper before he starts working in here."

Ella shrugged, trying to appear as if it was no concern of hers. She'd told Maude what had happened when Nate had returned from Lampasas, and Maude had insisted pain had made him irritable after his trip and that pride was now keeping him away. "Men can be incredibly stubborn, can't they? He'll come around, full of sweet apologies. That man loves you, Ella. I'm sure of it."

Ella allowed herself a disbelieving sniff. "We'll see about that," she said. "If he wants to stay angry, I'm sure there's nothing I can do about it. I'll be content if he just finishes those cabinets and the countertop like he said he would." But that was not all she wanted, and she knew it.

"Oh, I imagine he's going to keep his word on that. Haven't you seen the boards stacked up out back?"

Ella stared at Maude, then went to the back window next to her stove. Sure enough, freshly sawn boards were neatly stacked there. "They must have come when I was so busy cooking at noon."

She hoped Maude was right, and Nate would come early and have supper with her before he set to work. Surely, if she apologized for her shrewish words, all would be well between them again.

But when it came time to close the café, Nate had not shown up.

Lighting her lantern—for it was now October and fully dark—she pulled her shawl off its hook, put the closed sign in the window and shut the door behind her. Knowing Nate was going to come during the night, she didn't lock it. No one would bother to steal furniture.

Her footsteps echoed hollowly over the bridge as she crossed Simpson Creek, and a cool gust of wind blew up her skirts. She started as a stray cat, no doubt hunting night creatures for its dinner, crossed her path as she stepped off the bridge and onto the road that led past the church.

Perhaps she should get a dog, Ella thought, a big dog that could walk home with her on these dark evenings so she wouldn't feel so alone. She imagined Mrs. Meyer would fuss about the idea, though, even if the creature spent its days at the café and only returned at night when Ella did.

Perhaps in time she would have made enough money that she could have a cabin built behind the café, and live there, and she could have as many pets as she wanted—and chickens, too, she thought, thus saving the cost of eggs. And perhaps a milk cow, as well. She'd still have to buy meat at the butcher's, though, for she knew she would not be able to slaughter the creatures she spread feed for every day.

But Ella knew instinctively that however nice it would be to have her own house, she could not exist in such solitude, with only animals to keep her company.

Her interactions with the others who lived at Mrs. Meyer's boardinghouse fed some need within her.

Ella wondered if Maude would be willing to come live with her if she had the cabin built big enough. Such an arrangement had worked very well for Prissy and Sarah, she'd heard, until Sarah married Dr. Walker.

But Maude might get married someday, too. It had always surprised Ella that her pretty friend was one of the last unmarried members of the Spinsters' Club. What if Maude agreed to share the cabin with her, then got married and left? Ella would be happy for her friend, of course, but she'd be just as lonely as she had been before.

She was getting way ahead of herself, Ella thought as she turned down the alley that led to the boardinghouse. Her café had only been open for one day, and while she'd made a handsome profit, she knew many of her customers had come only to encourage her. She'd have to see what her average daily take would be before she could think about anything further.

Nate watched Ella walk past from his room above the saloon. It hadn't occurred to him that she would be returning from her café alone in the dark, and he didn't like the fact one bit. Maybe he should get her a dog—a big, fierce but loyal dog—as a parting gift. Then at least he'd know she had a protector once he was gone. He had no idea where he'd obtain such a beast... But wait—when they'd been riding after Salali, hadn't Jack Collier mentioned that his ranch dog had had pups a while back? Maybe he'd check with Collier. Ella probably wouldn't accept any gifts from him, but if he left the dog tied to one of the trees beside her café...

But he'd better stop woolgathering and get going

now that she was safely back at the boardinghouse. He had a lot to do during the night. He was going to start with one of two sets of shelves built against the wall. He'd have to be sure to be gone before she got there in the morning. If he knew Ella, she'd probably be there before the sun rose.

"I'm going to the café," he called to George Detwiler as he passed through the half-full saloon.

Detwiler looked up from the glass of whiskey he'd been pouring for a customer and waved. He'd already expressed his opinion twice since Nate had returned from Lampasas, after Nate had explained why he'd be building Miss Ella her cabinets and countertop at night rather than during the daylight hours.

"You two are the most prideful pair I ever did meet," Detwiler had said only this morning. "Why don't you be the bigger person and go tell her you're sorry for what happened and for what you said? You know you want to, and I'm telling you, she'd forgive you. Miss Ella ain't one t' hold a grudge."

"Says the confirmed bachelor who's never spoken to a woman long enough to get her mad at him," Nate had mocked. "Maybe I'm just not the type to settle down any more than you are, George."

Detwiler had rolled his eyes at him. "Oh, I'm plenty settled down, all right. Been livin' in Simpson Creek all my life, haven't I? I just haven't found a woman who'd put up with me. Go apologize, and at least then you wouldn't have to be eating meals at the hotel."

Nate had shuddered at the memory of the food the old cook at the hotel had set before him last night. All grease and gristle. And the woman herself was getting odder and odder. There was something in her eyes that wasn't quite right.

"I could explain the situation to Ma and you could stop in at the house for meals till you get things patched up with Miss Ella," Detwiler had offered then. "She'd be right glad of the company."

"Thanks, but one of you nosing into my business is enough. I'm going to get done for Miss Ella what I said I would, then I'm heading for California like I planned— after I testify at Salali's trial, that is."

Detwiler had shrugged. "You're both making a big mistake, but I guess it's yours to make."

As Nate made his way down the darkened road toward the café, carrying a heavy canvas bag containing a saw, a hammer and a sack of nails, he figured Detwiler was probably right. It was a mistake to let pride stand between him and Ella. But he didn't know how to bridge the gap.

Lord, if you want Ella and me to be together, show me the way.

Chapter Twenty-Two

"So he didn't come after I left yesterday?" Maude asked the next morning while she cracked eggs into a big bowl at the café. She'd come along this morning to help Ella with breakfast, "just for something to do," as she called it.

"No, he didn't," Ella said, keeping her voice even. "That's probably enough eggs to start with for now."

Helping out at the café was evidently Maude's way of ensuring Ella would be a captive audience today while Maude nosed into her business. Ella had avoided her last night at the boardinghouse, going straight to her room while Maude was still helping Mrs. Meyer with the dishes, so now her friend evidently meant to make up for lost time. Ella hated to reprove her friend, but perhaps she needed to make it clear that the subject of Nate Bohannan was off-limits.

There had been shelves on the far wall this morning, all of them varnished. These would be for the supplies that would go there—flour, sugar, salt, cornmeal and canned food—though she couldn't put those things on them just yet. Bohannan had left a note scrawled on a scrap of paper—*Let these dry today. OK to use tomorrow—N*

"You know what you should do…?" Maude mused aloud.

"What's that?" Ella responded, assuming her friend was about to make a suggestion about serving breakfast.

"If Nate doesn't come today while you're still here, you should go back to the boardinghouse, put on your prettiest dress—that burnt-orange one with the dark green trim—brush your hair out loose on your shoulders and put on some of that rosewater perfume that you're always saving for a special occasion, and come back here. Oh, and save a piece of that pie you're planning to make today," Maude said, her eyes distant and dreamy. "Bohannan will be here tonight, working away, but then you'll come in, all prettied up… With the two of you alone, it'll be the perfect time to kiss and make up," Maude concluded, a grin spreading from ear to ear. "Isn't that a good idea?"

"No," Ella said in what she hoped was a quelling tone. "I declare, Maude, you must have been borrowing romantic novels from Caroline Collier or Violet Masterson again." Both women were known for their collections of books.

"Not at all," Maude retorted in a breezy tone. "I draw my inspiration from the book of Ruth, in the Bible. At least you wouldn't have to go to the lengths she did to show Boaz how much she cared."

In spite of herself, Ella felt a blush creeping up her neck, remembering the story of how the biblical heroine had covered herself with Boaz's robe on the threshing floor at night. "Nate Bohannan is hardly 'kinsman redeemer' material like Boaz," she told Maude. "I know you mean well, dear friend, but enough meddling, all right? As president of the Spinsters' Club, shouldn't you be setting up social events to enable matches to be made?"

"As a matter of fact, I've been doing that, too," the irrepressible Maude said. "There's to be a harvest festival later this fall, the date as yet undetermined. We'll talk about it at the next meeting."

"All right, then. But now we'd better get down to business," Ella said. "Here comes Mr. Calhoun and Mr. Wallace, and we don't even have biscuits out of the oven yet."

The morning became very busy after that. Even as she flew around the kitchen, taking orders, removing biscuits from the oven and putting more in, scrambling eggs and flipping pancakes, Ella could not banish the image Maude had placed in her mind of her returning to the café in her prettiest dress, her hair loose on her shoulders and smelling of rosewater. Nate would be there, hammering or sawing away on a piece of wood. He would look up and behold her standing in a circle of candlelight, and be unable to resist the appeal in her shining eyes....

Why not? Nothing ventured, nothing gained, right? But she didn't tell Maude that she'd decided to go along with her suggestion, just in case she lost her nerve.

Her friend left in the early afternoon, after the crowd at midday had thinned down to a customer or two, and it seemed that she took Ella's courage with her. She'd been silly to listen to Maude's romantic fantasies, Ella thought as the day wore on and fatigue stole her optimism.

There was no guarantee that Maude's idea would result in the romantic reconciliation Ella hoped for. Indeed, it might make things immeasurably worse! What if Nate took one look at her and uttered scornful hoots of laughter at the idea that he could ever think of forgiving her, let alone having tender feelings for her again? Or what if he forgave her, and they declared their feelings for one another, and she got anxious and afraid when he started to kiss her again, as she had that night at the mill? No man would want to commit himself to a fearful woman like that. Or worst of all, what if he got the wrong idea about her coming to him like that, and took advantage of their solitude?

Suddenly she was back at the asylum again, and Mr. Antoine had taken her into the pantry on the pretext of finding the rye flour that he claimed was there, but which Ella had been unable to find...

"No!" she cried as someone took hold of her arm.

George Detwiler let go of her arm as if it burned him. "Miss Ella, are you all right? Why, you're pale as a sheet! Sorry, I didn't mean to startle you, I just wanted to point out your pot is boiling over."

Yanked out of her nightmare, Ella stared at Detwiler's familiar face as the present time surrounded her with reassuring familiarity, then she whirled around to see that, unattended, the pot of homemade noodles was indeed boiling over onto the black surface of the oven top. "Oh! Thanks!" she called over her shoulder, and flew to wrench the pot away from the heat with the aid of a dish towel.

Detwiler studied her, his face concerned. *Please, Lord, don't let him ask me what I was thinking about.*

"Just didn't want you burnin' my chicken and noodles," the saloonkeeper said with a grin.

"How is it you're here asking for supper to take back to the bar?" Ella asked. "Is your mother out of town?" She knew Detwiler always ate supper at home.

"No, Miss Ella, I just miss your cooking, and I didn't make it over here at noon… Be sure and make that a big helping, will you? You can charge me double, I don't mind."

Ella was suspicious. Could George be secretly taking the food back to Nate? Very possibly. After all, with the way things stood between Nate and her, he didn't have anywhere else to eat except the hotel, and Mrs. Powell's current odd behavior was the talk of Simpson Creek.

The idea that Nate still preferred her cooking rather appealed to her. "George Detwiler, why won't you come right out and admit you're buying this for Bohannan. I won't charge you if you fess up—as long as you don't tell him I figured it out." They were alone in the café, so no one else would tell Nate, either.

Detwiler looked sheepish. "It *is* for Bohannan, Miss Ella. He just couldn't stomach Mrs. Powell's vittles no more."

"So he put you up to fetching his food from my café without me knowing about it?" She assumed an arch tone.

Detwiler looked uneasy. "He told me not to tell you it was for him, Miss Ella."

"I have no objection to feeding Mr. Bohannan," she said. "After all, he *is* performing a job for me." She pointed at the new shelves behind her. "It can remain our secret, if you like."

"Yes, ma'am," Detwiler agreed, looking relieved at her easy acquiescence. "Miss Ella…I purely don't like the way things are between Bohannan and you. Isn't there some way—"

She shrugged. "I think that's up to him, George. If he doesn't even want me to know he's eating my food, he apparently isn't ready to make amends for the way he spoke to me that day he returned from Lampasas. I admit I was a bit…tart with him, too, but he evidently isn't ready to forgive or ask for forgiveness."

Now Detwiler looked as miserable as he'd looked relieved a moment before. "Yes, Miss Ella. I won't tell him that you know. I'll be sure and bring your dish back," he added as she served up a generous portion of the chicken and noodles and put a glass cover over it. Then he made his escape.

Well, that settled it. She wouldn't act out Maude's suggestion. If Nate Bohannan was too proud to make the first move, it shouldn't have to be up to her. He had time to change his mind if he wanted to.

As soon as the last supper customer had left and she had finished washing the dishes, she put the closed sign in the window and headed for the bridge. Perhaps she'd heat some water for a bath once she got back to the boardinghouse. Tomorrow was Saturday—it would be interesting to see how much busier she'd be on a day when folks from the outlying ranches came into town for supplies. While she soaked, she could plan her menu for Sunday, too. Now that the café was right across the creek from the church, business was sure to be brisk. She'd better ask Maude if she'd help her later today and tomorrow—for pay, of course. If her profits continued to be good, she could offer her friend a permanent job.

Yet she couldn't help remembering when Nate had helped her, and how much fun that had been. Shoulders drooping, she headed up Main Street to the boardinghouse.

Nate had left his tools in the large bag in the back of the café that first night, so all he had to carry were the extra lanterns he needed to use, along with the ones already in place in the café. One thing was for certain, he'd never take daylight for granted again.

Tonight he planned to start on the first of the two cabinets. With any luck he'd get it done by the time he left in the morning, varnish and all, since she hadn't asked for anything fancy.

It had taken all of his self-control not to come out and call to her an hour ago, when she'd come up Main Street heading for the boardinghouse. He could have used the pretext of complimenting her on her chicken and noodles, he told himself. Ladies liked to be complimented on their cooking, didn't they?

But that would mean admitting that he'd been the one eating her food, not Detwiler. He might have actually gathered his courage and done so anyway, but just then Sheriff Bishop rode by on his last patrol of the streets before heading for home and leaving the care of the town to his deputy, and stopped to chat with Ella for a moment.

None of us will stand for you breakin' Miss Ella's heart, the sheriff had said. He didn't want Bishop to see him approaching Ella, especially if she wasn't ready to talk to him.

Suddenly a knock sounded at the café door, startling Nate so badly he hammered his thumb. He smothered a yelp.

Who could it be? Ella? By some heaven-sent chance, had she decided to forgive him, and come to tell him when there would be no one to interrupt them?

The notion evaporated as soon as the caller knocked again. *Fool—why would she knock at the door of her own building?* "The café's closed," he called. Had some cowboy, too intoxicated to remember how late it was, seen the light and figured the place was open?

The knock sounded again. He suppressed a growl of irritation. He was going to have to go to the door and send the fellow on his way. Taking up one of the lanterns, he went to the door and opened it.

No drunken cowboy was there, however. Unfortunately, neither was Ella Justiss. His lantern cast an eerie light on Mrs. Powell, standing there with a covered dish.

"Ma'am, Miss Ella's is closed," he said, not knowing what to make of this weird visit. "I'm just here working on her cabinets."

The old woman peered at him through cloudy, pale eyes. "I know it's closed, dear boy. This isn't for Ella. You forgot to come for supper tonight, and I was worried that you might be hungry." She held up the dish.

He took it, not knowing what else to do. Knowing Mrs. Powell had it out for Ella, he couldn't very well tell the old woman he wasn't about to eat what passed for a meal from her restaurant when he could have food cooked by Ella.

"But wait, I brought you silverware, too," the old woman cooed, fishing in an apron pocket and bringing out a knife, fork and spoon, which she held out to him also.

Taking them required setting the dish down beside him, for he held the lantern with his free hand.

"That…that's very thoughtful of you, ma'am…" he said. "You didn't have to do that. I'm afraid I don't have any money to pay you," he added, patting his empty pockets, "but I'll take it to the hotel later." And he'd tell the hotel proprietor about her strange visit and tactfully suggest it wouldn't be necessary for her to come again.

"Nonsense, you come on into my restaurant when you finish work and I'll cook you breakfast," Mrs. Powell said with a tremulous smile. "Doesn't matter how early. I sleep in the kitchen, so you just knock on the back door anytime."

Nate wasn't about to encourage the woman, but he didn't want to argue with her, either. The poor old thing wasn't quite right in the head. "Yes, ma'am. You'd better go on back now. Why don't I walk with you and make sure you get there all right," he suggested. He was loath to leave his work, but it wasn't gentlemanly to allow an addled old woman to wander in the dark. She hadn't carried anything to light her way.

"No, thank you, dear," she cooed. "I'll be fine. I can see you're busy." Then she shambled away with surprising speed, and in a moment he heard the *clump clump* of her heavy shoes as she crossed the bridge.

Bemused, he uncovered the dish and lifted the lantern so he could see what was in it. It looked as if had started out as some sort of beef and mashed potato dish, but the beef had been cooked till it was nothing but a blackened lump.

He wouldn't have been remotely tempted to try it, even if he hadn't eaten Ella's chicken and noodles just hours before. Perhaps the half-wild tomcat that had been hanging around the place would like it, if some other wild creature didn't find it first. After checking to make sure the old cook hadn't circled back, he dumped the mess out back and went back to work.

Should he speak to Bishop about the old lady, or Reverend Gil? Detwiler had already told him about Mrs. Powell's strange appearance at the café raising. Someone needed to be aware that the old woman was falling further and further into some sort of demented state. He couldn't imagine she'd be keeping her job at the hotel much longer if she was acting this strangely there.

* * *

Yet when he told Bishop about the strange visit, later in the day after he'd slept, the sheriff didn't make too much of it. "I've been telling Mr. Kirkwell his cook was as crazy as a lizard with a sunstroke for a long time now," he said. "I'll take that dish back for you, if you'd rather not encourage her by showing up there," he said, reaching for it. "Kirkwell knows he'd have to pay any other decent cook twice as much, so he lets Mrs. Powell stay," he said. "By the way, I was going to come find you today anyway," he said, reaching for a piece of paper on his desk. "Sheriff Teague says the circuit judge has arrived and they'll be ready for your testimony Monday morning first thing. He'll put you up at the hotel there, but he said you should only need to stay the one night, unless you want to stay to hear the verdict, of course."

"No, thanks," Nate replied. He didn't need to hear the judge's word to know that Salali was going to end his life at the end of a noose. "I reckon I'll need to borrow that horse again." He sighed. The news meant he'd have to spend Sunday riding back to Lampasas, rather than working at the café.

He'd still work tonight on the second cabinet. He could turn in early when he got to Lampasas, which would fill the empty hours better than sitting in his hotel room wondering how to make things right with Ella.

If the telegram hadn't come, he had been thinking about showing up at the end of dinner Sunday. Ella would be in her glory after the full crowd she'd no doubt have after church, and maybe in more of a mood to be generous. Perhaps, if he found her alone or waited until she was, he could talk to her about how wrong he'd been.

Chapter Twenty-Three

Saturday when Ella arrived at the café, a sleepy Maude in tow, she found the second cabinet completed, but with the same sign on it advising her not to use it until the varnish was completely dry the next day. As with everything Nate had made for her, he'd done a painstaking, careful job, and the result was simple but beautiful.

Her lips curved, glad that she could return the mismatched tables, trunks and the hutch she had been loaned. Then her smile faded as she wondered again if Nate would be gone as soon as he had fulfilled his promise to her.

It wasn't long before the customers started streaming in, and Ella had little time to think about Nate—or anything but the next order of bacon, eggs and grits or pancakes. Saturday was a big day in Simpson Creek, for ranchers and their families came into town for supplies or sent their foremen for them. Some would stay over for church on Sunday, but all of them now seemed to find Ella's café a necessary stop either for breakfast, dinner or supper. Her restaurant was a success!

As evening drew close, she started thinking about the fact that the next day was Sunday. She would hold to her policy of not opening for breakfast so she could go to church, but what of Nate? He should be able to attend church, shouldn't he? Wasn't he needed to play piano? Surely if they worshipped together, a reconciliation between them would be that much easier.

Accordingly, when Detwiler stopped in for a piece of pie in midafternoon, she made it a point to suggest, oh so casually, that since tomorrow was the Sabbath, it would be all right with her if Nate skipped working on her cabinet tonight and came to the worship service Sunday morning instead.

Detwiler looked down at his plate. "I dunno if he plans to work on your cabinet tonight or not, Miss Ella, but I do know that he's been notified that he's to testify in Lampasas Monday morning, so he's got to travel there Sunday."

"I see." Ella did her best to appear unaffected by the news, but her joyful anticipation of Sunday dimmed.

On Sunday, Ella hurried across the bridge to start Sunday dinner as soon as Reverend Gil said the final amen. Her second cabinet and a note were waiting for her: *Will finish countertop and all final work when I come back from trial. I should be back sometime Tuesday at the latest.*

"All final work," she murmured aloud. It sounded so dreadfully…final. Like he couldn't wait to have the project done so he could leave Simpson Creek—and her.

That was it, then. Ella wished he was already done and gone. Maybe once she knew for certain he had left the state, she would stop hoping every footstep at the door was his.

Having worked all night Saturday and setting out for Lampasas as the sun rose, Nate was exhausted by the time he reached it. Sheriff Teague directed him to the town's one inn, the Burleson Hotel, a vastly inferior place compared to the one in Simpson Creek. It didn't even have a restaurant, not that it mattered. He found his room and fell asleep across his bed with his clothes still on.

He woke sometime in the middle of the night, muscles cramped from the awkward position in which he had slept. Further sleep would be impossible, he knew.

Having gone without supper, he devoured the sandwiches that Detwiler had sent along from Ella's café. Now there was nothing to do but think about her and wait for the trial in the morning.

Nate wasn't sure why his testimony was needed—the murder Salali had committed here was enough to send him to the gallows, and it didn't matter how he had been captured or by whom. He was all for doing his civic duty, but he resented being called away from Simpson Creek just now simply because Teague wanted to make the case against Salali as airtight as possible.

He wasn't looking forward to facing a doomed man across a courtroom—not because he was afraid of Salali, of course, but because he could imagine what it felt like to know that one's days were limited, and would end at the end of a rope, without the surety of heaven as his home. Had Salali given thought to what he'd said about getting right with the Lord?

It was useless to fret about it. As soon as he testified, he could go home.

Home. He'd thought of Simpson Creek as home. But Simpson Creek would have been just another Hill Country Texas town without Ella Justiss in it.

I must find a way to make things right with her.

And then he thought of what he would do.

* * *

Despite her near certainty that Nate would soon be out of her life, he was on her mind as Ella went about her routine Monday, cooking meals, serving customers, cleaning up after the breakfasts, dinners and suppers. Would Nate be allowed to testify early so he could leave, or would he have to wait till the judge thought his testimony was needed? What would it be like to testify against a man he'd once trusted, she wondered, a man who had assaulted him and left him for dead, a man in whose capture he'd then played a decisive role?

"There are seats outside, sir, since the inside ones are full," she told a customer. "You can place your order and Maude will bring it to you soon as it's ready."

All of the furniture that had been lent to her had been returned, and Mr. Dayton, the lumber mill owner, had constructed a pair of simple rectangular tables and benches for her overflow customers to sit at outside. They would have to be stored during the colder months, of course, and during the hottest parts of the summer she doubted anyone would want to use them, but for now customers were taking full advantage of the extra seating.

Tuesday afternoon, when Detwiler came down for a late-afternoon cup of coffee, he brought with him the news that Nate had returned from Lampasas in the middle of the night and planned to build her countertop that night. He was sleeping now.

"But what of the trial?" she asked. "How did that go? Is it over? Was that dreadful man convicted?"

"It was nearly over when Salali cheated the hangman. He had a heart seizure right in the courtroom and died," Detwiler said.

Ella couldn't suppress a shudder, remembering how

amusing she had found the flamboyant Salali when he'd been hawking his useless elixir. She couldn't have imagined him a potential murderer then.

There was no use thinking about it anymore.

"Penny for your thoughts," Maude murmured sometime later.

"Hmm?"

"You've been kneading that bread dough like you're trying to squeeze it out of existence, but then you went all still with the most faraway look in your eyes," her friend said with a laugh.

"I'm going to do what you suggested," Ella told her. "Tonight. I'll come back later, once Nate's working here. I'll wear that dress you suggested, my hair down... Oh, Maude, are you sure this will work?" she asked in an agony of uncertainty. After tonight she'd be either the happiest woman in Simpson Creek or the most embarrassed.

Maude grinned. "If it doesn't, Nate's a fool. But it *will*," she said. "Don't forget the rosewater."

With any luck, Ella thought, she could close early tonight, run back to the boardinghouse and commandeer the bathing room with its claw-foot bathtub, and have plenty of time to bathe, wash her hair and let it dry on her shoulders. Maude would be willing, she knew, to help her slip out the back door without any of the other boardinghouse inhabitants seeing her. It wouldn't do for one of them to get the wrong idea and spread rumors about what Ella was doing, going out at such a late hour dressed in her best.

Luck was not with her, though. Tonight, one straggler after another showed up at the café just before she wanted to close, and dawdled endlessly over their meals. She began to consider the wisdom of leaving the dirty dishes to soak and coming in early to wash them the next day. But a mess of dirty dishes wouldn't contribute to a romantic atmosphere.

Finally, as the last customers departed, Ella put the closed sign in the window. Checking the watch pinned to her bodice, she groaned. Eight o'clock already. That balding drummer who'd been staying in the boardinghouse the last few days was no doubt ensconced in the bathtub by now, and in any case there wasn't time to heat enough water for a bath. Well, she could use the basin and ewer in her room, and dress quickly... But what if she encountered Nate on her way back to the boardinghouse, walking toward the café?

She began to wash the last of the dishes.

The knock on the door startled her so much she had to stifle a shriek. *Good grief, is Nate already here? I look terrible, and probably smell of grease!* And she didn't want to appear at the door holding the carving knife she had been washing when the knock sounded. Absently, she dropped the carving knife into her apron pocket and went to the door.

It wasn't Nate who stood on the café threshold however, but Mrs. Powell, leaning heavily on her cane. If Robert E. Lee himself had chosen this time to visit her establishment, she could not have been more surprised. Or dismayed.

"Mrs. Powell... I was just leaving. I'm sorry, but the café's closed," she said, wondering why the old woman was here.

"Nice establishment you have here," her former bully murmured, as if Ella hadn't spoken. Her avid gaze wandered the room. "Very nice. I heard your pecan pie was exceptionally tasty tonight, and I thought maybe you might have a last piece to spare for me? Normally I treat myself to a piece of cake at the hotel restaurant of an evening, but when we closed tonight there wasn't a morsel left. So I just thought I'd pay you a visit and see the inside of your place and ask if you had a bit of pie left to satisfy my sweet tooth. You remember, I have a sweet tooth." She laughed as if her taste for sweets had always been a subject of amusement between them.

"I… Sure, I have a piece of pie left," Ella said, thinking quickly. She had been saving it for Nate, but if dessert was the price of getting this woman out of her café, she'd sacrifice it gladly. "I'll have to wrap it up for you to take with you, though—it's getting late."

"Of course, of course," Mrs. Powell agreed. "I don't mean to delay you, dear…"

Dear? Ella would have laughed at the endearment as well as the false courtesy coming from this woman, but she didn't want to prolong the conversation any more than she had to. "I hope you like it," she said, going over to where she had left a plate over the last piece of pie.

To Ella's annoyance, the woman followed her. Maybe she wouldn't have taken the liberty if the new countertop had been in place, dividing the public area from her work area, but Ella doubted it.

"Nice cabinets," the woman said, following her and peering at them with the inquisitive eye of a rival cook. "Did your fella build them for you?"

How infuriating of the woman to speak to her as if she and Ella had always been confidantes. "Nate Bohannan built them, if that's who you meant," she said levelly. She wasn't about to discuss her private business with this woman.

Mrs. Powell looked hurt. Perhaps she was being too harsh, Ella thought. What if the batty old lady had only been seeking a private time to try to repair their relationship? It wasn't a convenient time for Ella, of course, but she should be willing to forgive, shouldn't she?

"This is on the house, Mrs. Powell," she said, turning away from the woman as she wrapped up the pie, "to thank you for all you taught m—"

She never saw the blow coming, but suddenly there was a crashing pain in her head and a black crepe curtain fell over everything.

Carrying a lantern to augment the faint light of the quarter moon, Nate headed for the café. The countertop was the last piece he had to construct to fulfill his promise to Ella, and then he would be free of any obligation to her. If he stayed, it would be because they had made things right between them. He'd prayed hard about the matter, and the peace he'd felt encouraged him to think that God would bless his efforts.

If she wouldn't listen to him, he would travel on, and this time he wouldn't depend on anyone but himself to get to California.

Perhaps, if the project took him till dawn, he'd just wait until she arrived to start preparing breakfast and say his piece. But maybe that wasn't the best idea—Detwiler had told him that Maude was helping Ella at the café, so Ella might not be alone then. She might not think it fair to leave breakfast preparations to her friend while he took her aside for a heart-to-heart talk. No, better to leave before she came, sleep awhile, then go to the café at its closing time. He'd be rested then, and less apt to state his case clumsily.

He'd have to take the borrowed tools back to Dayton when he left the café in the morning, he thought as he crossed the bridge over the creek. It was fortunate that the lumber mill owner had been willing to lend him the necessary hammer, brace and bit drill, chisel, rasp, plane and saw. He hadn't known the man that long, of course, but from what Detwiler had told him of Dayton's character, the man must be mellowing not to charge him for the use of the tools. And Dayton had thrown in a selection of nails, wrought-iron drawer pulls and buckets of whitewash, to boot, in addition to making the crude benches and chairs for Ella's outdoor customers.

Yes, the man was definitely mellowing. Maybe Dayton thought that the nicer he was to Nate, the more apt Nate would be to stay and go into partnership with him.

Whether he stayed or left Simpson Creek, though, had nothing to do with the crusty mill owner's unaccustomed generosity and everything to do with a petite café owner whose black hair gleamed with brown highlights in the sun and whose dark liquid eyes had unlimited depths.

Light flickered through the café window, casting a faint light on the short path between the road and the café. Had she left on a lamp for him, knowing he'd be arriving soon? How considerate of her, but she shouldn't waste her precious lamp oil when he'd brought a lantern of his own.

Then he thought he saw the shadow of someone moving within the café. Had Ella stayed to see him? Could she possibly want to make peace between them, or did she merely want to give him grudging thanks away from curious eyes?

Curiosity sped his steps. In a few short strides he pushed the door open. "Ella, are you here? It's me, Nate."

But the figure that came toward him possessed nothing of Ella's lithe grace. It was heavy and lumbering, and leaned on a cane, blocking the doorway. "Yes, she's here," Mrs. Powell said, showing yellowed, uneven teeth as she pulled her lips back in an attempt at a smile.

It was all Nate could do not to groan out loud. *What is this woman doing here now? Has she come to make peace with Ella, too? Of all the times to do that...*

He tried to look past her to spot Ella, but Mrs. Powell was too tall and broad. How quickly could he get her to leave so he could talk to Ella?

"May I see her then?" he said, trying to mask his impatience.

The old woman stepped aside to let him in, then gestured toward the shadows at the back of the café. "I fear the rude girl couldn't stay awake to greet you proper-like." She cackled, and pointed a gnarled finger to a crumpled form sprawled on the puncheon floor.

Chapter Twenty-Four

It wasn't a natural slumber, it couldn't be—not the way Ella's limbs were splayed out, as if she had fallen instantly asleep and dropped to the floor. "Let me past," he ordered the old woman, pushing her aside as gently as he could despite the alarm bells ringing in his head.

"Sure, sure," Mrs. Powell murmured, allowing herself to be moved. "You come right on in an' see if you kin wake her up. Maybe with a kiss, like the prince in that old fairy tale," she added with a cackle.

Nate ran to Ella's side, threw himself down to the floor beside her and began pulling on her arm. "Ella, what's the matter with you? Are you hurt? *Wake up!*" He patted her cheek with increasing force. Gingerly, he felt her head and found the soft lump at the back, just above the neat knot she always twisted her hair up into when she was cooking.

"Do you know what happened to her?" he demanded without looking at the old woman. When no answer seemed to be forthcoming, he said, "I have to get her to the doctor, so you'll have to hold the door open for me—"

Mrs. Powell stood just behind and to the side of him,

he saw out of the corner of his eye. Her cane lay on the floor. Now she held something large over her head—a chair?—but before he could wrench himself aside, she brought it down on him with amazing strength.

Instant, blinding pain. He fell to the floor, arms and limbs unable to answer his order to move, to seize the old woman and subdue her.

She is insane...

As consciousness faded, Nate heard her cackling now as she walked away from him.

Must stay awake. Must help Ella. Get her away. Must...

Ella wanted to remain in that misty, murky land where the thundering pain in her head was only a distant, throbbing echo, but the stinging in her nose and a distant shrieking were too insistent. Flashing light battered her closed lids. A crackling noise assaulted her ears. Tentatively, she slitted one eye open just enough to see what was making such a ruckus.

What she saw had her bolting upright in alarm, only to sway dizzily from the blow to her head and the stunning realization that her nightmare had returned.

By some horrible means, she had been transported back through the years and was once more in the asylum on the night that it had burned to the ground. She could hear a thumping somewhere beyond the wall of flame nearby—the thudding against the door of a dormitory full of helpless children, trying in vain to alert someone—anyone—that they were trapped behind a locked door.

The cavernous room was filling with smoke. Part of the ceiling was alight, glowing a sinister orange-red above them. She could hardly see the children pounding at the door now through the gray clouds between them, could barely make herself heard through the roaring of the flames when she screamed at them. "Come this way—we'll get out through the other dormitory! Follow me!"

Two or three turned around, blinking at the smoke that stung their eyes, as she pointed to the door that led to the adult dormitory next to them. This had been the portal through which her nightmarish tormentor had entered the children's dormitory and crept unerringly to her bed so many nights. She could picture him clearly now—not one of the crazy old men, but Mr. Kimberly, the superintendent of the asylum.

Now, though, that door might mean their salvation.

Then the portion of the roof over the children pounding at the door collapsed with a tremendous crash, and she could no longer see them, just a writhing, dancing inferno where they had been.

She had to get out! She could no longer help the others, but perhaps she could save herself. There were no guarantees that the adult dormitory was not entirely afire, but when she felt the door, it wasn't hot. She pushed it open.

The other room was impenetrably black with smoke, but she could see no flames. There seemed to be a few inches of relatively clear air at her ankles, so she dropped to the floor and began to crawl, dodging the shapes of cots and men and women awakening to the horror of the smothering thick smoke. She had to find the door—and then she did, and scrambled through it. The corridor was only a little smoky, and she ran through it, coughing until she reached the door to the outside and retched in the cold night air.

She began to run, unaware that she wore nothing but

a sooty, singed nightgown. She never stopped until the fiery asylum was a distant torch behind her.

But something was wrong. She wasn't free. She hadn't escaped. Ella still smelled the lung-strangling smoke, saw the flames around her. She hadn't outrun them the way she had that night.

The years fell away again, and Ella knew that this nightmare was real. *Dear God, the café is on fire!* Red tongues licked the wall behind her. A curtain of flame lay between her and the door; another arching, writhing, spark-spitting red-gold line separated her from the west wall that faced the creek.

Mrs. Powell had done this, Ella realized—had knocked her insensible and set the fire to rid herself of her competitor *and* her competitor's establishment in one fell swoop. Perhaps the woman's odd behavior of the past few weeks had been only an act designed to allow Ella to trust her just enough to let her into the café when everyone else had left. Night would cloak the flames from the town until the place was nothing but a smoking ruin—and Ella's body with it.

Where had the woman gone? she wondered. Was she watching from a distance among the trees that lined the creek? Or had she crept back to her little room in the back of the hotel, so that morning would find her feigning blissful ignorance of the tragedy that had befallen Ella?

She didn't have time to speculate about Mrs. Powell. Flames caressed a portion of the ceiling above her now, showering the floor with sparks. A couple of them landed on her skirt and smoldered. With a shriek she beat at her skirt until they were nothing but blackened holes in the fabric.

She had to be calm, had to gather her wits and get

out. Panic was useless and lethal. She'd survived a fire before, she could do it again.

Her only possible exit was the window at the back, the one she looked out when she washed dishes. She could clamber up onto the table and escape from her burning café.

But the table was gone, and she dared not waste precious time in the smoke trying to find it. It would be awkward getting out of the window without the table, but she could do it—had to do it, and quickly, before the ceiling fell in on her the way it had on those poor luckless orphans at the asylum. She'd land on her head and hands, but with any luck she wouldn't break her neck...

Then she heard the thumping again behind her, past the line of flames, and realized it hadn't been the children in the asylum. Someone was in the burning café with her, beyond the writhing line of fire. Was it Mrs. Powell? Had she fallen victim to her own trap? Ella had to try to help her get out.

The fire bowed low for a moment, and she saw that it wasn't the malicious old cook but a man. A man whose hands and legs were bound with rope, whose mouth was gagged by a rag tied around his head. *Nate!* He was thrashing against the floor with his legs, trying desperately to free himself—that had been the noise she'd heard. He'd come to finish his work, and somehow that evil, crazy woman had managed to lure him inside and knock him unconscious, too.

"Nate!"

He heard her yell, and twisted around in his bonds to see her. The words he tried to speak were incomprehensible, of course, but the anguish in his eyes said everything he needed to. He was afraid they were both going to die in this fire.

"I can…get out!" she cried, then paid for inhaling the smoke with a fit of coughing that brought stinging tears to her eyes. "Th-through the window—then I'll come around and get you loose!"

The smoke hid the doorway from view, but she saw no flames in that part of the ceiling, and thought that fire hadn't reached it yet. Of course—Mrs. Powell had left herself a way out. She'd set the fire at the back, hoping it would kill Ella and Nate before consuming the rest of the little building.

She looked back at Nate. Through the smoke, she saw him shake his head. He was telling her to save herself, not to expose herself to more danger by trying to save him, too. Of course. He was not her father, who'd thought only of himself and abandoned her. Nate was putting her safety, her life, before his.

She couldn't wait any longer. The heat was unbearable. Any moment now she'd miss a spark landing on her clothing, and her skirt or her blouse would catch fire. The fire was creeping closer, not only to where she stood but to where he lay, and overhead, too. What if the roof collapsed over him before she could struggle out the window and come around to the front?

Lord, save us!

With a smothered cry, she lunged for the window. But she couldn't raise it! Had Mrs. Powell rigged it closed somehow, or had the heat in the room swollen the wood? Quickly, raising the thick twill fabric of her skirt, she wrapped it around her fist and, closing her eyes, struck at the glass. It cracked, then broke, raining shards of glass outside. She struck frantically again and again until most of the glass around the frame had fallen out. She'd still probably get nicked by the remainders of it as she went through, but her clothing should protect her to some degree.

She threw her arms out the window, then, clutching the outside wall, pulled herself farther out, her high-buttoned short boots scrabbling at the wall inside, trying for a foothold. When her waist hit the window, something pressed against her abdomen from inside the apron. She didn't have time to wonder what it was. A forgotten spear of glass gouged the top of her head. She ignored the pain.

Precious seconds of struggling later, she had pulled herself out of the window far enough that her weight took her the rest of the way. She fell in an ungainly heap onto the ground below, her back scraping against the rough bark of the big live oak closest to the window.

Was Mrs. Powell waiting out here, she wondered, ready to bash her over the head again? Ella peered around, but she didn't see her. The fire had roared to new life behind her, as if frustrated that it had lost its prey. *Has it already killed Nate?* She could hear nothing but the crackling of the flames within.

Now that the little building was a blazing inferno, would anyone in town see the smoke that Ella guessed rose above it like a tower and raise the alarm? The parsonage was closest, but it was the middle of the night. Before anyone was roused by the fire, it would be too late.

She scrambled around the side of the building, dashed to the door and pulled at the handle, and when it wouldn't move, threw herself against it. It gave way and she fell heavily on her shoulder just over the threshold.

There—there was Nate! The fire hadn't reached him yet, though it sprinkled sparks all around him. Leaning over, she pulled at his lower legs, but she couldn't budge him.

Aware she was there now, he jerked his head toward the door, making more of the incomprehensible noises that were all the gag would allow him. Then his gaze went to the ceiling.

Her gaze followed his. The ceiling was entirely ablaze above them now. He looked back at her, and once again jerked his head toward the door. As clear as anything he could have said without the gag, he was ordering her out, ordering her to leave him to his fate.

She wasn't about to do that, though she had to clamp her jaws over the shrieks of terror that threatened to escape her lips. *Help us, Lord!*

Then she remembered the object that had poked at her belly when she'd clambered over the window ledge. *Can it be...yes!* She still had the carving knife she had carelessly dropped inside her apron when she had first heard the knock at the door. It was a wonder it hadn't fallen out when she'd gone headfirst out the window.

No, not a wonder—an act of God.

She pulled out the knife, and Nate's eyes widened. Glancing at the ceiling again, she saw that they might have only seconds before it would come crashing down on them. Running out of time, she cut the bonds at his feet—he could run out with his hands still tied.

Hands shaking, tears pouring down her cheeks, coughing so hard she could hardly breathe, she knelt by his side and sawed at the rope around his legs.

It seemed to take forever, and she was afraid she'd go too far and slice into his skin, but then the knife cut through the rope and he was scrambling to his feet. He was clumsy because he could not use his hands, but at least the old woman had tied them in front of him, and

Nate was strong enough to lean on his bound-together wrists and use them, along with his newly freed legs, to lever himself up off the floor, which was beginning to smolder around them.

Once outside, they ran to the road, far enough from the café that flying sparks couldn't reach them, and she cut the rope between his wrists, then, holding the cloth carefully away from his cheek, slashed through the gag. He spit it out.

He threw his arms around her, pulling her against him.

"Oh, Ella," he said. "Thank God you're safe. *Thank God.*"

"Thank God *we're* safe," she said against his soot-smeared torn shirt, but his heart was beating so hard she wasn't sure he could hear her.

As if it had been waiting for just such a signal, the roof of Ella's café crashed in just then, and all four walls were alight.

Behind them, past the creek, the bell of the Simpson Creek church began to toll, and she heard distant shouts.

Chapter Twenty-Five

"You saved my life. I love you, Ella Justiss," Nate heard himself telling her as they clung together, barely conscious of the chilly October night at their backs. "I was going to tell you so later today, and let the chips fall where they might. I was going to tell you how sorry I was for the angry way I spoke to you when I came back, and to tell you that I wanted to stay in Simpson Creek—if you'd have me, that is. Don't know why you'd want a fellow who changed his mind so many times about whether he was going or staying, though."

He felt her sigh against him. Then, incredibly, she said, "Oh, Nate, I love you, too. Of course I'll have you. Do you think I'd let you get away if I had a choice?"

"You just saved my life," he said once more against her forehead, before lowering his lips to hers for the kiss he'd been waiting for all his life. And this time she didn't get scared or pull away but kissed him back as fervently as he was kissing her.

Probably the fire had drained all the "scare" out of her and she wasn't able to resist him. She'd change her mind later, he thought—he was honor-bound to let her come to her senses. Until then he'd wallow in the happiness of knowing she was his, no matter what else had happened tonight.

They heard running feet coming toward them, and looked up to see Reverend Gil, followed closely by his wife and Sheriff Bishop. "Are you two all right? We saw the fire— How'd it start?" the sheriff demanded.

"You can talk to them later, Sam," Faith said. "Right now they must be in shock and chilled to the bone." Then she was draping a blanket over each of them and leading them away, murmuring about getting them into the parsonage and out of the cold wind.

As they crossed the bridge, Nate saw more and more townspeople run past them, buckets bouncing at their side, to form a line from the creek to the raging inferno that had been Ella's café. The building was gone, but Nate knew they needed to put out the fire so it wouldn't spread to the meadow and start a grass fire that could burn for miles if the wind was right. It might even leap the creek via the trees and destroy the church again.

Faith ushered them into the parsonage's parlor, totally heedless of the sooty tracks they left in their wake. "I'll make you some hot coffee. Guess I better make a lot of it for all those folks outside, too," she said, then left them mercifully alone.

Soot smudges became Ella, Nate thought, and kissed the one that decorated her nose. She gazed up at him in the soft light of the parlor lamp.

"When I was in the café, in the fire, I remembered everything, Nate. From the asylum…what happened to me. I—I've been… I'm not innocent, Nate. You need to know this."

He'd suspected what had happened so long ago, of course, from her reaction the other time he'd kissed her.

"You *are* innocent, Ella. *Nothing* that was done to

you was your fault, do you hear me? It's all in the past, and it need not matter to us." He thought maybe she'd already begun to realize the truth of this when she'd kissed him a few minutes ago.

Her eyes shone with tears. "Oh, Nate."

"So, will you marry me, Ella Justiss?" he asked. "Dayton gave me the idea of setting up a furniture shop in town, so I reckon I'll have a way to make a living here in Simpson Creek and won't have to be hanging around in the café, pestering you while you cook," he told her with a grin. "Unless you get any more rowdy cowboys trying to take liberties, that is," he said, remembering the way they'd met.

She'd had a radiant smile until he mentioned the café, but now she stared at him as if he'd gone mad. "Nate, did you get hit in the head too hard? My café is *gone.* The church drained their benevolent fund to give me the one that just burned down!" she cried, collapsing into his arms. "All that work, theirs and yours, and it's all ashes!" She began to sob against his chest.

He rubbed her back, letting her cry out all the anguish that remained in her. "It'll be all right, I promise you, Ella, you'll have your café again—and we'll have each other."

"I love you, Nate, and I'll love being your wife."

"Good. Then that's settled."

"I suppose George might let me use the back of the saloon again, though it'll take a while before we could buy a stove…"

"That'll work until we can build you a new place, but it won't take so long—not since I have this to sell." He pulled the gold watch out of his pants pocket.

Her eyes grew round as dinner plates. "But… I thought that was stolen…"

"Salali didn't get this when he robbed me," he told her. "It was my father's. God only knows why he didn't sell it and put a permanent roof over our heads, but he didn't, and when he was dying, he gave it to me. When Salali knocked me out, I fell flat on my face, and he never thought of searching my front pockets."

"So you could have sold it and left Simpson Creek as soon as Bishop let you out of jail," she said, blinking at the realization.

He shrugged. "I could've, but I felt bad about the saloon and your café being wrecked, so I thought I'd wait till I'd repaired what I could. Then I...kinda didn't want to leave so much. This pretty cook behind the saloon had snared my heart, you see."

He was about to kiss Ella again, when Faith came in with cups of steaming coffee, then said she was leaving to take coffee to those working to put out the blaze.

"If I sell this watch," he went on once they were alone, "we'll have enough to rebuild your café *and* build a house in the back for us *and* my furniture shop right by it, too. I'll be too busy making furniture to pester my wife in her café—except at mealtimes, of course."

"But, Nate," she protested, "I don't want you to have to sell your father's watch. It's all you have to remember him by."

"I have my father inside me," he said, and for the first time he knew that it was true, and valuable in a way that he had never realized before. "In all the skills he taught me, not in a *thing*," he said, pointing at the watch. "I kept this not because I need to know the time at any given moment, but knowing someday I might need to sell it to accomplish something important. I thought 'something important' was getting to San Francisco and becoming rich and powerful. Now I know 'something important' is starting a life with you."

"Nate," she murmured, "I love you so much." Then for an endless time they were lost in each other, until one by one, the members of the bucket brigade filed in to see them and assure themselves Miss Ella and Nate Bohannan were all right.

Sheriff Bishop eventually arrived to get their account of what had happened. They told him how Mrs. Powell had knocked each of them unconscious in turn, tied Nate up and set the fire—probably with the kerosene out of the lamps.

"I don't know what happened to her after that," Ella told the sheriff, appreciating Nate's warm arm around her as she remembered the terror of waking up among flames and struggling to get out, knowing she might not be in time to save Nate.

"We found Mrs. Powell in the creek," Bishop said grimly. "She must have caught her dress on fire, 'cause a lot of it was burned away. I figure she must have jumped in the water to put out the fire and hit her head on that big rock that sticks out on one side below the bridge."

"Is she dead?" Nate asked as Ella clutched his arm.

Bishop nodded. "It's probably a mercy, as bad as her burns looked."

Next to her, Nate sighed, and Ella knew he could no more rejoice in Mrs. Powell's death than she could, despite what Mrs. Powell had done. *The poor demented soul.* Having felt so insecure about her own future before, Ella knew how insecurity could fuel a person's actions.

Those in the parlor cheered as they learned Ella's

café would be rebuilt and Nate would be staying in Simpson Creek as Ella's husband. It was impossible to be sad anymore.

A fortnight later, Ella still hadn't changed her mind about marrying Nate, much to his relief. Dressed in a beautiful dark green dress, which had been made up with skillful haste by Milly Brookfield, Ella Justiss became the bride of Nate Bohannan.

The wedding dinner was held at the hotel and prepared by Daisy Henderson, the new cook. She'd been promoted by the hotel owner because of old Mrs. Powell's demise.

"Delicious." Ella sighed as she tasted her first morsel of wedding cake. She sat next to her handsome groom, who wore the silver brocade vest and black trousers he'd been wearing when she'd first seen him, along with a new white shirt and a black frock coat lent to him by Nick Brookfield.

"Not bad, but she doesn't cook as well as you do," Nate whispered into his bride's ear.

"You're just saying that because you want me to keep you supplied with cake all the time, Mr. Bohannan," she accused him with a wink.

"I won't deny it, Mrs. Bohannan," he said, grinning.

They would be living in a little cottage on the grounds of Gilmore House, the mayor's palatial mansion, until their new house could be built. The café would be rebuilt first, rising again on the site of the old one. Nate's shop would be built after the house, but it could wait because Dayton had offered to let him use the workroom at the mill again until the shop was constructed.

Mayor Gilmore made a point of taking out his new

gold pocket watch, which Nate had sold to him for a very nice sum indeed.

"I think it's time the groom made a speech," he announced, and everyone began to clink their glasses in agreement.

"Aw, I'm not so good at speeches," Nate protested, reddening as every guest's gaze fell on him. "Wouldn't you like me to kiss my bride again instead? I've found that's one of my new skills."

Beside him, Ella felt herself flush, but she didn't mind her new husband's suggestion a bit.

* * * * *

Dear Reader,

Welcome back to Simpson Creek, where the ladies of the Spinsters' Club make matches to achieve their "happily-ever-afters." This Hill Country town has become a dear location to me, full of old friends and new characters asking for their own stories. I hope you like them, too!

As with all authors, I'm often asked where I get my ideas. In Ella's case, I'd already decided she would be the next heroine in my series, but while deciding how to deepen her background, I attended my granddaughter Olivia's school play, *Annie*. In the program, I read about the development of orphanages, and how at first, orphan children were placed in asylums right along with indigent and sometimes insane adults. That was what had happened to Ella, I decided, which made her occasionally unsure and feeling as if she had been damaged.

And who would be the most apparently unreliable man for her to fall in love with but a jack-of-all-trades who was helping to sell snake oil in a medicine show? I admit I have a weakness for "jacks-of-all-trade" since my own husband is one of those men who can build or fix seemingly anything.

And so the story began. Thanks for choosing *A Hero in the Making.* You can contact me via my website, www.LaurieKingery.com, or on Facebook, or Twitter—@lauriekingery.

Blessings,
Laurie Kingery

Questions for Discussion

1. Have you ever been subject to repeated nightmares about a particular subject? How did you deal with it?

2. Describe Ella's and Nate's reactions when they first meet. Do you think this is love at first sight?

3. How is their meeting different from when you met your husband or significant other? Do you believe in love at first sight?

4. How is Ella different from the career-oriented women of today?

5. Have you ever wanted to go into business for yourself, as Ella does? Did you do it? Why or why not?

6. How does Ella's childhood influence the woman she has become?

7. Did you want to be just like one of your parents, or, like Nate, the opposite of one of your parents? Did you become like your mother or father? Why or why not?

8. What do you think of the Bible-theme verse, "Be not forgetful to entertain strangers, for thereby some have entertained angels unawares"?

9. Have you ever met a slick con man like Robert Salali? How did that come about?

10. When we first meet Ella, she is insecure and determined to trust no one, especially men. How does she change?

11. Have you ever developed a plan, as Nate does, only to have God lead you in a different direction?

12. Ella and Nate both have secrets. Ella's, of course, is her asylum upbringing. What is Nate's?

13. Do you have a confidante like Ella does, whom you can be "real" with? Why is that important?

14. How does Maude show support to her friend Ella?

15. Maude's story will be next in the Brides of Simpson Creek series. What kind of hero would you envision for her?

REQUEST YOUR FREE BOOKS!

2 FREE INSPIRATIONAL NOVELS
PLUS 2
FREE
MYSTERY GIFTS

Love Inspired
HISTORICAL
INSPIRATIONAL HISTORICAL ROMANCE

YES! Please send me 2 FREE Love Inspired® Historical novels and my 2 FREE mystery gifts (gifts are worth about $10). After receiving them, if I don't wish to receive any more books, I can return the shipping statement marked "cancel." If I don't cancel, I will receive 4 brand-new novels every month and be billed just $4.74 per book in the U.S. or $5.24 per book in Canada. That's a saving of at least 21% off the cover price. It's quite a bargain! Shipping and handling is just 50¢ per book in the U.S. and 75¢ per book in Canada.* I understand that accepting the 2 free books and gifts places me under no obligation to buy anything. I can always return a shipment and cancel at any time. Even if I never buy another book, the two free books and gifts are mine to keep forever.

102/302 IDN F5CN

Name	(PLEASE PRINT)	
Address		Apt. #
City	State/Prov.	Zip/Postal Code

Signature (if under 18, a parent or guardian must sign)

Mail to the Harlequin® Reader Service:
IN U.S.A.: P.O. Box 1867, Buffalo, NY 14240-1867
IN CANADA: P.O. Box 609, Fort Erie, Ontario L2A 5X3

Want to try two free books from another series?
Call 1-800-873-8635 or visit www.ReaderService.com.

* Terms and prices subject to change without notice. Prices do not include applicable taxes. Sales tax applicable in N.Y. Canadian residents will be charged applicable taxes. Offer not valid in Quebec. This offer is limited to one order per household. Not valid for current subscribers to Love Inspired Historical books. All orders subject to credit approval. Credit or debit balances in a customer's account(s) may be offset by any other outstanding balance owed by or to the customer. Please allow 4 to 6 weeks for delivery. Offer available while quantities last.

Your Privacy—The Harlequin® Reader Service is committed to protecting your privacy. Our Privacy Policy is available online at www.ReaderService.com or upon request from the Harlequin Reader Service.

We make a portion of our mailing list available to reputable third parties that offer products we believe may interest you. If you prefer that we not exchange your name with third parties, or if you wish to clarify or modify your communication preferences, please visit us at www.ReaderService.com/consumerschoice or write to us at Harlequin Reader Service Preference Service, P.O. Box 9062, Buffalo, NY 14269. Include your complete name and address.

"We used to count the stars at night, Jack. Remember that?"

Oh, he remembered, all right. They'd look skyward and watch each star appear, summer, winter, spring and fall, each season offering its own array, a blend of favorites. Until they'd become distracted by other things. Sweet things.

A sigh welled from somewhere deep within him, a quiet blooming of what could have been. "I remember."

They stared upward, side by side, watching the sunset fade to streaks of lilac and gray. Town lights began to appear north of the bridge, winking on earlier now that it was August. "How long are you here?"

Olivia faltered. "I'm not sure."

He turned to face her, puzzled.

"I'm between lives right now."

He raised an eyebrow, waiting for her to continue. She did, after drawn-out seconds, but didn't look at him. She kept her gaze up and out, watching the tree shadows darken and dim.

"I was married."

He'd heard she'd gotten married several years ago, but the "was" surprised him. He dropped his gaze to her left hand. No ring. No tan line that said a ring had been there this summer. A flicker that might be hope stirred in his chest, but entertaining those notions would get him nothing but trouble, so he blamed the strange feeling on the half-finished sandwich he'd wolfed down on the drive in.

You've eaten fast plenty of times before this and been fine. Just fine.

The reminder made him take a half step forward, just close enough to inhale the scent of sweet vanilla on her hair, her skin.

He shouldn't. He knew that. He knew it even as his hand reached for her hand, the left one bearing no man's ring, and that touch, the press of his fingers on hers, made the tiny flicker inside brighten just a little.

The surroundings, the trees, the thin-lit night and the sound of rushing water made him feel as if anything was possible, and he hadn't felt that way in a very long time. But here, with her?

He did. And it felt good.

Find out what else is going on in Jasper Gulch in
HIS MONTANA SWEETHEART by Ruth Logan Herne,
available August 2014 from Love Inspired®.

LIEXP0714

Sonya Daniels heard the sharp crack and saw the woman jogging four feet in front of her stumble. Then fall.

Another crack.

Another woman cried out and hit the ground.

"Shooter! Get down! Get down!"

With a burst of horror, Sonya caught on. Someone was shooting at the joggers on the path. Terror froze her for a brief second. A second that saved her life as the bullet whizzed past her head and planted itself in the wooden bench next to her. If she'd been moving forward, she would be dead.

Frantic, she registered the screams of those in the park as she ran full-out, zigzagging her way to the concrete fountain just ahead.

Her only thought was shelter.

A bullet slammed into the dirt behind her and she dropped to roll next to the base of the fountain.

She looked up to find another young woman had beat her there. Terrified brown eyes stared at Sonya and she knew the woman saw her fear reflected back at her. Panting, Sonya listened for more shots.

None came.

And still they waited. Seconds turned into minutes.

"Is it over?" the woman finally whispered. "Is he gone?"

"I don't know," Sonya responded.

Screams still echoed around them. Wails and petrified cries of disbelief.

Sonya lifted her head slightly and looked back at the two women who'd fallen. They still lay on the path behind her.

Sirens sounded.

Sonya took a deep breath and scanned the area across the street. Slowly, she calmed and gained control of her pounding pulse.

Her mind clicked through the shots fired. Two hit the women running in front of her. Her stomach cramped at the thought that she should have been the third victim. She glanced at the bench. The bullet hole stared back. It had dug a groove slanted and angled.

Heart in her throat, Sonya darted to the nearest woman, who lay about ten yards away from her. Expecting a bullet to slam into her at any moment, she felt for a pulse.

When Sonya turns to Detective Brandon Hayes
for help, can he protect her without both of them
losing their hearts?
Pick up HER STOLEN PAST to find out.

Available August 2014
wherever Love Inspired books are sold.